In the year 1900—on the afternoon she suspects might be the last of her long, eventful life—Emma Garnet Tate Lowell sets down on paper what came before, determined to make an honest account of it. It is a story of family secrets, of inglorious war, of courage and sacrifice, of the sorrows of a divided heart and the consolations of enduring love.

Like America in the mid-nineteenth century, young Emma Garnet Tate Lowell is at war with herself. Born to privilege on a James River plantation, she grows up more and more aware that her family's prosperity is inextricably linked to the institution of slavery, and she is determined to escape the domination of her bullying, self-made father, Samuel P. Tate. In the company of her mother and adoring brother Whately— and through the wisdom, vigor, and kindness of Clarice, the family servant—Emma manages to survive with her heart and mind intact. She secedes from the control of her father to marry Quincy Lowell, a surgeon and member of a distinguished Boston family, and they settle in Raleigh on the eve of the Civil War, bent on creating the ideal happy home.

But then comes the Civil War—described by Emma as "a conflict perpetrated by rich men and fought by poor boys against hungry women and babies." Emma works alongside Quincy, assisting him in the treatment of wounded soldiers, witnessing scenes that will be engraved in her memory. And, before she can begin the long journey of her own reconstruction, she must face the shame of her relationship to her "servants" and learn the terrible secret that shaped her father's life.

Sprawling in its scope but heartbreakingly exact in its depiction of a family torn apart, *On the Occasion of My Last Afternoon* is a great and unforgettable novel in the great Southern tradition.

(more praise follows)

"Deeply satisfying…Gibbons' most fully realized novel to date…
a muscular narrative that humanizes all sides
of that bloody conflict—North and South, black and white,
male and female…a robust novel that deserves
to be set on the shelf alongside *Cold Mountain.*"
—*Orlando Sentinel*

"Gibbons' depiction of the war's impact on those who fight it
and those who suffer it is masterful. She has a gift for focusing
on the telling detail, the seemingly trivial incident that suddenly
explodes all the rhetoric about freedom and states' rights
and noble causes…Kaye Gibbons has crafted a vivid portrait
of a woman who, despite—or perhaps because of—
the sorrows weighing down her life, has truly lived.
Emma Garnet is, finally, a woman to be envied."
—*Richmond Times-Dispatch*

"A fascinating story…Kaye Gibbons goes back to the days
of the Civil War to depict the life of another extraordinary woman…
A reader couldn't ask for better company than Emma."
—*USA Today*

"A vivid account of a gentle woman who desperately wants
to put her brutal childhood behind her but finds her life
ripped apart by the Civil War…Gibbons is a masterful writer,
one of the country's best…[Her] novel provides a realistic picture
of nineteenth century Southern life and the horrors of war."
—*Greensboro News and Record*

"Gibbons is continuing the fine tradition she established with her
previous novels…Like Eudora Welty, Gibbons captures the
cadence of a time gone by, yet she makes the characters seem
entirely modern. Like Welty, Gibbons never blinks when looking
at some of the horrific madness of the day…The message is well
worth the effort it takes to slip into a more refined time that was,
ironically, the nation's bloodiest."
—*San Jose Mercury News*

"A novel that will have been worth the wait for Gibbons' fans or anyone else with a passionate interest in the Civil War."

—*Portland Oregonian*

"Haunting...a rare jewel...Kaye Gibbons has gone from being a wonderful, fascinating novelist to a national treasure...Gibbons' measured cadence, the confidence of her narrative, and the power of her main character's growth, reflection, and realization of self all amount to a rare achievement... There isn't a single weak sentence in the entire novel."

—*San Antonio Express-News*

"Brilliant...Gibbons does a masterful job of portraying the realities of the war years and what they did to the human lives that were consumed by them...There are so many moving moments and passages that perfectly capture the heart and soul of Emma and other women of her time in this novel that it is fairly impossible to put it aside without finishing it in one sitting. *On the Occasion of My Last Afternoon* is a treasure. And Kaye Gibbons is as much of a gift to the world of readers as Emma Garnet was to the women and men she knew all those years ago."

—*Milwaukee Journal Sentinel*

"Gibbons has evolved a distinctive narrative style based on the poignant eloquence and acuity of young female narrators struggling to transcend the moral and spiritual failings of their troubled families. Emma Garnet Tate Lowell, her newest creation, fits the mold but with a subtle twist: she's telling her tale at the end of her long and tumultuous life, a life derailed, as so many were, by the Civil War...Gibbons has gone back to that still-smoldering conflict and imagined it from a wholly personal and female perspective, concerned not with politics but with blood and suffering...[Gibbons is] unflinching in her effort to convey the madness of that time and the havoc it wreaked on people's souls."

—*Booklist* (Starred Review)

Also by
Kaye Gibbons

On the Occasion of My Last Afternoon

A NOVEL

KAYE GIBBONS

HARPER
PERENNIAL

HARPER ⬤ PERENNIAL

A hardcover edition of this book was published in 1998 by G. P. Putnam's Sons, a member of Penguin Putnam Inc. It is here reprinted by arrangement with Penguin Group (USA) Inc.

P.S.™ is a trademark of HarperCollins Publishers.

HarperCollins books may be purchased for educational, business, or sales promotional use. For information please write: Special Markets Department, HarperCollins Publishers, 10 East 53rd Street, New York, NY 10022.

First Bard edition published 1999.

Reprinted in Harper Perennial 2002.
Reissued 2005.

Designed by Marysarah Quinn

Library of Congress Cataloging-in-Publication Data is available upon request.

ISBN-10: 0-06-079714-2
ISBN-13: 978-0-06-079714-0

05 06 07 08 09 ❖/RRD 10 9 8 7 6 5 4 3 2 1

FOR FAITH SALE

The Queen of Love and Beauty

I thank those who rescued this novel and me when we faltered: David and Barbara Batts, Robert Bilbro, M.D., Jerry Cashion, Jane Clendenin, Jeffrey Crow, Liz Darhansoff, Jonathan Davidson, M.D., Perry Dowd, Miss Mary Lee Edwards, Anna Jardine, Susan Nutter, Harry Pillsbury, Al Purrington, Benton and Emma Garnet Satterfield, Aimée Taub, W. W. Taylor, Jr., Kelly Thrower, John Ulmschneider, Charles Wallace, M.D., Mary Alice Ward, Richard Weisler, M.D., Sarah Ward Whiteside, the staff at the North Carolina Department of Archives and History, the North Carolina State University Friends of the Library; and Alice Ward Farnham, for giving me a place to rest and think, and Robert Farnham, M.D., for helping me kill people.

For the model of sustained excellence, I thank Louis D. Rubin, Barry Moser, William Friday, Grace Paley, William Leuchtenberg, Studs Terkel, William Kennedy, Barry Hannah,

Elizabeth Spencer, Eudora Welty, Kirkpatrick Sale, Cleveland Amory, Shelby Foote, Joe Blotner, and Charles Portis.

Mary, Leslie, Louise, Victoria, and Frank III deserve Purple Hearts for all the times they heard, "As soon as I finish this book . . ." The girls bore the strain of having a nocturnal mother, but they are wise and somewhat self-sufficient. And they know already, at their tender ages, that a writer is obligated to do more than "slop words on paper."

And to my husband, Frank P. Ward—*Quick now. Here now. Always.*

IN MEMORIAM
Charles Seymour
(1944–1997)

Cursing only the leaves crying
Like an old man in a storm

You hear the shout, the crazy hemlocks point
With troubled fingers to the silence which
Smothers you, a mummy, in time.
ALLEN TATE, "Ode to the Confederate Dead"

Shaw's father wanted no monument
except the ditch,
where his son's body was thrown
and lost with his "niggers."

The ditch is nearer.
There are no statues for the last war here;
on Boylston Street, a commercial photograph
shows Hiroshima boiling

over a Mosler Safe, the "Rock of Ages"
that survived the blast. Space is nearer.
When I crouch to my television set,
the drained faces of Negro school-children rise like balloons.
ROBERT LOWELL, "For the Union Dead"

On the Occasion of My Last Afternoon

one

I did not mean to kill the nigger! Did not mean to kill him!

This my father shouted out loud on slaughter day of 1842. I heard him from the kitchen, where I was shaping sausage into little rounds, a pleasant job for a girl of no domestic training. I ran to the kitchen door at his bellowing and wondered at his raging, bloody presence, but I did not go to him. His arms were uplifted as though he were prophet to the clutch of Negroes who stood about him, a hand still holding a blade. I recall, fifty-eight years thence, my extreme horror of recognition that the man standing underneath the spready sycamore had probably done wrong, that he had probably murdered with vile intent, and that all my night-fears of atrocities incited by the Turner rebellion would come true now—for vengeance, my family and I would be slit ear to ear in our sleep. That was the class of talk we heard those days, all I overheard through closed parlor doors. Even among the children of the James a rumor abounded, repeated as hard fact, of a Negro who had murdered a farmer and then dipped the man's wife and children in his blood. I was of an impressionable nature, and my heart quailed within me each time I heard the tale told. *The servants will rise, and they will cut our throats, and they will laugh and drink red whiskey and go about with our bloomers on their heads.*

Weighing the two, my surety that my father had indeed meant to kill whoever had ailed him and the prospect of Negroes murdering us all in the moonlight, I had more faith in the Negroes, more trust in their inherent and collective sense of right. Even then, at twelve, I knew that my father was a liar. Although he had served two terms in the legislature and was known all over Virginia to be an honest, upright, hearty, and earnest Episcopalian, I knew he had a dark secret. Children see into the recesses of the soul. They are rarely fooled, seldom duped save at rummy and shell games, so it was not extraordinary for me to stand in that doorway, while my father demanded of God and a brace of Negroes that they acknowledge his innocence, to see that he was lying to all, for I knew him. I was not now struck down in sudden disillusionment of a beloved parent, for I had heard him delivering my mother his fury in the nights.

Like the servants, we, his children, were beneath him, and so we were left oftentimes standing with his lies in our hands like baffling presents, not knowing what we were to do with this collection of things, his words, whether they should be used or displayed or hidden like a broken toy in a corner of the nursery armoire. *I did not mean to kill the nigger!* Was I to trick the words apart the way a patient mother will sit and tease the knot out of a tangled necklace? Were they to be left for when I was older, the way so much of my life then was lived, in a knowingly, deliberately superficial fashion, until I could nurse the time and free peace of mind to revisit and decipher what was happening to me and around me? I heard Clarice, the chief cook and housekeeper, behind me moaning, heard as if in half-sleep, "Oh my God, oh my God, oh my goodness," but I could not arouse any response, any spoken word. I felt heavy in my body, and over and again in my head, one idea whirled a dervish—I do not know what to make of this now, because I am too young. I am too young for this. I did not believe I would ever forgive my father for making me withstand more than I could bear.

Always, in a moment of import, such as the day memory has now furnished me, Father seemed to speak the utter and ardent truth because he was so very loud and so commanding in his bearing and demeanor. His style was bullish, though he never seemed desperate that he be believed. On that awful day, and at every other time when his method or intent might be questioned, he struck a tone of extreme willfulness, steady and wrathful, without any urgent pleading or begging to be understood, to be followed into whatever mendacious reckoning he might construct. And that is what he was doing as Clarice and I watched him. He was constructing, building a notion of thorough blamelessness that whoever had witnessed the killing or might hear of it later would let him own as a certain verity. No, he did not mean to kill the Negro. Perhaps, even, the Negro asked to be killed, by his insolence or indolence or impudence, the three faults that Father trusted to be at the heart of the reason why the race was inferior and not included in the tenet that all men are created equal and seen as such by the eyes of God. But still, he found it necessary to say again and again to the people who ganged about him underneath the spready sycamore— *I did not mean to kill the nigger!*

When he was tired of hearing himself say it, tired of waiting for what did not come—the Negroes to say, "Of course you did not"—he told them all to go to Hell and then jabbed the knife into the tree and strode toward the kitchen. He had on hog-killing clothes, wool and muslin with a skin over-jacket, and they were bloody with the gore of man or pig—I could not tell where one stain started and the next began. He came blowing in hard through the door, like a tempest raging into an open window.

"Tell Lazy to come clean that Goddamn baby," he shouted to Clarice, though she was in a flurry at the zinc fixing his wash. Clarice, Bertha, and Suzy had been cooking cracklings in big pots by the hearth, jumping back now and again when the grease spit, calling me frequently to taste one while it was hot, promising to fry a nice pig tail as my treat for helping. The frying was all I could smell, that and the sausage and thyme and sage, but Father said, as he stripped to the waist, that the air was "pluperfectly putrid with baby doings." He announced an intention to gag, said he had not sired a child to sit around in his own filth. I thought it odd that a man so profane as to swear with such habitual ease in front of his family and servants, a man who might have been killing hogs for three days, who had just flourished a bloody knife, would not simply line out in direct language what little John had done in his breeches. But he was unaccustomed to the workings of the house, the perpetual inevitabilities of soiled baby napkins and dropped jelly jars, flies in the milk, mealworms in the flour. He was an interloper, in fact, in the kitchen. As I studied him, I made a note to myself that the hearth was the only feature of the room larger than he. He could have fit in it, racked on a spit.

Before Father had entered, I had been about to change John myself and fetch the water to rinse his napkin, for Lazy, his nurse, demurred, butted her head against all grades of work with her sweetgum-snapping obstinacy, had to be haggled with over every issue of the day. And so now, with Lazy doing her job and Father holding his arms over the zinc and telling the Negress to fumigate the baby, I patted at the sausage, watching and listening to Father and Clarice with great interest, for she was the only person, Mother included, who was not afraid of him. She had known him when he was worth two acres, then two hundred, then two thousand, and she knew where his heart ached. Because she kept his confidentials to herself, she held sway over him. And plus, she was free, not bound to him by any shackle other than her own unwillingness to tell all of her mind. In rare and necessary bursts, she would say that there was something to tell. We should know that, simply know. I heard her confide to someone once, when I was just old enough to know that what I heard was of worth to me, "I knew Mr. Tate when he was what he was before he became what he is. I know why he wears stockings two weeks to a time, and I know a fat budget of stories, oh yes, oh yes."

My sweet mother was far down the river road at the Carters' on what she called an escape holiday. On these three and four days a year when the house was overrun by dank odors of chitterlings on a boil, when Negroes threw lungs out from the barn for the foxhounds that howled when the ground was empty, Mother would run. These days were not pleasant for her, so she would take off with a Scottish wrap, a huge satchel, and her Negress in a basket phaeton, driving herself at top speed the five miles to Shirley Plantation, for she loved a winter wind. The Carters always slaughtered the week before we did, and so the meat would have been put away, the grounds cleared, field Negroes back in their settlement. Life there would have returned to the sort of order that Mother admired. She loved quietude. For her, there was nothing like hours on end of no hurry, when coming holidays would be planned with ease and joy. Alice Tate lived her each day as it came to her, never thinking the next might be better than this. "Live today for memory tomorrow and for pleasure now. Always," was the motto she spoke whenever a child wanted to take leave of the moment. She did live well at the Carters', so far away from Father in the kitchen. Mother and the many Carter sisters plugged clove oranges for Christmas, needlepointed, tatted, and, when weary, perused *Godey's Lady's Book* until sangaree time. I never begrudged Mother her pleasure there, all of which she would recount to me on her return. If ever one is deserving, it is a woman of nightly-broken spirit. It is a miracle that he did not destroy her utterly. To look at her, to see her tatting by the fire, to see her weep as she took the Eucharist, filled us all with her goodness.

So Mother was not there to pull me away from grown-talk, from Father's ranting. As he was washed, he repeated his yard remarks. Clarice stopped swabbing his arms and said, "Now listen, Mr. Tate, you need to say who it was. You know he gots a name. Ever'body gots a name. Just tell me who it is laying there gone."

"Who the devil knows it?" Father was not impatient with her for asking. He sounded as if he honestly wished he could have given her an answer.

"If I have to go out there and see who it is," she said, "I'm liable to be wicked. You need to talk to me."

He swiveled his head around on his neck, slumped his shoulders like a child set on the verge of a whine, like my sister Maureen when Clarice or Mintus, the butler-cum-driver, would catch her eating cornmeal, to which she was a-frenzied addicted. "I don't know, Clarice," he said. "He was a bluegum, just a Goddamn bluegum, loudmouthed field nigger. It hardly matters. Except for the money I've lost on him, it just does not matter."

"It does matter to somebody." Father remained indifferent, would not reply. Clarice splashed the box lye into the water, left him there with his arms coated in a burning lather, and went to the door to holler, "Who it be? Who it be dead?"

A young woman trotted to her and whispered in her ear. Clarice told her to wait while she cut her a slab of souse to take to the Negroes who had not stopped work at the five or six boiling kettles in the yard; they had to keep the fires stoked and stir the roiling fat with boat paddles. When she went back to Father she did not help him. I understood, as did he, that he was to suffer the humiliation of cleaning the rest of the blood from his arms and chest and all the way up to his beard. And then she would make him wash that, too, himself, all because he had belittled one of her own, not only by the heinous act of simple killing but also by not knowing his name, not admitting that he might have had enough humanity to have been given one at birth or at sale. In Father's mind, though, the dead man had never been born but merely bought into existence.

I knew that Clarice would be handling Father, manipulating the fate of his day, something I was highly curious to see. I was already of a mind that studied the manner in which people of varying classes dealt with one another, and I was rarely a witness to Father's daytime doings, being by myself reading or at other plantations much of my time. And so I had even more reason to sit by that hearth with my table of sausage and thyme and sage before me and mix and pat and listen without making a mite of sound. I felt that I was watching an exciting drama, not at all like the sleepy-making plays that we had seen on the Grand Tour.

Clarice ripped a piece of the muslin we had used to make bouquets garnis, and thrust it at him, motioned for him to dry his arms, saying, "He had a name and it was Jacob. He had a woman on Mr. Throckmorton's place, too. She's a goomer and will be over here to you screeching, soon as word hits. It gone hit soon and what you like to call a nigger mess will come calling and you'll be out there with a sackful of pennies to hand her if you smart, on account of goomer with a kilt man is a mean flora-dory. She'll burn the house down with you in it and then jump in the river and die laughing." Although Father did not believe in trick Negroes, he did rid himself of them as soon as they were found out, for they fomented fear in some of the others, those who did not attend Bruton Parish Chapel on Sunday afternoons. Whenever I heard that one was on Seven Oaks, I policed the grounds for piled bones, checked the thresholds for hairballs, huddled as I wondered aloud about the tale, my pet nightmare, of the Negress who had squirted chloroform through a keyhole and killed five babies.

Clarice would have kept ruminating on our demise had the baby not started crying because Lazy had wrapped his napkin too tight. He was running loose and ricketing about, pulling at his pants, headed for my table, thus the nearby fire. Clarice snatched him up, went over and slapped Lazy. Then Clarice retied his cloth. Father watched her activity in seeming astonishment that she could run a kitchen and his life with such a deft hand. He seemed eager, too, for her to tell him how to thwart this trick Negress from setting up an irksome and maybe even dangerous roost of incantation and lighter wood on our front landing.

"If I had meant to kill him, I would go right now to Throck-morton and find the woman and make a peace, but I——"

Clarice stopped him. "Oh, let me hide and watch you go give

that woman a sack of pennies. Ha!" She resumed drying his chest with the rag piece, as if his heart needed to be massaged back into use. She dried and talked, both hurriedly. Father was caught in a sort of standing-still hysteria, waiting for Clarice, who could crawl all over him and leave him hassling, the only woman he would allow a riposte, to tell him how to manage an affair. She finished with him and told him to go upstairs and dress and not to wake the twins, who took late-morning refreshers. The twins were Henry and Randolph, age three. After Whately, who was seventeen, came me, then six-year-old Maureen, then the twins, and finally baby John, who was eighteen months. Three of us were dead. And so up Father went, and I asked, for that was my nature, not to push but to inquire at critical passes in a story that was playing before me, "What is going to happen now? Is somebody going to kill Father? Is somebody going to cut our throats?"

"Chee-chee-chee," Clarice laughed, for she did so between tiny teeth. "Your father did that, and now you worry on it coming back." She armed up the bucket of water and threw it out the door, scattering the chickens. I dared to go to the zinc when she came back in to clean it out. I told her I was indeed worried, yes, because that is what things did. They came back.

"And if they do not come in the night to Mother and my brothers and sister and me, won't the law come, won't the constable come and take Father and make him walk the thirteen steps?" I tried to finish, to say "hang from the neck until you are rendered dead," but I could not, for I had attached myself to her ample middle, and I was howling. She did not stroke my hair, did not soothe me, for she was not made of such gentle temper, and she was not at that moment of any temper that would admit a simpering white girl concerned about her Lord's retribution when it was her kind, her family of racial kin, who had been killed by a man she had seen grow into hardness and venomous spite since he was a boy. She admitted to me later that she had herself whipped him with a wire brush because he had torn the shell off a live turtle to have a Lancelot shield.

She told me to straighten up and find some paper for a note to send Mintus with to Mr. Throckmorton; her hands were wet. I wrote: "Please let Jacob's woman come here for the time being. I'll look out for her. Clarice." I ran the note to the main house and gave instruction to Mintus.

When I returned to the kitchen, Clarice said, "Come on 'way from here with me," poking her finger toward the barn. I said nothing but followed her out past where the Negroes had been rendering lard and cooking cracklings. It was a dreary walk and cold, the barn a world away from the main house, a true journey. Only the girl stirring Brunswick stew, the one who knew the dead man's name, was left to tell, when asked by Clarice, that everyone had gone to see after the trouble. Her mama, the girl said, had told her not to leave the stew, which was annually the Negroes' treat at hog-killing days. Clarice told her to put out the other fires. "You ruin his lard, burn down this place, and see who Mr. Tate kills next time!"

The barn was made of butter brick, as were the main house

and all the dependencies, built by Germans Father had brought from Potsdam and berated into finishing the entire place in six months. They liked the weather and moved house to the James, staying not with us but with Mr. Carter, who was the pink of kindness and courtesy. Surely the Negroes, the thirty-odd of them who were gathered in that barn, wished that Mr. Carter had charge of them that day. We had to step over carcasses and pooled blood the color of calf's liver to get to where Clarice pointed out a clean place on the floor. The Negroes were in awe that a house servant had come onto their territory, and they made room for her, knowing, they must have, that she could tell them what to do now.

"Why y'all ain't got nothing over him? Cover him up, fool," she directed a young man. While he found some burlap and placed it over the body, she asked questions until she had heard enough answers, which they gave her with their mixture of field-hand English and Gullah, most being original Guinea Negroes I recognized as those Father had bought in Charleston in one lump the year previous. Negroes did not all look alike to me, the way I understood they were supposed to. I knew them by the quality of their faces, the way they held themselves, their voices, the same way I knew anyone on the James. From my earliest days I had heard Father's voice boom from the back door, where grounds help came with their needs, "Who is this talking to me?" and then I would hear some measure of what I happened to hear once: "Missa Tate, I's Matthew, same's as I always was."

As the men spoke, I regarded the body beneath the burlap. I

had not seen it before it was covered, but I had ample imagination to feature a near-severed head, for Father's hog-killing butcher knife was mighty, and blood soaked down to the man's waist. The certain unreality of the event was now protecting me from my earlier fear of retribution. I heard as though through water the collection of them saying, the best I could comprehend of their language *mirepoix*, that the man had been holding a pig for Father to kill, and he had had something to say about how Father should try for a cleaner bleed, that he was spoiling good meat. "And Missa Tate, he be lis'nen and lis'nen, and you could see him mad, and then he be saying, 'I be gone kill you, nigger, if you don't be quiet,' and that nigger, he be talking and talking, and Missa Tate, he say, 'Who you be gone tell me my bidness?' and, 'Don't I already tole you to shut up?' They be talking on, and going back and forth, and then Missa Tate, he be looking like he meant fo' the pig, but he reach up and swipe Jacob."

"And that is the truth?" Clarice demanded of them all as she walked around the body, inspecting its girth and dimension and ruminating about what to do.

They all nodded. Several of them joined in to say that Jacob had a woman and that she would go crazy, and Clarice told them she already knew and to hush. Then she turned to me as if I had set off a fire bell. She had to know exactly and immediately what I was doing in a cold barn without a wrapping. Did I not have better sense and it freezing? I thought for a moment, interpreting her, translating her. Then I knew why she had brought me out there, knew I was to perform for the good of my family. I was to right then call her Auntie, thus showing the Negroes that at least one Tate had respect for a Negro, and I was to say something on the order of I supposed I was ignorant, thus showing them that a Tate could be humble. When I had spoken, saying, "It is silly for me to be out of doors at all, Auntie. May I run back to the house?" Clarice snapped, "I reckon you might oughten to stay out here and freeze a minute," before she whipped back around to address the curious, who, by their sympathetic eyes and the way they were studying me, seemed to have noted that I might be witless and therefore perhaps innocent enough to spare the horror of their appearing in the night, gathered on the front lawn with blazing torches, rabbling for Father, breathing threats of slaughter. I set up a coughing frenzy, sounded perfectly consumptive.

She said to the Negroes, "Pay no mind to her. She just Mr. Tate oldest girl. Stays sick. He's got nine children. Six living and three dead. And what I say 'bout this one, *he* dead? I say, Let it go. I ain't saying to let it go on account of he had a big mouth and the world's better off. No. I say when Mr. Tate sends rat bait and flour and whole cloth and shoe leather out to y'all this evening, and he will, y'all take it and be glad to have it and send word back about how pleased you are. And next time he come out here, and it won't be today, he might act like he's king, and you let him go on and don't say nothing, and sure to God don't act like nobody wants to stand forth and hold him a hog. Everybody act like they want to help. Let him get his hogs put up. Jacob, he will keep cool off till Saturday. Then bury him, and don't be a fool over it. Just stick him in the ground and wait until Mr. Tate cools off himself before you drink whiskey and bang a pot and break up dishplates for the grave. Then somebody send somebody to the kitchen and I'll give you some side meat, and see if that don't go 'round plenty. See if all of what I told you don't make you feel better, 'cause you know what won't?"

Clarice waited big-eyed for them, dumbstruck as they were with her battery of instruction, to figure out exactly what would not make them feel better. I remember listening hard, too. With no answer, she continued. "I know what, and what it is is being taken to the burg in January and having yourselves up to the block, and having the man say, 'These niggers they all right, but they mad on account of they saw somebody get his throat cut and they can't get over it.' There's worse in the world than Mr. Tate. You smart niggers know it. Then see who has you. Somebody with a mean white man who don't own the place and all he's got on his mind is whup, whup, whup. Don't care nothing 'bout the money you folks is worth. Be proud to what you is worth. I ain't worth nothing but all I am. Chee-chee-chee. All I got to say else is keep yourselves to yourselves and pray Mr. Tate from now on he does the same. Now do his toes."

I was amazed then, perfectly stupefied at what they did. They formed a neat queue and, one by one, walked by, leaned over, and touched Jacob's toes. No, they did not take his shoes off, for there were no shoes. Of course, no shoes. They did not want to be molested by his ghost, so, without a word, they went about preventing it, the younger ones touching him quickly, as though he were afire, the older ones pausing, sighing or shaking their heads, all bowed down with trouble. When one glanced at me and murmured something I did not understand, Clarice poked him on and told him I would get the message. If they lingered too long, Clarice hurried them along in the same annoyed way she rushed recalcitrant goats through the gate. Otherwise, she stood silently while they moved by her, and when they were through, she said, "Now finish all these animals you got in the pens. Get with the killing, and I'm going to take this Miss ole baby girl to the kitchen and try up some lard that somebody might leave out by the dairy tonight." Then she laughed her "Chee-chee-chee," grabbed my arm, and pulled me out of the barn.

"What did he say?" I asked when we were about to take back up our jobs.

"What did he who say?" she asked, separating a head of sausage and stripped sage and thyme for me to work with.

"The man with the message." I was worried that she had forgotten, that I had lost some valuable chunk of information, and my genius already seemed to lie in the direction of finding out things I was not ready to absorb. I had oh so many bits of ideas waiting for the years to align into some pattern of logic, to be synthesized so that by my adulthood I would have what I often termed to my children as quick-marrow, the living sense, the core of knowledge about the way the world works.

"Oh, he said he's sorry about your papa," she whispered, and then she popped my hand, not in a way to hurt me, but to tell me not to mox in the sausage without washing. But I was not going to the pump without hearing her say why I should be sorry about my father, even though I knew full well why. I had to hear her say it. I wanted to remember in her words what I knew to be a coming sorrow. That way I knew the words would keep better. They would be of some definite and direct use to me, for she was a supreme pragmatist, and I had my mother's bent toward daydreaming. Albeit I was a curious daydreamer, and there is a good in that, but we must put to purpose what we find, even if we use hanks of poetry, as I have done, to soothe and entertain us in our old age. That is how Clarice lived, with objectives, little missions for her days. And so what was I thinking just then of Father, of what she would say? That he could not help being a hard man. I lost myself for a moment, remembering the witching-hour voices through the walls, the sounds of Mother's pleadings. Clarice saw me thinking hard and stopped me.

"You don't worry, Emma Garnet," she said softly. "All that man meant was he's sorry you have to see. That's all. He's just sorry you have to know."

She left me alone and told Lazy to take John to the main house for his sleep. While she worked humming by Bertha at the hearth, I washed my hands and went back to my job. I did not think, See what? Know what? All was evident to me. See my Father and know him. And so 1842 was the year the sausage had an odd addition, though no one but me would have known, for it was rolled around and around in my hands, sprinkled with thyme and sage, and bound whole by tears. *He said he's sorry about your papa. He had a name and it was Jacob.*

t w o

In the days after the killing, Father maintained a solemn phiz, keeping mainly to his rooms, sending Mintus on several trips to the burg to fetch books that he had ordered from Vickery and Griffith's stall, as part of his campaign to master Italian and German. For a hard man, he did have a love of language that confounded those who feared him. On our trip to Europe he had said he felt like a "bumbling foreigner" because he could not comprehend the languages, and he could not tolerate the inadequacy he felt on the sunny afternoon we spent floating down the Rhine as he nodded agreement at everything an elderly German gentleman said to him. *"Ja, ja."* A nod to the perplexed man. Then more, *"Ja, ja."* So while he hid from the Negroes and the varieties of ways they might have looked twice at him, admitting only Mintus and Clarice to assure him that the year's meat had been well put up, the Negro buried, his woman no trouble, he read aloud Dante and Goethe.

He had that accentuated vanity that a self-made, self-educated man carries about with him, but he had as well what I now see as a plain jealousy that he was not given the same opportunities he had given my brother to go off to school, where, he told Whately, "pointy-headed professors can make a stale-bread living teaching you the Latin I learned at midnight after I'd come in from yanking these first hundred acres out of the ground, and you don't appreciate it? You have the stupid singularity of mind to sit there and tell me that it is inconsequential to you to learn and make something of yourself so you can have something to be proud of? Are you an idiot? Did I raise an idiot?" Oh, the voice so loud in that room. "Did I?" *No, Father. You did not raise an idiot. I love my books. What you fail to see is that I do. I'll pay the debts. I'll pay.*

Until the shame of the killing wore off, and that took about a week, Father came down the stairs only to eat, and then he did not lead his usual table-talk, designed, he said, to aid in the flow of digestive juices. No, for good, he ate and left the table, giving us the first respite in years of harangues. Mother actually chattered, described patterns she and I would cut for spring dresses, delighting me by listing what I could wear to this or that birthday party, how prettily an eyelet collar would set off my face. She knew which Baltimore merchants sold the best grade of grosgrain, and she told me how she and the Carter ladies had drawn intricate pictures of skirts and blouses, and maybe, if I was a good girl, she said with a wink, she and I could wear matching dresses to the soon-upon-us party of my friend Sally Willcox, and there, since it was so very far, we would need to spend the week. Maybe Whately could take a few extra days off for the holidays and stay there with us. Would not that be grand? Oh, how she prattled on and was happy, and I wanted to know more about her, what she had been like as a girl, and less about my father as a grown man upholding the tyranny of his favored God, that of the Old Testament, not my favored, the God of forgiveness and light.

What we usually endured—what Mother and I, Whately when he was home, listened to—was a tension-making oration on the Protestant, that is Episcopal, work ethic, and the glory of life on the James as the reflection of God's splendor. Father would turn his whole big body to whomever he was addressing, and if the stepping-babies had been allowed in the dining room, I often wondered whether he might have offered them early lessons on our family's chosen status as recipients of blessings, "rained down," he would declaim, "even when this country is in economic chaos. Buy nothing save with true money. Owe no one. Live by that, and leave God's green Earth a wealthy man." We heard that oration nightly.

I dreaded when Father looked my way, moving his chair closer. I would think quickly of some acceptable reply to whatever catalogue of atrocities he might furnish me—willfulness, treachery, conspiring with Whately to make Father's dotage a horror. He sometimes accused me of being "in league with your buffoon of a brother," but more often I heard that I was taking preliminary though calculated steps outside the woman's sphere and was destined, if I did not work harder at my china painting and pianoforte, to be an old maid in the home of the more sensible Maureen, who did not keep company with the help. Maureen, who was six at the time of the killing and not yet allowed at the adult table, was fair of face and not plagued—as was I—by ambition for things beyond a gentlelady's ken. I was, as Father suspected, too eager to know matters that would do me no good in making a marriage that would be, for the both of us, propitious and prestigious.

After Father finished delineating my weaknesses, for which I always regarded as the acceptable reply a simple, straightforward apology, the kind he admired, he usually turned to Whately, when he was at home, and to Mother when he was away, criticizing her son by proxy. My stomach knotted around his allegations and suspicions that he swore could be substantiated by any barkeep in Lexington, where Whately attended Washington College. Mother sent me up to my room when Father became over-invigorated, and on the way I would collect John or one of the twins, for rocking a baby gave me comfort, still does. With John or Henry or Randolph, their bodies freshly dressed for night, I could listen to their first words, help them make more, words that would drown out Father's noise. When the fighting sounded ominous, when Father's rage over a predictable range of irritants, from Whately to Mother's coddling of the servants to the state of his gout, was not of the class that would expend itself and leave Mother be, I would knock on their bedroom door and, hugging a baby to my hip, say that he felt hot. The first time I play-acted, Father stood aside and let Mother come to us. When, in the nursery, she could detect no fever, she showed me how to hold my palm on the baby's neck, where true heat rests, so I would know better next time.

I said, "Mother, I already know better. I had to stop Father. That is why I came."

Taking a moment to regard my ingenuity, she said, "Come again."

That was all I needed to hear to make me pad down the hall and present a baby to her. When the children grew older I would take their hands and lead them, drowsy as they were from their nursery beds, to Mother's room. Father would moan that "a man cannot finish saying his piece without a sick child interrupting," and then he would retire. Mother always thanked me and put the children back to sleep. In my dream-fantasies of those bad nights, I was a member of the burg's fire brigade, running back and forth to save calves from a burning pasture.

Although the supper-table strife did not occur every evening, the episodes spoiled my hopes for any pleasant times we might have passed had Father been capable of seeing that a healthy family was a greater heart's blessing than the material attributes that marked our life—the rich, alluvial soil, the bounty of slaves, the fat squabs in the dovecote, the icehouse on the river, Thomas Sully's portrait of Mother, the elegant Arabian horses, the loyal, silent manservant who slept on a hemp pallet by Father's bed, who shoved Father's gouty feet into his boots each morning and removed them at evening, the sixty-foot marble-tiled ballroom on the west side of the house, a room that was not, until my coming-out, put to merry use save by little wild playmates from up and down the river who delighted in taking turns at running and sliding into the paneled wall, hitting just underneath the Gainsborough that Father had bought from a gentleman—I cannot to this day name him—who had not hoarded money like salt during the Revolution, who had not courted interests in the legislature and marled his land and dammed ponds on neighbors' borders. When this man went under, Father was there to catch not him but his things. He took three Negroes and Mintus to the southeast banks of the river, where the man's estate lay, and I see them in my eyes now, returning from the legalized pillage, another Panic sale. Mintus was in the back of the wagon, reclined on a brocade chaise like Cleopatra up on her burnished throne, sleeping as usual, while about him sat the three Negroes with as many paintings as they could hold. Romulus, the wheelwright, gripped, as if under life-threat by Father, Copley's study of his younger brother with a pet flying squirrel. As for the Copley, Father did not have to admire a man's politics to lust after his art.

When Mother expressed dismay at having "disappointed paintings" in her home, Father told her that he was merely filling in gaps he had left "yawed open" when he had bought like a crazed man in Paris, while simultaneously enabling "that poor blighter to pay his tax assessment and stay shy of the workhouse." Then he handed her Mr. Wedgwood's Portland vase, saying, "Find somewhere noticeable for it," before he ushered the other pictures into the house and directed their immediate hanging. During his Saturday-afternoon segar rounders, he would escort a legislator from the provinces, which was to Father anywhere west of Charlottesville, through the grand foyer and on into the ballroom, where he would gesture toward the Gainsborough with the solemnity of a country rector pointing out the grave site of a beloved lord. Father would need comments, questions, but as I saw happen when I peeked in so many times, the visitor would stand before the huge painting, frozen, perplexed, ready at that moment to hand over all powers of Commonwealth government to a gentleman who could see into the soul of Art. Once, though, that one time that sent me rollicking out to the kitchen to shout for Clarice, he was showing off the Gainsborough, describing the deft brushwork and so forth, when his guest had a question yet did not want to interrupt.

"But no, please," Father begged.

The man wanted to know one thing only, and that was about the other painting, the Copley portrait.

"Yes," Father droned, and pulled on his segar. He knew, I know he knew, that the man would want to know how much it might be worth, discounting the hard times and the value of a dollar. Then Father could mumble something about a recent appraisal, whisper the price in his ear, and see him fall back with wonder of the order reserved for sights of shooting stars and newborn babies.

The man faltered, then finally found his words: "How in the Hell did they get that squirrel to sit still?"

Father could have struck the man down, ridiculed his naiveté, cut his throat, for I know what he was capable of when challenged, but he knew his name as a politician would not withstand anything other than a jolly, "Well, they swiped his arse with molasses!"

They had a fine laugh, which Father well knew would carry over with the spittoon brigade, but he was probably wishing the swain had never darkened his door and reminded him, for Clarice was the only person allowed to do so, that he had not always had great paintings or high walls to hang them on or Negroes to drive the nails, that twenty years earlier he himself might have asked similar questions about the squirrel. Rarely, when provoked, Mother could make him face himself, but the penalties, the ones I heard him pronounce on her, were worse than her having to listen to him crash his way through those homes of the Quality through which she moved with the welcome and ease of one of their own.

I knew of her origins before I suspected his, for when I went with her to the Carters', she did not knock. She went in cheerfully, calling, "Woo-hoo!" and Negro and white, mingled as though thoroughly confidential, whished around us, taking us in to them. If Mr. Carter was about, he would ask how Tate was faring, and Mother would chirp, "Fine!" Then we would sit around the quilting loom, the other girls and I given bits to practice with on our laps, and I would hear how thrilled they were to be alive. Mother, at first tentative, would soon lose care of her troubled son, of her grasping husband, and she would come check my stitches and say, "Oh, Emma Garnet, aren't we due this very good time?" Mr. Carter did not enter and curse, did not stomp his displeasure upstairs, did not say "nigger," a word that was expected of the coarse, never mentioned by the gentility, who said "Auntie" or "Uncle," "the servants," "Cuffee," or "the Negroes." And certainly never "slave," though our world would have died in a day without them. I have learned through time and the War and eighty-five people to the count dying in my lap that we cannot name what we fear we have made of our lives. For "slave," there was "servant." For the War-dead, the newspaper would head the column "Those Passed at Manassas," "Those Passed at Vicksburg," until my husband Quincy demanded of the editor that he stop "slopping silly words on the condition of death and disfigurement that we see in this hospital daily, more cold, hard faces of dead than you will ever see in your nightmares. So stop. Mothers and fathers need to know that an end has come, and they do. They are not stupid as you make them to be. The finality of death is said in its name."

What I do have of my father's spirit, of what I feared I would inherit, the need to look and not hide my eyes, helped me through the War, but I would not have gotten through, my sanity undisturbed, without my husband, Quincy Lowell—never without Quincy, who though born in Boston of a famous man did not hesitate to marry the daughter of an infamous one. If he and I had faltered, men whose hands we were holding would have died with nobody praying fast on their case at that moment when the spirit leaves and we are, this Earth's lot of us, lonely. The Gainsborough and the Copley eventually came to me as well, and when Quincy and I one day could not look at them another moment without hearing Father rant about what lunatics the "entire incestuous stew of Lowells" were, as if every Carter and Lee and Landon were not of history cousin and uncle to one another, we freighted them off to the museum in Boston. There all my dear Lowell family can go see the pictures and try to figure how a man such as my father could have found such things of beauty. I have wanted to tell them, but cannot, that the art came to them off the back of a broken man. I am too ashamed, but now this will be the telling. He did have some eye for art, such as in the selection of Sully for Mother's portrait. It is here over my mantel now, watching me in what I feel, more and more, to be my last days, last afternoons.

All these memories, fighting for the right to be heard, to speak an uproar over the stillness of this winter day. I envision Father surveying the walls of the long foyer hallway, his favorite and most populated gallery of ancestors who did not belong to us. He enjoyed the hallway also because it was where visitors might first see that he had in his safekeeping the treasures that others were forced to yield because of the Panic. Art was in his trust. Family legacies from Scotland and England, porcelain that had traveled from Sèvres to Boston to Williamsburg, were arranged on our marble-top tables by the time the banks opened again. He would stand before the fireplace in the drawing room and strike a pose. *Whately, if you were not destined to be such a wastrel, you could take all this right now. By God, if I had a son I could bank on, he could have it. I might leave it to Mintus or Clarice. They have more appreciation in their thumbs. No counting on Henry and Randolph. Born weak, barely breathing, sorry fate. Sad to say for their dear mother.*

My mother's being in the room did not seem to count for him, and she would slip away, go to her bed, fall across the counterpane and cry. Clarice, whose genuine appreciation was not misplaced, for she had laid it at the feet of a woman who loved her as another woman, simply as another good woman, would hurry up to her with a cool cloth. I would hear Mother's sadness as Father intoned the evening's lesson from the Prayer Book, and he might stop now and again to ask me whether I planned to inherit my mother's constant state of the blues. The question always alarmed me, for if I inherited anything from her, was it with any plan at all? Could I control who I was to be by taking this or that from the array of inherited offerings, the way Mother and I chose items from the menu at the eating house in Washington? Could I be less him and more her? Was I waiting to "turn out a fool," a phrase Father used to decry how Whately's mind and features were configuring themselves? And was I not already somebody? Maybe not yet? I would lie in bed and touch my face, better to feel who I was, and I would graze the inside of my arms, sense that particular chill, and wonder whether I would spend my years weeping for Mother and Whately, apologizing to

Father, loving Negroes in secret, saying that I broke the rake handle to save Romulus from another slapping. Or, I thought as I fell down in the dark, I could be kidnapped by Transylvanian Gypsies and buried alive. Father would pay a fortune's ransom, sell the precious Gainsborough, convey land and people, bankrupt himself for the child he had once in a time jostled in his lap and called (as my mother confided) "my first baby girl, my first little woman." In those early days I gathered the impression that those tender words spelled my name.

Young as I was at the time of these remembrances, I felt an ancient history, a pull back, back to wherever Father had been born, to the way he was raised, into details of his story that were not mentioned except at Thanksgiving, when he included "Martha, Luther, Dodges, and that villain, that incubus Bartlett and that sibilant sow Beatrice" in an after–Prayer Book blessing that would send them all to Hell. Mother would put her hand on his vulnerably shaking one and, as she did at every meal, say, "Thank you, my Lord, for the Negroes. And bless my dear husband, on whose back our lives are made. Amen. Whately, Emma Garnet, up straight." I close my eyes this afternoon and see the dining room hung with aubergine velvet curtains, hear the clinking of Waterford. Then: *Clarice! Yessir, Mr. Tate? Bring me some more biscuits! You ain't et them ones yet! Eat what you got. Bring them on, Clarice. I might not eat them all right now, but you know I like to see them before me. Yessir, Mr. Tate, you ain't gone 'round hungry in a long time. Shut up, Clarice!*

Had Whately and I not survived meals with him, which despite the oft-repeated strophes and antistrophes never became routine, we might have been able to listen to Father's ardent prayers and his fervent thanks and dream ourselves into thinking he was indeed the just and upright man we had read of in the newspapers, the champion of a lower tariff, a leading light in the struggle against the electoral college, which he believed would undermine the authority of the populace. And he was, for the public, a man of some political acumen who enjoyed a reputation from Baltimore to Savannah, the poles of the universe so measured by Southern planters. Father was a fire-eater, predicting in a wild and full-reported speech from the floor of the legislature first the Panic, then a string of calamities and foolish elections of "absurd nonentities" who would destroy the doctrine of states' rights and usher in changes that would see "niggers licking pencils at the polling places." The Carters must have put their heads in their hands when he shouted out loud "niggers" in the halls of Jefferson, who owned slaves but, as Roberta Lee told me once, "did not like it a bit."

I remember Father saying that the Virginia Whigs were devils, their leaders intriguers who lacked the brains to keep their stories straight. Well, he knew how to take charge, by God. Mr. Jefferson's ironies did not challenge him, annoyed him for certain; he took what he needed from the *Notes on the State of Virginia* and left the rest alone. Father's frequent correspondents—in the main South Carolinians with ultra views—had pushed him to offer for governorship of the Commonwealth in 1840, but he would not. He dilated in the newspapers on his desires to effect change in the South as a common man, an ordinary citizen. During these difficult days when the North's insistence on the damnable tariff had corroded the morale of all Southerners, he was needed at home, as were all men. Yes, he would remain a force in "the workings of my beloved Commonwealth," but he did not need the "head-miseries and back-stabbings that go along with high office." He would be "first and foremost" a God-fearing family man. One editor praised him for the tenor of his speech, his "able and characteristic honesty and humor." I could see our neighbors reading that and howling the sentences aloud to one another, then stopping, shaking their heads, astonished that Mother could endure the arrant fraud of life with him. I remember reading those words myself, over and over. They could not be missed, for Father had pasted them with some of Clarice's gum arabic to the front of the family album and pointed me to them, saying, "See how a great man declines his office." Then he strode off magnificently, leaving me to read alone and think, Who is he? What is this man? After more thinking than a child should do without fond guidance, Mother having taken to bed with her own sick head-misery, for that is sometimes how she had to endure the arrant fraud, I concluded that my father was a dangerous man. That was two years before the killing. As said, I knew my father was a liar.

Our new neighbor, General Harrison, was taking a drubbing in the newspapers when it was made known that the same man who ate off gold chargers and scented his whiskers with French perfume was actually from quite modest means and had lucked into quick wealth. Although Father despised the General's politics, he softened to learn that a man whose taste, save for the perfuming, he admired and emulated at Seven Oaks—with his addition of chinaberry trees sent from the territories and the chargers that arrived one day from Philadelphia, as well as other accoutrements of a well-turned life—and who might become his compatriot was not to the manner born. Father took frequent rides to the Harrison home, Berkeley, but usually he was back before long, saying the General had entertained "all his chief notions on the method of this nation's recovery, admired them despite his Unionist flappings," and so forth. Mother need not have listened and asked interesting questions about the feminine aspects of the home, but she did. She was that generous and forgiving. And then on the day that Mr. Harrison composed his inaugural address at Berkeley, Father insinuated himself into the president-elect's library and, according to gossip passed along the Negro wires, offered to rewrite his speech. The Harrison Negroes, who were accustomed to their master's cold regard that connoted contempt, reminded the General that he had, according to Clarice years later, "something on the order of one thing or another" to tend to immediately. In Mintus's memory, a Negro burst into the room and reported that the General's mule had her head stuck in a fence. Father must have felt unmasked when he was abandoned for a mule. General Harrison left a chambermaid to show him to the door. His embarrassment at having been dashed off by a man who could have expected no good due to come of Samuel Tate sitting in on his inaugural address writing, sitting in his library at all, soon belied itself. By the time President Harrison died, a month after taking the oath, Father held him in the lowest contempt. "Bastard thought he could out-will a chill wind. See here now, I reckon, what the temperature is in Hell." Yes, I thought, Father, see here.

three

I have always maintained my own opinions. I am fortunate to have married a man of a splendid liberality of thought who gloried to hear me speak my mind on any subject. Quincy and I were in voice with each other. Together of a still night we would sit on the veranda and discuss things on a range of importance from his inventive ideas for the ligation of femoral arteries to my sadness over the root rot caused by a servant's soaking my prized African violet. Some evenings the turns of phrase might be sheerly of our love and the faith we shared in a union that had withstood Father's outrage at our leave-taking from the wedding celebration, the anger and my final vision of Mother in our wake. While Herodotus put out the streetlamps, Quincy would unpin my hair and comb it with his fingers, listening to me retrieve memory, and then, as they do now, memories would breed in the wee hours, and there seemed no stopping the accretion of past wrongs that did and did not go reconciled and exorcised.

Even in those early years of our marriage, he helped me drag the past into the present, and when I could not maneuver amongst the ruins, he held me steady and helped me step along the roughest places. When I stumbled and fell, he took my matters in hand, and I felt relief wash over me like the lavender water Clarice would pour over me in calming baths. By Quincy's end, he had taken care of everything. I suppose now I am left with ghosts of memories, remnants of trails that lead back through the War, past cedar-kneed swamps, past Williamsburg and the Bruton Parish cemetery, down the river road to Seven Oaks. I have closed the curtains against the harsh late-afternoon light that assaults my eyes, for it is in dim light that I see best, mind and eye. Then I have before me again those nights on the veranda. We did not care that nice people did not sit out all night, that a lady did not let down her hair except in her chambers. Quincy would work a plait steadily and skillfully, entwining loose tendrils, promising as he worked that he would adore me in double measure, once for my merits and again for my mother, who was due love and made to go wanting.

As he berated just-married Quincy and me for "stealing Clarice" on the way out of his house, this the last in his barrage of accusations, Father repeatedly struck his cane at the carriage, and thus brought Mr. Throckmorton and Mr. Custis to restrain him as they might have subdued an outlying bandit. Although they held him tightly, he lunged forward when Mother left the company of her ladies and approached my side of the carriage. She gave me one more kiss and slipped me, out of Father's notice, her velvet purse, wherein later I would find a thousand dollars that she must have obtained from Father's compliant solicitor. She knew I would wonder of its origin, for the note that was wrapped around the bills read, "Please do not ask in a letter. He may see. Mother loves you."

While Mother and I talked, Quincy told Clarice, who sat squirming across from us, crammed as she was in a new costume, that he was about to defend my honor. I had to listen to him and to Mother both. She was explaining to me again how to tell the quality of English tweed, that I should stay away from herringbone, for it swelled the hip regions. When daughters are on the way from home, be it for the afternoon or a lifetime, a loving mother will disguise her agony with trifles. Whenever I left for any event, she would follow me to the door, sometimes out the door and to the carriage, and as I mounted, then would come the catechism. But I did not mind. From her I learned the ways a mother shows care, warns and protects even after a servant has already scrutinized, made a young lady turn this way and that, loosened a bustle, yanked up a bodice. It does not matter who has given the approval. A mother must ask and be told—Do you have your handkerchief? Is your nose still running? Do you have the gum I gave you in case those stockings tear? I should have made you wear lisle. How are the slippers? Perhaps you should have worn the coral Moroccans. Your bun is too low on your neck. Here, sweetheart, let Mother fix it. For a mother not to trot behind a daughter with those questions and concerns is to send a toddling child into the snow with no mittens.

All the while, Quincy was debating the merits of putting Father "on his rumpus" with Clarice. "Is that not what Southern gentlemen do? I can practice on Tate. I have to make my peace with him." He moved to leave the carriage, but Clarice told him that Father would spit in his face.

"Stay still," she said. "Let him fume. You be the one dignified. You know that. Let me think of what to say and let me do it that way."

Quincy took my hand and worried with my ring, leaning forward to hear what Mother was saying. "Are you going to fare?" he asked her.

She told him she would get along very well indeed, that she would see his parents off. She apologized once more for the dinner.

"Mother is not a well lady," he said. He was afraid that the event had addled her permanently.

His parents had spent one night the week previous at Seven Oaks, one meal exposed to Father's wrenched-up performance, before an early-morning departure to the Carters', who must have kept a tally of all the guests and workmen who over the years had used their home as a rescue shelter.

Father, I suppose, felt that he had not adequately abused them during the main course, with his talk of the "thugs" in the White House and of Mr. Calhoun as the "nonpareil blow-hard of this era." Tyler, though a cross-the-river neighbor at Sherwood Forest, was untrustworthy, prey to the dictates of his "nefarious intrigues." Mr. Calhoun spoke for the states' rights and sound reason now that it was to his advantage, "the chief *modus operandi* of the university set."

Dr. Lowell, whose family had witnessed Harvard's birth in 1636 and remained part of the school since, tried to banter with Father, always a mistake, by laughing and saying, "But perhaps the problem is that Calhoun is a Yale man. He is wrong in his newly assumed opinions, but he is brilliant. Would you not concede that?"

Father never conceded anything on the issue of Southerners' rights. "Calhoun," he said, "thinks too much to hold the office of Postmaster. We need men of action. A university man sits costive, cogitating his next move until he petrifies in his seat."

Dr. Lowell ignored the criticism of university training by changing the topic. He told Mother that the tenderloin melted in his mouth. He had never tasted new red potatoes, and Mother offered to have Clarice hash them for breakfast. I glanced at Father, who, angry at the thwarting of a burgeoning argument, seemed in a mind's retreat, scheming his next sortie. When the table-talk hushed for a moment as Mintus cleared the plates, Father held forth. "So is it true," he asked, thumping segar ash into the plate as it arose, "that the ladies of south Boston harness themselves up with buggy straps to be whipped up and down the streets by Negro men?"

Dr. and Mrs. Lowell were mortified. We all were. Quincy rose from the table, with his parents, Mother, and me behind him. Father was calling for Mother to stay where she belonged. "You won't get up and leave this table," he commanded. But she had left already and did not swivel to return. I worried that she would pay, but I was too disorganized in my thinking to regard fully the risk that Mother assumed when she followed two gentlemen who were above responding to a man she knew could speak so coarsely and then fall into sleep with a volume of Voltaire on his chest.

We went into the parlor to repair Mrs. Lowell's reason. Walking down the hallway, she had begun vibrating her head as though her hair were infested with ants. Mother and Quincy adjusted pillows for her on the lounging sofa, her husband saying that his dear wife was not one to weather such calamity. Then he closed the door for her peace. She admired the peacock feathers that Mother and I had arranged as a summer fan for the fireplace, and I knew her mind was furnishing her with an escape from the notion that her son would now be a part of this calamity. In a small opening for truth that her mind allowed her, she said, "Emma Garnet, you and your mother are so pleasant and so very kind, but if there is another place for me to stay, I would appreciate a removal." Mother suggested the Carters, who were known of by Dr. Lowell, who appeared to know every American of eminent worth and intelligence. Both the Lowells and the Carters were of Revolutionary memory. Their Revere services were personal gifts for kindnesses shown the patriot and for courage displayed by brave sons at Saratoga and Trenton, not objects of incessant desire scrambled for in Philadelphia shops, brought home and set on the library mantel and fondled when esteem faltered, or taken up and flourished for impressionable visitors.

Even with the parlor door closed, we could hear Father now laughing uproariously over his feat of degradation. I expected to hear Clarice chastise him, but curiously she did not. She could have asked why he never mistreated his fellow planters, those of heritage equal to the Lowells'. In few words, he needed our neighbors, not for political standing, elected and supported as he was during his legislative terms by those men who used him to speak their fears. The families whose ancestors had disembarked at Jamestown were necessary to complete the picture he craved himself part of, just as he had paid dearly for a visiting, reluctant artist to touch up a fox-hunting scene and place him on the one riderless horse. And then there Father was, all of a sudden on the library wall, in the lead on a race across a Scottish moor, wearing a full kit. He also had the man render a coat of arms of the Tates of Edinburgh, the place he fancied that he belonged to have come from had his family—as I found out from the greasy letters of passage sent to me when one of his kin died—not swabbed steerage of vomit and human refuse from Liverpool to Mr. Oglethorpe's debtors' colony in Georgia.

He must have been stroking a new image of himself as a man of circumstance since the day his father, run out of Georgia, took him to Arlington and hid in the bushes while Father begged at doors for money. Because his father could not stay in the lane, Clarice had to drive the sorry mule cart to Alexandria, where old

Tate could deposit the money at a tavern. Waiting outside in the cold with a buggy blanket over her legs and Father's, she heard as she fed him a supper of fatback and stale biscuits what Father had seen in the few minutes it had taken the servant to fetch some silver. In those moments, the boy had stepped into the foyer and gorged himself. *Shiny things everywhere, Clarice. Things the color of the new purse change the nigger gave me. Flowerdy chairs. And bedclothes all over the floor.* Clarice told him that the bedclothes were rugs, called carpets by nice people. When at Christmas she lovingly wove a rag rug for the side of the straw cot the boy slept on, he pronounced it inferior. It was not like the ones at Arlington. He wanted those, and no rag rug made from the cast-off clothing of the families Clarice did wash for so he could eat meat once in a while would suffice. He threw it in the fire.

Father would have been satisfied with the surfeit of money he accumulated, with the docile servants, the distinguished-looking Mintus, and the handsome wife he acquired with unbelievable gall and calculation from her cotton-factor father in Savannah. He cared not so much what she was right then, graceful but penniless, he cared more for what she could turn out to be, an elegant hostess, a Tidewater lady who could ease his path uphill, impress others when he failed at courting them, apologize for whatever rough edges he did not hack off himself. But the children who followed their marriage were a problem, for young children develop characters and wills and consciences. They buck authority. They want shortbread instead of split peas, and when they are of age, they long for fulfilled dreams instead of dashed wishes.

I had helped Quincy write a letter to Boston before the wedding, a warning missive, but I felt the need to say I was sorry for Father's boorish behavior. His parents were gracious and did not accuse me of overstating Father's charms. Why, I thought, could he not have been gored by a bull at my infancy and left me to be raised by Mother and Clarice? In a moment Clarice herself appeared in the parlor and asked permission to sit awhile with "sane people." Father had danced on her last nerve. She plopped into his favorite chair, not on the short-legged hard stool he made Mintus use, and peeled the apple she had brought with her, teasing Dr. Lowell to bet on whether she could work it all of a piece.

"I got a pumpton tart in there, full of these apples, and when Mr. Tate goes to bed we'll eat it." She assured the Lowells that their Irish girl, the only servant they had brought, was happily eating in the kitchen, where, I knew, Bertha was asking all grades of questions. Lazy, who was putting the children to bed, had interrogated her earlier in the day, fascinated at a white girl in a servant's costume. Clarice had explained that the girl was Irish and instructed them to leave her alone, which they were not about to do. Later I learned that they made her pull up her dress and show them that she was indeed white all over.

Clarice turned to Quincy, who had folded his handkerchief onto his mother's forehead, and said that he would need to wait until she could fetch her some chamomile tea she looked to need. "I go out. Mr. Tate comes in," Clarice said.

Mrs. Lowell said she would parch first. Even Mother allowed herself a snicker at Father's expense.

"And Dr. Quincy," Clarice continued, "you did right not giving him something to push up against."

Mother told the Lowells that Clarice knew Father very well. And oh she did. She knew his habits and his ways, and I had seen her translating them for nonplussed guests, once for a senator's wife whom Father had questioned about her dress. He wanted her to leave it at Seven Oaks, go home in something of mine, so he could have it copied for Mother. After Mother took the lady aside and said that she admired the dress but thought the style did only someone of slender proportion justice, the lady asked how she was to answer Father. Mother told her she would take care of Father, and she did so by consulting Clarice, who then announced while serving the next course that she thought she had seen something like that dress on a "high-yellow" in the burg. The dinner guests nearly choked, but the lady went home with all her clothing. The only person who laughed was Whately, who was about fourteen then and on one of his leaves—I treasured them all—from Warren Academy. Later I heard him being backhanded, his shoulder knocking down a picture frame, and he was backhanded again for breaking the glass.

"There is much," Mother now told the Lowells, "for which my husband needs forgiveness. You know, he is very religious. He baptized all the Negroes. But he does not always attend to matters in a way that pleases others, or me."

"Yes ma'am, ah Lordy," Clarice added, and took the coin she had just won from Dr. Lowell. Quincy told his parents that in his experience Clarice was always right.

Dr. Lowell took a slice of Clarice's apple and addressed Mother. "If I may, then, why are you sending her with Quincy and Emma Garnet? Do you not need her?"

I knew he meant that he recognized Clarice might protect Mother from Father's storms, and wasn't she afraid to be alone in the house with him?

Mother explained that when Quincy and I were through traveling and setting up house, Clarice would return. "Emma Garnet will need someone familiar with her to help her. Neither of us has a hand for the house."

Feeling better, Mrs. Lowell asked Clarice, "So this is your home, where you are from?"

They had not asked about my parents' backgrounds, for they were not that sort of people, but had they been curious in that way some of their station are, Mother would have said, "Oh, Savannah," and asked if they had tasted mushroom catsup and would they like a jar to take with them. Not the James River ladies, who knew and loved her, but other visiting wives took home many a jar of catsup. After the luncheon the day following my coming-out, when ladies from other parts of Virginia were exchanging tales of their debuts, the question of Mother's lineage and debut arose in turn. She froze. Mrs. Custis, knowing that Mother's ubiquitous catsup would not save the day, furnished her with a glorious past and told of the event herself, for Mother, she said, looked worn. What came forth was a tale of a ball not seen in Savannah since Lafayette's visit, when the truth was that mother's father went bust in the cotton business and could not finance the parties and dresses. That is when Father stepped in with his "one less mouth to feed."

Mrs. Custis delighted all her listeners with Mother's story, and when she was finished, Mother, entranced herself, swept up in what she wished might have been, cooed, "Oh, that sounds lovely, perfectly lovely." Mrs. Custis looked wide-eyed at her, smiled, and said, "Yes, Alice, dear. I know it must be so gorgeous for you to remember. All that candlelight and taffeta." Nobody on the cotillion committee had asked Mother to present social credentials, as is the rule now for mothers of aspirants who are not of readily apparent standing in the community. Her credentials had been assumed. And nobody, thank goodness, asked Mother to expound upon Mrs. Custis's wistful remembrances. I could tell by Mother's eyes, set on the make-believe past, that the slightest inquiry Mrs. Custis did not catch first might do her harm and make the ladies wonder more about her besides why she had married Father, who had mangled his way through the first dance with me the night previous and set couples within our sight to rollicking sport, pointing at us, calling out directions over their shoulders.

So I found need for Mother in another room. There I thanked her again and again for all she had done, sewing cascades of pearls on my gown with her own delicate hands, watching me sit and stand, walk to the end of the room, curtsy and turn about until I could do so without looking at the floor, listening to me deep into morning, when I could not help gleaming and gushing over "this doctor name of Quincy Lowell" I had been introduced to. He had told me that my slippers looked too small, that many a lady presented herself to society one evening and blistered toes to her doctor the next day. In a fit of sudden intimacy, I asked him to follow me onto the porch, where I showed him my toes and testified to their comfort. Mother had squealed, "Your feet? You showed him your feet?" I told her I had been seized by the moment, and she took me into her arms and told me she could see the days that were before me, days of "bliss and rose salve, both prescribed by the same gentleman." She helped me concoct an intrigue to see him again, but I did not have to. A few hours after the luncheon, Quincy appeared with salve and told Mother—Father, for good, was not there—that only a trained doctor could apply it.

As for that evening with the Lowells, Clarice was thinking hard on what she might call a home. She chewed and spit seeds into her hand, finally to say, "It's sometime like living in the lunatic asylum, but it's home. He's worn himself out now. I can hear him being quiet, listening to hear if Dr. Quincy wants to get rough. In a minute I'll divide the tart."

We agreed that a nice dessert would calm our shattered nerves. With Clarice joining us in the dining room, we heard Father's boots hit the floor upstairs. Mintus would be hearing about how Father had gotten the goat of the "ninnyhacker," his pet name for all doctors who did not apply leeches anymore. When Quincy and I married, there was not an evening when he came into this house late from the hospital and placed his shoes gingerly on the floor to spare me a startle that I did not come to half-waking and recall sitting with his parents that night, wanting to go upstairs and smother Father for making the chandelier shake as though a marching band were taking route.

Those boots thumping to the floor after Father and Mintus had fought them off, and then the cane on the carriage. Father was always so very loud—he had to act out for us at every moment the raucousness that churned inside him, or we might lose interest in him. If he was quiet for a second, we might forget that he was Samuel P. Tate, man of means, by God. Sitting in the wedding carriage as Father railed against us, I thought, Soon, very soon, I will be far away from the noise. Maureen, who stood in the yard, twirling her hair for the sake of young Landon Carter, tossing up and again the tussy-mussy she had cajoled me into throwing straight to her, seemed carefree to the extreme of appearing dim-witted, thoroughly immune from Father and this attack on her sister. "Why are you so mad at Father?" she had always wanted to know. I rarely answered her. And now she could have him. She would do as he wished, be the child who did not take up her brother's books and "coagulate the blood by reading out of your sphere," as Father said I had done.

I wanted to fly out of the carriage and tell them all, Mintus and Maureen and Father and the gaggle of trusty male servants he could call by name, those who shuffled for him, those who stood watching him humiliate me, that if they allowed harm to come to Mother before I could take her, if they did not step between them when he went to hit her, I would destroy them all most assuredly. But I sat and spent exquisite time with her for the simple reason that I chose her company in those last moments, not theirs. I could not leave my seat, not with Mother gripping the edge of the window. When we did finally drive away, I took off my glove and touched the moist place she had left, and heard Clarice saying to me, "But she'll be fine. We'll be back. It is no reason to cry."

As I took Mother's hands in mine, I promised to come for her. "I'll make a room for you." Over and over I said that I would make a room.

She shook her head and smiled the way that had always signaled to me a retreat into the bliss of denial, and said, "He loves me, Emma Garnet. I have to stay."

Quincy put his hands on mine and Mother's, telling her, "No. We'll be here to get you. When we bring Clarice back, you will come."

Mother did not argue with him, but I knew that face. She would go nowhere unless dragged, but I had just married a man with power enough of mind and spirit to help me make her go when the time came. We would carry her off in the night and set Father off howling at sunrise. Clarice could tie him to one of his blessed Queen Anne chairs, stuff a rag in his mouth, and hold forth on why his wife was gone. We would somehow get her. I was imagining her tucked safely away with me, when, wordlessly, she kissed me again and then backed away and stood by Father, who had shaken off his neighbors and now pressed his weight on his cane, his gouty ankles unable to support him and so much impacted fury at once.

He shouted, "Let me say one last thing!" and then he pronounced a curse on my new house, my "exiled self," and the "gang of yard apes" that Quincy and I would no doubt raise.

"This is it," Quincy said. "I'm going to brain him with his own cane." Sitting across from me with her satchel in her lap, Clarice sputtered, "Yard ape? Who he calling a yard ape? You let me do it, Dr. Quincy. I can take his brains out without drawing blood."

Clarice worried her hands all up in the air, said something else about how ready she was to get started on her way to Paris and London, our honeymoon destination. She asked Quincy to give her room, and threw open the carriage door. The guests became quiet. Her handling of Jacob's woman—who had been managed and subdued, and went home whistling without giving the Negroes time to finish hanging witch-proofing pennyroyal around their doors—had made Clarice a woman of formidable reputation beyond the James. Word had spread of how she saved our household from a trick Negro who had been bartered from another plantation and reformed into the Episcopal church before she had a chance to give vent to the Negroes' festering desire for retribution over "Tate's mishap in the barn." Now those who had heard of her wanted to hear her reply to Father. Quincy held on to her hips so she would not topple over.

She pointed at Father, who stood up straight on his unsure ankles, knowing by her glare that he had crossed her line in demeaning my mother's grandchildren yet to come. I watched the way he studied her face, his eyes sinking into their common past. I hope he was taken all the way back to the night on which she saw his deepest secret, when he was a boy whose father had just made him scratch a grave from the hard clay, the butt of a shotgun kicking into his back when the spade did not move fast enough. And there was Clarice again, watching him again, not from behind a tree this time, not with the compassion that would make her take up house with them the next day so she might help the boy make some sort of life after the deed she had witnessed, comb the nits out of his matted hair, drive that mule cart to Alexandria, weave the rug. The governor was as transfixed by her presence as Father and all the others, shoeless field hands included, who had gathered at the pecan trees to send their regards to us. As they had waited in the barn when I was twelve, they waited again five years later for some message on how to get along with Father without her kitchen-door guidance.

Keeping her finger trained on Father, whose dyspepsia must have been gripping his stomach, she dealt first with the Negroes who had their trust in her. "Y'all keep grabblin'," she advised. "A brighter day is coming. And Mintus, you sleep on my cot in the kitchen now. I oughten to leave you on the floor but I'll pull you on up. Miss Alice, I worship the ground you tread and take your gifts to my heart. And you, Mr. Tate, you watch for her heart. You already taking a load with you to the grave. Do not need to plus it with laying a name on a precious baby, one not even thought up yet. But that first grandbaby won't be name of Tate or Samuel, neither one. I might name it Calhoun, boy or girl. I know how you appreciates the man. I know, too, how you love the Ezekiel," she continued. "So listen when He say, 'A new heart I will give you, and a new spirit I will put within you . . . and cause you to walk in my statutes and be careful to observe my ordinances.' You made me put that to memory when I took the church. You remember that, and you remember that these are all fine days that the Lord has made. Amen and be glad. And now I am set to go. Remember, you touch a hair on her head . . . I ready for you to reel me in, Dr. Quincy."

They all clapped as we left, save Father, who turned quickly to go inside, crushed. I could tell by his gait, and I was glad to see him hobble up the steps. And what of my mother? She stood waving with the boys, who had torn loose from Bertha and Lazy, until we lost sight of each other.

On those nights Quincy and I talked until dawn, he would soothe me, whispering in the darkness, "You didn't know. Oh, my Emma Garnet, you didn't know." Even after years passed, my father's debt reconciled, I would wonder aloud to dear Quincy why God in His infinite wisdom and knowing did not send me back to the James, why I let a new life keep me away, why I had let myself leave in the first place. Simply and regrettably, my mother was the price I paid for finally being able to lie down in peace. Oh, those nights of my Father's rained-down spite of her, when I did not set aside my terror and take a baby to her, when I did not want to get hurt in the crossfire. I would clamber behind a wall of fear and leave her in open pasture. Let me now, in this dying light of my dying days, put them to rest, those nights I remained in my safe bed. *Alice, you Goddamn schemer. You think that quack won't turn Emma Garnet against me? She's already turned against you. You take care of that every day she stays here. I will not have you say that. She's seventeen with no sense and no values, and betrothed to a nigger-lover. This is what my life has come to. Then why did you give consent? Why, Samuel? Because they deserve one another. Made of a cloth. Got everybody on the James eating out of his hands. Fixing niggers' busted heads. And her? She's spent her entire life spying on me. If I'd jerk open a door, she'd break her neck. Lurking, always has to know too much. Her and her brother. Their smug-faced superiority. Look at you cry. Listen to you. You want to cry? Don't, Samuel. Please don't. Hold still. I told you to stay. Shut up and stay.*

I left her there. I left my mother with a fiend, went to Paris, strolled down the Champs-Élysées and ate *petits fours*. I am ashamed.

four

When Quincy, Clarice, and I got to Raleigh, I had to overcome
the horror dealt me by the pious arbiter of Raleigh society before
I could try for the bliss that Mother said would come with the
salve and the doctor to administer it. Name of Miss McKimmon,
she died last year, and now, recovered from the memory of Father's cane, *thwack thwack thwack*, on the carriage and all the
precipitant pain that it caused me in the night, I can tell how she
welcomed her new neighbor. Quincy had had the temerity to
have a Northerner, Mr. H. H. Richardson, who was later to de-
sign the beautiful Trinity Church of Boston, as our architect, and
the tongues that particular decision set to wagging were quieted
only when I let a troop of ladies tour the rooms and pass com-
ment on Clarice's suite and the copper bathing tub, a great deca-
dence in their minds. Blount Street, the address Mr. Richardson
and Quincy had chosen, was close to the governor's palace, and it
was early in 1849 that we were invited by Miss McKimmon to be

her special guests at a party there. Although she was aggressively plain in the face, Miss McKimmon appeared innocuous enough in the way she invited me to inquire of her later of any ladies I wanted to especially know. She did say that she knew "everyone good society can merit." I thought the remark a bit snobbish but then did not give it another thought.

Arriving at the party with Miss McKimmon, who effused through the front door and into the arms of everyone simultaneously, we were noticed right away by Governor Manly, chiefly because of Quincy's appointment as director of the Mary Elizabeth Hospital. Fresh from medical school in Philadelphia, he had been asked to come by Dr. Burke Haywood, who introduced us around the room, saying to his listeners that Quincy was a fine, sensible man, temperate and thoroughly averse to low associations. Burke did not mention to anyone that Quincy made him await his arrival in Raleigh so that on his way from Pennsylvania he could start a training school and pharmacy for the free Negroes of Virginia, that he had been waylaid even further by love and a honeymoon. The *Weekly Standard* had hailed Quincy as "a coming" in a lengthy article that ran some time before the party, and I was never as proud to be his wife as I was that evening, when a gentleman asked whether Quincy's "leanings" would allow him to treat Southern boys as his "own kind" if the secession that South Carolinians were agitating for brought about conflict.

"Sir," Quincy replied, "everyone is my own kind." He was roundly toasted, and the admiration expressed him was not in any way false. It was so wonderfully sincere and heartfelt, in fact, that the next week we were delivered the invitation to another engagement, a dinner given by Miss McKimmon, who had since the governor's party sent me trinkets daily—fresh butter, finely milled black pepper, a globe basil, pear soap from a Charleston shop, and, finally, three fat live ducks. I heard Clarice at the back door on the morning of their arrival, asking incredulously of Miss McKimmon's servant, "Ducks? That what white people in North Carolina give each other? I heard y'alls is backwards, but ducks?" Before Clarice could do much more damage, I had Miss McKimmon's girl put the ducks in the chicken yard and wait while I wrote a note for her mistress about what toothsome receipts Clarice had for duck, how fine one would be that very Sunday. Clarice told me that if I wanted those ducks eaten, I would be cooking them. Reading over my shoulder, she had me go back and write that a duck would be fine soon, no one Sunday in particular. "Suppose she sits out after church and waits for the odor to drift to her nose holes?" Clarice was adamant that I not commit her to the ducks, and so I obliged her, knowing as I did that I would soon be forcing her to cook those ducks, a fashionable delicacy that Father scorned for being as "freakish and ungodly" as fruit served out of season.

My cooking anything was out of the question, as was training Mavis, her new assistant, to do anything Clarice did not tell her to directly. Not that I was not willing to cook, but Clarice saw me as ignorant beyond salvation, said many times she would rather feed me than fool with me. Quincy had bought Mavis's freedom, along with that of a housemaid, Martha, and a butler and driver, Charlie, channeling their papers through the medical school. We let the servants think that Clarice owned them rather than have word of more than one free Negro in the Lowell household send spasms through Raleigh. They readily accepted the notion of ownership by Clarice, for the practice of Negroes owning one another was not that uncommon in Warren County, where we had found them. I promised them good pay, rooms inside the house, plentiful food—a much more comfortable way of life than they had known. Both Quincy and I agreed that they would be better off with us than as indentured field hands on a struggling tobacco farm. As for keeping mum news of Clarice's freedom until Quincy and I could establish a place for ourselves, she told everyone who would listen. She acquired friends among Blount Street servants immediately, soon handing out petty loans, preaching toothbrush rules up and down the block, and making herself so scarce that at times I had to hunt her down.

Frances Haywood, Burke's wife, told me that if anyone found fault with Clarice or anything about her, it would be Miss McKimmon. The fact that my imperious neighbor had not contacted me—that and the butter and basil and pear soap and ducks—made me think that I might have a new friend in her. I would have been wise to consider the dab of sense in one of Father's mottoes: Next to God and money, trust only yourself.

I remember writing to Mother about this generous lady who had accepted us, how I might not be so lonesome after all if I could find more like her for a hand of whist every now and then.

Each day I posted a letter to Mother, making my news sound as cheerful as I could, making long hours Quincy was away seem full of wifely purpose, when all I actually did was take strolls with Clarice and read novels and Whately's old textbooks while Clarice lifted my elbows from the tables to dust, picked up my feet to mop. Every once in a while she would stop to ask me what I was learning. When I told her that I had just read in Mungo Park's *Travels* that in Africa, Tuareg brides dyed their faces with indigo, she gave me my hat and told me to have Charlie set me out downtown to shop about, a "better waste of time." I credit her with giving me my love of browsing in the dry-goods stores that were just beginning to appear, and I credit Quincy with giving me the idea that a ready-to-wear hat might be pretty on me, and was not, as I had heard at Seven Oaks, a ruse by Satan to keep "white trash employed in some gainful industry." I still do appreciate a hat that I do not have to blister my fingers trimming. But however lucky I have been in this life to have money, I never wasted it. I never threw my husband's money about, as do these young brides who live to ride the streetcar and who do not remember that the store where they now buy shoes used to be a grocery that, by late 1864, had a sign on the door that read: "No chickens today. Only rats. And them two dollars per pound."

As for my letters to Seven Oaks, when I was with child, soon after we moved onto Blount Street, I let Mother think that my morning hours were replete with restful contemplation of the upcoming blessing, not with agonizing sickness. I promised that I would come for her and the children when the baby arrived and

I had not the pressing need for Clarice. During that first hard, hard year, when Quincy was working the hours of an intern even though he could have come home at noon and treated people out of the side-room office, I would often sit by his tub at night, read to him the latest letter from Mother, and laugh over her constant closing line, "Father sends his very best wishes and love to you and Quincy." Then I would read to him chief reports from the newspaper and fill him in on the quotidian, what Clarice had said, what Charlie had torn up with the hoe.

We loved the regularity of our life, the run of little satisfied expectations. He would tell me of the latest reports in his medical journals, describe how black inside he had felt to watch a baby die before she had been held. I would tell him what I had learned about the Sandwich Islands or the Orkneys or the canals of Venice, on which I was something of an expert. Though I loved Venice, its ribbons of water, I had refused to go there on our honeymoon, or to Prague, Budapest, St. Petersburg, or Athens, places spoiled for me by Father, irredeemable even by fast love. On my family's visit to Venice in 1839, we had been drummed out of a restaurant by a waiter whom Father had asked, in perfect Italian that he later rendered in English, whether the fish on the menu was infested with any of the same filthy rubbish he had seen floating earlier by our gondola. Clarice and Quincy and I kept to Paris and London, places Father had not thoroughly trampled, defying gout and reason in his thunderous quest to tour a wife, new babies, children, and a bevy of borrowed servants around Europe in time to be home for the laying-by of his crops. All the sights were fresh and new to Clarice, who had been kept home by Father because she was the only person, besides him, who knew everything that went on and could nab the hired man if he tried to take unfair advantage.

And so after talking with me, after praying for Mother and the coming baby, Quincy would put his ear to my middle and rest there where his baby girl was sleeping. I had much to be grateful for, but those nights of serenity in our new home seemed remote, impossible even, in the terrible days after Quincy pulled my chair away from Miss McKimmon's table, only for me to try to stand and then fall on her floor, to be scooped up and carried home by the governor, who would not let my husband take anything but my gloves. When I was safely home, Governor Manly returned for Clarice, who, I later learned, could be heard up and down the street, throwing rocks at the McKimmon front windows, screeching wild threats to poison her ducks. If only she had not sent all those gifts that had made her seem so motherly to me, I would not have suffered, would not have terrified Quincy and caused Clarice to make me take a Bible oath never to alarm her again. If I broke my word, she would tell Mother everything.

Miss McKimmon's question had seemed very simple, and I thought that I would replicate my husband's social success indeed if I answered it as honestly as he had his. I did not have to be like my father to be honest. I could be sweet and forthright, an amalgam of both my parents. Until that evening, I had never been asked a serious, thoughtful question in public, and so when she asked if my mother had treated her servants with the same "forbearance" I showed Clarice, I did not hear in it the insinuation that I was not worthy. Clarice, who had been standing in the next room with other servants, would tell me later that she heard exactly what was meant, even though she did not know the definition of the word "forbearance." Quincy heard, as well, and so did the governor. They jostled over each other trying to speak for me, but I hushed them and said, "Yes, very much. My mother loves her servants. She doted on Clarice." Quincy squeezed my knee, hard, but I pushed his hand away. I would talk for myself.

I said that my mother, just before the wedding, had cut a nasty splinter out of a maid's toe, cleaned the wound, and kept fresh bandages on. I said that being a lady, to my mind, did not exclude giving proper care to servants. I continued to say that Mother blessed them each night and taught us children to be gracious to them, scolded us when we ordered them about. Each member of the trash gang, I reported, received a candy cane at Christmas, and when women married, Mother furnished them out of her pantry and root cellar. So yes, I had inherited my mother's forbearance, and furthermore, if war came, white ladies might be working alongside Negroes, so it was in the interest of all to develop a mutual respect by then if not sooner. "Men of both colors will be busy," I concluded, pleased to have addressed the state of the modern lady.

Miss McKimmon asked Quincy what he thought of all this. He told her that my mother was the most compassionate lady he had ever known, that although she had never had the burden of minding a household alone, she would not merely sponsor a knitting charity if war came. "She is the backbone of her establishment and would teach herself or readily learn what the servants know," he said. "She has given my wife the gift of intelligence without stridency, and that is why she can speak her mind so gracefully." He then asked Miss McKimmon if she thought she had heard quite enough. As I was busy thinking, How unlike Quincy to manifest such unvarnished impatience, he kissed me on the cheek and spoke brusquely into my ear: "Say you're sick. Now, Emma Garnet."

But I felt marvelous, and did until the moment Miss McKimmon sighed deeply and asked, "Do tell me, Mrs. Lowell, what do you hear of your brother?"

I blanched. My hands went numb. As I fell off the chair Quincy was pulling out for me, I saw the soap, the pear soap. It was from the Charleston concern. Somewhere in the distance, Quincy was shouting, ". . . dead, you well know! What did my wife do to you?"

What had I done? Nothing save adore a brother whom I had not yet grieved, who had died in unimaginable horror. His legacy to me was my love of the English language, an appreciation for its myriad uses. Some people might balk at my refusal to step around words that are base and common, but those are the same fools who would drape *The Raft of the Medusa* and place fig leaves over Adam. The portrayal of death and sin, and I have seen a surfeit of both, requires that I employ the more direct language of Hawthorne than the circumlocution of Walter Scott.

I have reported rough language that no Southern lady, no Miss McKimmon, would approve of my setting down, even if it has been to show my father's character. I have seen myself thanked for honesty with calculated brutality, and there is no reason to think Blount Street residents will ever read my words and thank me less. But I care little. No, I care nothing. Having survived my father and the War, I am capable of anything. Making an honest account is what, everything, I want to do and must do. Although I am a Southern woman, my life has not been cast in that romantic ideal of Scott's. Many fools I know have assumed possession of his language, and when I hear them drone on about chivalry and glory, I have wondered that we are of the same place.

I engage only in the truth of my life for the sake of my girls, so they will know before the end what I hold right and just and dear.

Dear Quincy had to hear more from our wedding until his own end than most husbands are asked to hold, for he was not only my salvation but my confessor and confidant. He does not look down upon me now and tell me to watch my language. No, rather, as I write I hear him: *Say the truth. Say it as you spoke it to me. And say what happened after the dinner, the one that marked you. Speak of the South's rebellion and your own.* When I join him in the rock-frozen New England ground, I have to be able to tell him that I depleted the store of our memories and found for us a peace that will outlive the ages, leaving my love and me together on still nights again, past the time that the stars and moon close their eyes and God flings open the clouds to receive us and those we have loved. Oh, my helpmeet and Mother! I feel in a rush when they come to me, but there is time yet for me to spend here before I can meet them. Before the day closes, I must follow my heart, and Quincy's, and tell of the memory that one dinner forced me to face, of the carnival of destruction it wrought on my soul. You may hear that I tried to kill myself, but my children will know that to be untrue. I did put myself into a laudanum-induced stupor and threaten my baby's life. That is the terrible truth of it. When Mary was born healthy, I thought as I listened to her cries, Such a mother does not deserve you. As I lay insensible in a room full of the governor's flowers, Quincy keeping sleepless vigilance by my side, made to take a meal every now and then by Clarice, I would bob up once in a while and touch his shirt. I tricked the fabric the way Falstaff did before his death. I was trying to take hold of something that mattered, to will myself to fight my way out of the sweet languor of forgetfulness.

Quincy did fall asleep at some point, and when he did he began dream-talking. He woke me up talking, and I was glad, for I heard, "Emma Garnet, come around. I need you. I want some popcorn."

He knew that popcorn was all of something satisfactory to eat that I could make, and though my head pounded I went downstairs, lit the fire and popped corn. Clarice and the servants slept through the cooking because God meant for them to. He let me be very quiet, did not let me bang the pan or fall up the stairs. I awakened Quincy with my surprise, and together we enjoyed the corn and lay down on a bed of kernels. He fought back his tears, and then he went along to act as though we did this all the time, as though his wife habitually dosed herself with laudanum she stole from his bag, slept for three days, and then got up and made popcorn. At no time during the night did he remark on how thrilled he was that I was better. To hear him express joy would also have been to hear the other, unspoken words, "You disappointed me." He knew I had been wrong to endanger my life and the baby's, but he would not bore in on me, not ever.

Quincy stayed home with me that next day after I came around, even though I tried to make him go to the hospital. He stayed so that he could test my resolve by sending me on a morning mission, one right down the street here, where he knew I would meet my persecutor. He believed that I would prevail. All I had to do was walk by her but once, and I could meet her gaze thereafter at any dinner, any party, any tea, anytime, for the rest of my life. He did have me practice a disarming smile until it reached a semblance of genuine regard. She did not know the truth of what I had done to myself. At the time, only Clarice and Quincy knew. Charlie and Martha broadcast my affairs later, when it was to their benefit, and I blame them for that as much as anything else, deeds born of rampant misunderstanding. The neighbors thought I was sick in bed with embarrassment over Whately. Only the governor and Quincy's close friends cut Miss

McKimmon, swiping past her at every social moment they could, and that kept her miffed until the day she died, may I say, of liver failure. She hiccuped through her final days.

Quincy peeked through the curtains and sent me on my way when the right moment came. He said for me to go out and let her see me carrying on with the ordinary business of my day. I was weak and looked it, and there was a steady drizzle coming down. If she could not honor my family's privacy, she could respect my rebounded constitution. *Go out and be what you are. I'll be watching from the window. I love watching you. I love my life with you.* And so now, how can I not respect the wishes of a man I still see by that window, urging me on. *Walk on out. When time eventually arrives, say it. Say it all. Remember your brother again without flinching. Face it all dry-eyed. But if you must run, run to me. My arms still hold you.*

five

Whately was put out of the house an hour after he walked in on the afternoon of December 20, 1842. Father had emerged from his hibernation, not groggy, but blasting back into the family's life after having justified to Mintus and himself his murderous act as a "mishap," for so he was always to name the deed, when word of the hideous incident spread up and down and over the river. Mintus had wrapped Father's ankles in mustard and vinegar, so when he came down the grand staircase with all the dignified bearing of a just-coronated king, Clarice, whose uplifted apron was full of snowbirds bound for the nursery fire, could say, "Mr. Tate, the meek don't inherit the Earth. That the way it go now?"

"Yes, Clarice. The meek inherit Georgia, and the strong inherit Virginia. Where's Alice?"

My parents had not seen each other since my mother returned from the Carters'. She and I were in the sitting room, where we could hear the news of Father's emergence. We had been sewing silk and fringe onto the scarf that she had knitted to warm Whately in his chilly rooms at Washington College. As she rolled the scarf to put aside for another day, she sighed. "Your father has acquitted himself."

When I asked what "acquitted" meant, she told me, "Your father is a man of boundless appetites. When he eats what does not agree with him, he purges himself and eats more."

I thought at once of the rapacious Romans whom we had learned about on our tour, those esurient noblemen who retched without restraint in a common room, unashamed to gorge themselves while starving plebeian children roamed the lanes. I said to myself while I surveyed the carpet for bits of fringe, "Father eats people. He ate Jacob. Now, to his mind, it is all over."

Mother had heard of the killing while she was at the Carters', reported to that family by the tinker who kept a steady trade of copper kettles and gossip going along the James. He paddled a barge and frequently appeared at our grand entrance, which faced the river, not at the back door. I hated the fact that this unctuous rover was the messenger who had brought my mother the sorry tale. I remember her return from the Carters', the way she had thrown off her wrap, pitched it to Bertha, and then directed me to follow her out of the kitchen, where she, Clarice, and I put jars in a gunnysack and then smashed them with a mallet. She took the shards herself to the Negroes' cabins so that they could, as held a tradition, spread them on Jacob's grave.

Clarice was upstairs with the snowbirds, a delight for Maureen and the little ones to have roasted in the fire, when Mother and I arrived in the foyer. Father reeked of mustard, but he did not look like a man with sin on his mind, sorrow in his heart. I had seen Mintus toting upstairs countless jugs of Hot Springs water, and I assumed that the spirits were in part responsible for his renewed vigor. The last time I had seen him was after Clarice had washed blood from him, when he left our company with a flagging morale, evident even to a child, his shoulders stooped and gait slackened.

He asked Mother when she had returned from the "nest of vipers," the ladies he knew did not approve of him. He inquired after his wife's "viper" compatriots in a tone that was, in the narrow band of expressions he allowed himself, almost gleeful.

Mother ignored his commentary and replied jauntily that she had returned three days previous but had not wanted to disturb him. She asked if he liked her frock, deep green velvet with red grosgrain running like Christmas garlands around the skirt.

"I do, indeed, Alice," he said. He took a seat on the foyer couch and beckoned for her to sit by him. He asked me to sit alongside them, a rarity save during Prayer Book readings. I did, but on the edge, better to pop up and run to Clarice if I felt him drawing me into a web, luring me so that he could more easily grab my arm and chastise me for fishing with the Negroes or cavorting with the trash gang or reading novels that Whately quietly left for me on his visits. I was to read only the Book of Common Prayer, the Episcopal hymnal, the Old Testament. I worried that he might have found *The Castle of Otranto*, my fascination at the moment. My heart quailed within me, for just the night before, I had sat on my floor reading the pages as quickly as I could cut them, hungry for another thrilling chapter, eager for an escape into a world that, though dark and intense as my own, was far from a father who threatened to hack off his own "Goddamn, ever-loving feet" with his shaving razor.

But he did not scold me. Rather, he said that he was posting a letter to The Homestead, where we could escape the brutality of the hard February to come. The eclipse of the summer had pre-cursed seasons of heightened intensity, a bitter winter, a rainier spring, an oppressive summer. Father's gout required the indoor baths, and while he nourished his affliction with the minerals, Mother and I could drink Earl Grey and eat cucumber sand-wiches. I had never been to the resort with them, had always been left home with the other children.

"Emma Garnet," he said, "you have many errors of the soul that need correction, but it is time you make the journey. I have seen young girls of the highest caliber there, all comporting themselves as befits their station. Willcox plans to be there at the same time, and so you will have your friend Sally from whom to borrow dignity. I have observed her at worship. She is what you refuse to be."

Sally was not what I refused to be; she was everything I could not be—lithesome even when covered with layers of brocade and sateen, pleasantly ignorant of ideas. She did not put herself to sleep of an evening by riding the meters of the *Metamor-phoses*. I liked her because she did not mind the heresy I pronounced when I told her that each and every one of William Gilmore Simms's romances was dreadful. She was titillated, and when she asked where I learned everything I knew, I proudly said, "My brother. He tells me the world."

My father knew nothing of my declamations to Sally, who always kept my confidences when I swore her to secrecy. And she did sit calmly at Bruton Parish and follow the lines of hymns with her finger. She held her mother's hand as they left each Sunday, and curtsied to the priest. This was the kind of refinement Maureen was growing into, but she was too young for The Homestead. As I was considering what a more willing candidate she would make for teas and five-course dinners, Father set my mind for me.

"I would prefer to take Maureen," he told me, "for she has your mother's gift of grace already instilled. She may go when she is of appropriate age, but this trip is yours. You will go there and become what you need to be if a man worth a dime is to have you."

Mother asked why he could not stop comparing Maureen and me, to my detriment, and instead "dilate on the joys of our adventure."

"I compare them because the disparity rankles me," he said. "When has Emma Garnet fetched my spectacles? When has she taken a kiss from me without turning away and wiping her cheek? She will go to the Springs, act the lady, take open-air refreshment with you, and she will, by God, come home less of a hellion."

Mother replied sweetly, "Dear Samuel, you know she is hardly that."

He was about to hold forth again when we heard a carriage arrive, and went to the door to see dear Whately step down. He was a day early. "Well, now," Father grumbled, "watch out for a true hellion, home again, no doubt, to deliver me some fresh Hell."

Mother and I rushed out to greet him, but Father remained inside. The instant Whately saw us, he started weeping. His boy went to take his few bags from atop the carriage, but Whately motioned for him to leave them there. The boy shrugged his assent and then ran to see his mother, the weaver who toiled like Rapunzel to keep Father in brocade vests such as the one he wore for that day's descent down the stairs. He was feeling grand, all right, but his son was a shambles.

Whately clutched Mother and sobbed onto her shoulder, as I stood by needing to know what had happened. Had death taken the lame squirrel that he had rescued from Father's deer trap and kept in his rooms at Washington College? Had someone destroyed his beloved encyclopedias? I expected Father to burst outside and "slap sense" into Whately, as I had once seen him do when Whately, for no apparent reason, fell into a fit of despondency. But Father stayed his repugnance for tears and stood watchful at the door, letting Mother investigate. I recall that the day was bitter cold, yet I did not feel the weather, for all my anxiety, which will heat a body like a roaring peat fire.

When Mother pleaded for Whately to tell her what was so

very wrong, he mumbled into her shoulder, "Everything. I am done for."

Holding him apart from her and wiping his eyes, she said in that way a mother will when she needs to convince a sad child that the world is still turning, "Nothing is that bad. Nothing is too terrible. Anything can be corrected. You know that."

Mother could speak that way to Whately because she had seen years of thrust, *riposte*, and *tertio* between him and Father, the arguments, standoffs, and resumption of what, for Father and Whately, passed for normal activity. They existed by suffering each after those supper-table harangues, name-callings, requests by Father to "go to Hell or Lexington, it matters not to me, and stay there." It had become a tradition for Father to remind Whately every night he spent home from school: "You turned your back on Seven Oaks and all I stand for when Clarice was chasing after you with a snot rag, and now that you are older and out amongst the gentry, be sure to say when they ask of your origin, 'I am from nowhere.' " Father exaggerated the age at which Whately demurred when he had been offered "all this glorious land, the house, the niggers, everything." In truth, Whately was twelve, the age of accountability, when he told Father, "I do not think I will ever live here. If I take up your living, I will take up your Negroes. Thank you, though." They had been hunting quail. Father held a gun on him until he admitted that he was a weakling. Then they struck the bargain that Whately's tuition and expenses would be paid as long as he stayed clear of Father's sight and did not attend a Northern institution. I know all of this from Clarice, who was to offer a gloss on the parts of my brother's life I had call to understand. Whately would sit in the kitchen with her, before I was old enough to take his lessons, and recite sonnets, which she enjoyed, she said, because he made them sound like music, tender tunes. "He was a lonely boy," she would tell me, "glad, so very glad, when you got your first big tooth," the sign that a child is ready to read in earnest. I could, by Father's stern instruction, line out the Bible, but I wanted more, and Whately welcomed and satisfied my curiosity. Clarice also wanted more, and so he guided her beyond Bible verses and kitchen receipts, helping her read *Godey's Lady's Book* so she could discuss the love serials with Mother. He did us both great good.

Although Mother told Whately that anything could be made right, he said with all the sadness of this world, "Nothing can undo what I have done." Mother asked me if I should not go into the house, but Whately told Mother he needed time with both of us before Father demanded a reason for a grown son's crying on the front lawn. He squeezed my shoulder and told me to look in a bag that lay on the carriage seat. There I found wrapped gifts for Mother and me, and a rag doll marked for Maureen, whom he treated much better than I did. Once, he called me down when I chastised her for eating cornmeal so feverishly that she bit her tongue. I think I might have called her a little idiot. Whately told me that I should not lose temper over her foibles. Rather, I should feel sorry for "the way she will have to go through this world."

Knowing that I had heard Father berate Whately for taking company with the poor whites of Lexington, Mother then felt free to ask, "Whately, is it faro? Do you have a debt?"

"I wish it were gambling. That was bad enough, and now this." He held on to her again.

Father had branded him a wastrel because he had, the year previous, fallen into a crowd of young men who taught him to drink and throw dice. He did neither with much success. He accumulated debts that sent Father to his desk, grimly writing checks and letters of apology to the fathers who had sent Negroes the thirty miles from Lexington to Seven Oaks, all with approximately the same message. I would find the notes crumpled on the library floor. "Your boy owes me $10.00. Pay now." "Your boy took eight of my hard-earned dollars from my son. Remit at once." On his next trip home, Whately was asked by Father, in front of us all at supper, if he would like to wager which one of us would rot in Hell first. Mother, stunned, did not speak. Whately refused to honor the question.

"No," Father sneered, "will your mother, Emma Garnet, me, or you rot in Hell first? You love to gamble. I spent the past six months paying your way, so I ought to know. Now tell me, Goddamnit." He was inexorable.

Whately said he would not wager.

Mother trembled as Father shouted, incensed, "You will bet me a hundred dollars that your dear mother leaves this Earth first. And you know why? Because you are driving her to her grave."

Whately reached for Mother's hand during Father's sputterings about having sired a mountebank, rogue, fool, who somehow eased by in his studies, brought home the good marks, and still suffered from a moral lassitude that would see him through the "peripatetic life of all spineless wonders who have no skill, no ambition. You will tutor the sons of rich men like me," Father intoned. "You do have a brain. God did grant you that. And when you wear out the teaching, you will wander up North, where you belong to have been born, and die broke and dejected. And your legacy will be a pile of faro debts. Hide and watch."

Mother was again trembling as Father now strode down the steps toward the three of us, having surmised that ours was not merely the scene of a tearful reunion. He yelled for me to go to my room. As I left, still holding the gifts, I could not help myself saying to Father as I passed, "My brother is more sinned against than sinning." Had he not been so over-occupied with suspicions of everything that Whately might have done, he would have forced me into admitting that my brother had read the wisest parts of *King Lear* to me on his last holiday.

I went not to my room but to the nursery, where I informed Clarice of the trouble. She left Lazy with the children and snowbirds. Maureen grabbed the doll from me before she knew it was hers. Clarice and I closed the door to the nursery and went to the staircase, where we sat silently on the top step and waited.

Mother, Whately, and Father were in the foyer now. Father said, "I thought that you two might have been crying over something more than a joyous glad-seeing, but I wanted to let the fizz settle before I stepped in to find out what the truth of the matter was." When Mother bowed her head and thanked him for giving them some moments together, Father would not hear her out. "Be quiet, Alice. I want to know why a grown boy leaves his bags on the carriage and cries like a pluperfect baby on my front lawn. I want to know why he has to spoil every decent day of my God-damn life. Talk, Whately."

My brother sat down on the couch where I had just been promised a Hot Springs holiday that I now knew, already could tell, was doomed. I could hardly hear when he whispered, "A girl." He put his head in his hands and repeated, "A girl, Father. In trouble."

Father, without a word, knocked Whately off the couch. Mother went to help him up and through her tears begged Father not to strike him again. Clarice held my waist and whispered, "Your room," but I could not leave, and she knew it. I felt dizzy, and then I leaned over, laid my head on Clarice's apron and vomited, as silently as I could. Her lap smelled of the wet snowbirds. I restored myself and held on to the packages in my lap as though they were weapons. I was readying my defense. Of course, I did not know the meaning of "in trouble," but I understood that Whately had not run up a faro debt. He had not charged a load of books on Father's account at the Vickery and Griffith's. I had not long before seen evidence of Father's killing a man and thought that time the most horrific I would ever witness. And now I would have worry over the consequences of this event.

Whately sat up on the floor, with Mother kneeling beside him, brushing his hair from his forehead again and again, as if her only chance for sanity lay in that singular motion. She would worry over his hair and lose herself, take herself away from the brocade-chested man who was screaming and punching into the wall. "What in the Hell? What in the Hell hath God wrought? Sorry bastard. You sorry, sorry bastard." Father stopped pounding the wall and told Whately to go into the library. Mother was commanded to sit in the foyer and wait. I did not let her see me, for I knew that her worry would multiply by the number of minutes I had spent there with Clarice, seeing what girls were not born to see.

Father and Whately were not closed in for very long, and when they emerged, Mother moved toward Whately with that mixture of hope and dread that I have since seen on people's faces when Quincy approached them with the news about a loved one after a difficult surgery. She asked what was going to happen now.

Whately did not speak. He seemed to have shut down, all the light of his spirit extinguished. Always, he had had to work at keeping that light going, ever since he was eight, when Father dismissed him from Seven Oaks to Warren Academy. I now hear Whately telling me the story of how Father, who tutored him in Latin late into the nights, was walking through a canebrake with him one bright autumn afternoon. They were hunting rabbits. When they loved each other, they also loved to hunt. From nowhere, Father had erupted: "Start. *Fero.* Start, boy." Whately rested his gun across his arm and recited, *"Fero, ferre, tuli, latum."* Father demanded, "Haven't you been listening to me? It is *tulo.*" Then Whately made the tragic error. "It's simple, Father, *tuli.*" Father marched Whately home, and in a week he was on his way to the Academy. That day in the canebrake had been the start of their troubles, that incident of supreme embarrassment was another cause for Father to lash out at Mother for having loved a son despite his "smug-faced superiority." My father, afraid of a little boy.

Father poked at Whately and told him to tell Mother where he was going.

"Charleston," Whately mumbled.

Mother inquired why.

Father explained that he was sending Whately to Charleston to stay with Henry Hammond and sell marl. Whately could make an honorable living there. "He has ruined any hope of that here when he ruined the girl. A barmaid! For the sake of Jesus, a barmaid."

Mother wanted to know when Whately was going.

"Right now," Father said. Whately had been prescient in leaving his bags on the carriage. He had come home to see Mother and me and to confess to Father before the Lexington constabulary called at Seven Oaks. He had come to see Clarice as well, who had, the summer he read me *Lear,* purged him with lobelia when he was over-served at a barbecue, and met my parents' concern over his all-afternoon sleeping by explaining that he was "too pooped to pop and needs the rest, so leave him be."

Now that Whately asked Father to let him see Clarice and me before he left, he was given five minutes.

Clarice jumped up and scurried down the hall, and I followed. Whately caught us. He was a tall, lanky boy, but as he stood over me, I thought, My brother is a man. He seemed to be fighting for words, which I supplied him.

"You will be going away now," I said, conscious as I spoke that I was again being compelled by Father to bear witness to events for which my young heart had not readied me.

He knelt before me and said, "Yes, I will be in Charleston. I have business there. When I am gone, open your present."

Mother would put hers away, unopened, in a trunk until Old Christmas, for this was her habit. But I had to know, right then, what he had given her. Seeing me stare at her package, he said, "It is a Book of Days."

He asked Clarice to look after me. While he and I were talking, she had taken off her soiled apron. Nobody's servant now, stripped of that emblem of servitude, she was another woman of the Tate household, crushed to see a son taking his leave. She kissed his cheek and pushed the hair from his forehead in the same way, the very same way, Mother had done.

He left. He left Mother crying on the steps, to be ordered in and commanded to cease her tears by Father, who was in great haste now, charged with fantastic energy. She was told to find Mintus and awaken him. He frequently practiced his narcolepsy in the afternoons.

"Tell him I need clothes for three days," Father boomed,

"and then have a nigger fix me a tin of something to eat. Mintus will not be going with me. I'll drive myself." He considered for a moment and asked Mother what she had slipped Whately.

"When?" she inquired with clearly feigned innocence.

"When?" he snarled. "When you hugged him. You went into the parlor while he was upstairs with Emma Garnet and Clarice, and then you came out, put your arms around him, and did something that I could not see."

"Oh, Samuel," Mother responded. "I gave the boy ten dollars. Is that so terrible?" She was already near distraction, bound for a sick head-misery, but she managed the subterfuge admirably.

He told her that he had given Whately plenty of money for the Norfolk steamer and for continued passage for Charleston. "But never to mind," he said. "I have to start to Lexington before supper."

Mother asked Father to consider waiting until the light of morning, but he silenced her. He wanted his clothes and his ham biscuits and his carriage ready right now. She set about gathering for him to leave.

Clarice picked up her apron and said, "We done of listening. He oughten to be ready in a shag."

The house calmed when Father walked out, as though it were a living thing that needed to take in deep wind, sigh, and release its troubles. The children were happy with their snowbird suppers. Mother was napping. Clarice was warming soup for Mother and me. I went to my room, closed my door, and unwrapped Whately's gift. It was a copy of *The Deerslayer*, just printed. The binding smelled of fresh paste, and the pages were regularly, expensively trimmed. This was the finest book I had ever seen. Inside, a note for me read:

My dear, dear Emma Garnet—

The books in my room belong to you. Read them all eventually. But I think you will find greatest pleasure in *Tristram Shandy* (very comical), *The Pathfinder* (keen hero), and Irving's *Sketch Book* (a picture of the North). Remember all we spoke of. Remember Desdemona and Ophelia. Beware of Walter Scott, for he is a deceitful man, and his words lull the mind into sweet stupidity. Read and write as honestly as you can. Do not be timid (and do not let Father catch you with my books). Remember to use the Webster. Go to sleep tonight with the Chaucer.

Your loving brother—

Whately

It is ever and anon that I recall my time with Whately as if viewing a magic lantern show. Spots of that time that scrambled about in my mind in the moments, days, and years after his death now merge and align themselves. Without my brother, I would not have known to use books as a haven, a place to go when pain has invaded my citadel. His lessons, as well, have kept me company when I was alone and in need, simply in need, of companionship until Quincy got home. And finally, Whately's lessons found practical use in my life, for in the books he left me and in those I would later buy or borrow, I learned to be a better person, to everyone save Lucille McKimmon. Horace spoke that the end of literature is to instruct the mind and delight the spirit—Whately left my mind to receive both initiatives in full measure. Because of him, I have found joy in quiet hours, and direction on how to live through any trick hand dealt me. When my girls were tiny babies, oftentimes I would lull them to sleep with the purest language that Whately introduced to me:

> *Whan that Aprill with his shoures soote*
> *The droghte of Marche hath perced to the roote*
> *And bathed every veyne in swich licour*
> *Of which vertu engendred is the flour . . .*

We did not go to Hot Springs that February, because news reached us that Whately was dead. But the showers of April surely pierced the drought-shrunken roots of March. In Hell-reigning vengeance, God pounded Seven Oaks with torrents of water for seventy-six hours, and left Father asking a crowd of mud-wet Negroes who had gone sleepless to dam his floods, "Why me? Why in the devil me?" He spoke with the conviction that he was the only man on the James whose land had washed away. As though the Negroes might actually chirp up and say, "You know why it rained, Missa Tate? On account of you deserved it." But only Clarice would tell him, "The freshets came because of Whately. That is all. Because of the boy." He did not rebuke her or argue—he went to his room for a nap.

Whately was found at one of Henry Hammond's cabins on Sullivan's Island. Beside him on the bed was the note that Mother had hurriedly written to Mrs. Rhett and secreted to Whately when Father had supposed she was giving him money.

> Dearest Mrs. Rhett,
>
> You know my family from the old days in Savannah. Please see to my son Whately if he needs you. I will be forever in your debt.
>
> Sincerely,
> Mrs. Samuel P. Goodman Tate

Whately's body was wasted to a stick. He was so covered in running sores that the trappers who happened upon him wound him in burlap to take him across the river to the Rhett home. My brother lay bound like a shot deer in the bottom of a canoe. Henry Hammond was nowhere to be found. He was not an honorable man. My brother's right cheek was cut through with a hole the size of a half-dollar, evidence to Mr. Rhett that he had administered himself too much calomel. He had salivated enormously. In his mouth were found uneaten pills of blue mass. Places on his arms and legs lay open where he had tried to burn off putrefying matter. His eyelids were caked with mercurial ointment. I knew these horrid details of my brother's last days, of this syphilitic pox born of one night—or perhaps it was several—passed with a young woman he fancied, or maybe even loved, because Clarice pushed Mother to inquire of the Rhetts' doctor what had become of her boy. Clarice read the letter when it came and told Mother only what she believed Miss Alice could hear and still sleep at night. The doctor could not, by city authority, allow Whately's body to be taken from Charleston. He was buried with the Rhett family, and there he lies, just a boy who loved his books, among senators and war heroes.

When they told me that my brother was dead and buried in a place I could not envision, I screamed and was immediately slapped in the face by Father. Standing in the same foyer, right where Father had struck Whately, I knew that he would never let me grieve. I did not cry for years, did not feel Whately's presence again until Miss McKimmon's dinner. As for Mother, she was not allowed to grieve, either. She took the news, tried to cry, was stopped, and then turned and drifted ghostlike up the stairs. And then the rains came. God, Clarice said, was crying for us all.

s i x

I did not have to leave the comforts of Seven Oaks to have my vulnerable soul exposed to murder and mayhem, but in my sixteenth year my father announced that we were all in need of an excursion to Williamsburg, where we might be edified, made righteous, even holy, by attending a public execution. Lest I may convey the impression that he was unremittingly desirous that his family be tested for moral durability, I must explain that he did read aloud the news that Jack Robinson's Famous Circus would be set up across the square from the gallows. We were at supper, where Father sometimes shared morality tales gleaned from the Williamsburg newspaper. Henry, Randolph, and John were with Lazy at a small corner table, recently brought into the dining room after John scared us senseless by almost choking on a toy pewter spoon. Mother asked in her own quiet way that Father postpone his reading if the news was prurient. "Not designed for tender ears," is what she said as she laid her hand on his.

He would not hear her. "Hell no, Alice. Listen. 'The dual-rampaging highwaymen name of Lycurgus Barrett and Pink Pratt who outraged the fatherless daughter of a local sewing woman are scheduled to be hanged next Saturday in the usual spot. They have spent this last week in grand style, having sold their corpses to the medical school in Richmond to secure the steady run of tobacco and dainty food brought in to them by sundry cotqueans. They sing Negro tunes in the night. The sheriff despises them for this cavalier approach to their doom. They can be heard carrying on like there is no tomorrow. The young girl, whose ear was bitten off by Pratt, is still under the care of kind professors' wives at William and Mary. Recall that it was reported in this newspaper at the time of Pratt's arrest he had something that looked to be a dried fig hanging around his neck.' "

Mother told him she had heard enough. "This is the end. We will hear no more of it."

"Ask the boys if they want to hear it." Father did not give her time to inquire of them, for he shouted, "Boys! Lazy, shut them up and make them hear me."

John, who lived to have Lazy recount to him a story she proudly "thought up in my own head" called "The Indian with the Froze Arm," piped cheerily, "I heard you, Father. He bit her ear off and hung it around his neck for good luck."

Mother and I spoke together when we asked Father to consider what he was doing. When he revealed his intention to make an announcement, Mother asked Lazy to remove the boys.

"They will eat where they sit," Father told Mother. "Now listen to me. The report continues. 'Execution morn will begin with a sunrise breakfast of eggs and mutton chops served by ladies of the Methodist Church for a sum to be posted. They cannot decide yet. Then will follow speeches by several Englishmen who are here on holiday and wish to pass the hat for the chimneysweeps of London. Too-Whit-Too-Woo will perform a commemorative poem of his own making, and that should take us up to the preaching by Harold the Baptist. He promises that he will not drone on. Then the grand event at exactly twelve o'clock. After Barrett and Pratt are cut down and hauled off, a delight for children of all ages from three to eighty-three will commence. Mr. Jack Robinson's Famous Circus! All the fierce animals! Lions and tigers! French ladies riding ponies and throwing balls in the air. Italian ladies dancing across a rope. A Negro frying pancakes in a hat. Another Negro causing invisible pigs to squeal and other like feats of ventriloquism and legerdemain.' "

I do not recall that article by memory. Though I can still see the shape and number of bags on Whately's carriage, I have retained only swatches of Father's reading. I can give it now because I excised the notice when we returned home from Williamsburg, placing it in my copy of *The Count of Monte Cristo* to keep there forever. It was important to me that I have an account of the day, for my mind, so liable to imaginative forays, needed an objective touchstone, a lining out of the hours I might use if I slipped into forgetting what emotions the day accrued in its end, the strange, unaccustomed emotions of an epiphany. Life with

Father and life with Whately's books had prepared me to accept irony, the way of looking at the world with the head slightly cocked, buffeting against the wind, protecting. Yes, Father edified me, all right. This yoking of death and life, the hanging to be followed by pancakes fried in a hat, was an early lesson in the absurd. If we could not sometimes escape from horror into the realm of the bizarre, we would drown. Do not think that I see humor in death, for that cheapens the ground that holds those I have loved all my life as well as those young men I loved for the days or weeks I nursed them. During the War, when I would report for work at the hospital of a morning and hear the steward surveying for nighttime tragedies, singing out, "Anybody dead yet? Anybody 'bout to die?" I sometimes laughed to myself as I walked past.

Father put the paper down, finished his dessert, and said, "There," with great finality.

Mother said she was glad he enjoyed the syllabub, although she thought Clarice had put in too much lemon juice, but his liking it was all that mattered, and for the next evening she was proud to be serving his favorite, Solomon's Temple in Flummery, if we could find the Turk's-cap pan, which was probably in the nursery, where the twins liked to run about with it on their heads. I was astonished, had never heard her gush on and on to that degree. She looked exhausted, trying as she had been to postpone Father's inevitable intent for us to travel to Williamsburg, where we would stay with his friend Mr. Luther Edwards, Too-Whit-Too-Woo himself, and attend the execution.

"Alice, you make me nervous," he told her. She retreated at once and found interest in the pattern of oil that floated on her coffee. I sensed that the strain she would suffer over the coming weekend would put her to bed that evening with a sick head-misery, so I excused myself and walked through the muggy night out to the kitchen, where I found Clarice boiling dish-water.

"I am slick with prespiration," she said when she saw me. "Lazy behaving herself, or in there being sorry?"

I told her that Lazy was fine but Mother was soon not to be. "Mother," I told her, "is on the verge of a misery. I can see her eyes changing."

Clarice right away picked rosemary sprigs from the plant that flourished outside the door. As she rolled the sprigs and excited oil from them, she asked, "What he do? What he do this time?"

I told her about the hanging. "Father has not yet said we would be going, but the minute I go back in there and sit down he will. He needs his full audience."

"I give him an audience," Clarice said. "Come on." She told Bertha, who was stringing beans and had several, for some reason, upright between her toes, to finish the rosemary. On the way from the kitchen, Clarice grabbed Bertha's pan of beans. As we walked across the yard, she said to me several times, "You go on along with me now. You know how me and you always go along."

She hit the dining room in full stride and did not break her stride until she was at Father's chair. She slammed the pan down on the tablecloth beside him.

Mother jumped when the pan hit, but not for the surprise of it. No, she was not in any manner frightened. Rather, she was expectant. She knew that Clarice and I were about to "go along." I sat down and rubbed Mother's hand on the spot she always told me rubbing made her head feel better. In China, they will stick a long needle in you there, right in the fatty place between the thumb and forefinger, when any pain of the jowl or head is brought forward, and call it a cure. When I saw my mother so sick, moaning into her pillow, begging for opiates that her stomach would not tolerate, had I known of the needles I would have found a Chinaman to insert them. All I had was my hand just then, and hers, so I rubbed. She was making tiny grunting noises, and she leaned forward and blew out the candle in front of her. Hurry, Clarice, I thought. Mother needs this settled.

Clarice was taking her time. Sometimes if she glowered at Father she could make him alter his position before he stated it. But not tonight. His face organized itself into the grin of a thorough scoundrel. "What're you doing in here with a pan of beans, Clarice? You know I don't allow common goods in my dining room. Hurry up and say what you must. I have a statement to make."

"No, you don't got no statement," she said. "I been out to the porch, shelling these beans, and I hear this on and on about a hanging. I reckon you reckon on taking these innocent children and Miss Alice, but high-ho, they staying home."

He defied her. "Not only are they going. You are going, too."

She grabbed his English linen napkin and, reaching down

into her bodice, wiped perspiration. I pinched Mother's hand and made her look for that second of relief from her pain she might enjoy. I wanted to take her on to bed, but I knew she would not go. She would wait until nausea struck before she did anything to help herself. When I once observed to Clarice that Mother never got sick while we were at any of her friends' homes, Father, overhearing, accused me of plotting and made me go to bed without eating the supper that Clarice was to send up to me while he was snoring.

After Father finished tugging the napkin from Clarice, he threw it at Mintus and told him to go soak it. Mintus, not seeming to mind that he had been hit in the face with a dirty napkin, slunk out of the room. That is what he always did. He slunk. Clarice began to speak, but Father put his hand up and stopped her. Turning to the boys, he shouted, "Goddamnit, John. Let go of that sausage. Don't you sling it. You'll put Henry's eye out. Lazy, are you stupid?"

He did not wait for an answer. He continued once John's sausage was safely on his plate. "Boys, how would you like to go to a public execution?"

"Jesus!" Clarice yelled.

Father did not stop. "And boys, after they cut the men down, I will personally take you to the circus. Would you like that?"

They would very much indeed. They got up and danced around.

Clarice asked what she needed to do to change his mind.

"Nothing. It is decided. You will have this household ready to

go on Friday morning. We will stay at the home of a highly refined gentleman, so do not come into his dining room with a pan
of beans and wipe sweat with his Goddamn napkin. Make
Mintus dust his best suit of clothes. He looks like a nigger."

"He *is* a nigger, Mr. Tate," Clarice told him.

"You can *be* a nigger, and you can *look* like one. You know the
difference. Now get out of here." Father was finished. He pulled
out a segar and waxed it around his mouth, all around, up and
down.

Clarice left, but she came back in with the rosemary tea for
Mother, who was being told item by item what articles of clothing to take to Williamsburg. "Alice, I will not have you think for
a minute, either," Father said, perhaps reading her mind, "that
you will find just cause to trot off and take pleasure in that nest
of vipers and avoid going with us. And Emma Garnet, you will
go, and you will make yourself attractive to everyone you meet.
The poet has a son. You will take copious open-air refreshment
before Friday, so that your coagulated blood will course some
color into your cheeks and you do not look so much like someone
had tightened a noose around your neck."

"Oh Samuel, is this not enough for one night?" Mother said.
She was so tired that her hands shook when she picked up her
teacup.

Clarice took the cup from the table, motioned for me to stand
and pull out Mother's chair, and stopped Father from one last attack. "Yes," she said, "this is enough for many nights. Now
Emma Garnet and I will put Miss Alice to bed. She like to hardly

be walking. You look at her. Look at her walk on out of here. Tell Mintus he can wash the dishes. I will be with this one tonight."

Father took deep wind lighting his segar and did not say good night to us. From the stairs I heard him tell Lazy to clean off the table. Then he asked the boys to sit at "the big table with your father while he describes to you the wonders you are to behold."

Mother stayed in bed with the curtains drawn against light until Friday daybreak, when Father shook her awake, declaring that he was not going to Williamsburg without his wife. When he had opened the curtains, the better to "get you up and out of here," Mother asked if he had had the good grace to let the Edwardses know we were coming.

"Of course!" he told her. "You think I'm a rustic?"

She assured him he was no rustic, and he left her with direction to be downstairs for immediate departure. There was no time for breakfast. We would have corn dodgers in the carriages.

I helped Mother get ready. She was so limp that pushing her arms into her sleeves was like cramming mud into a glove. Her bags were already downstairs. Everybody's were. Father had had the servants pack us the previous evening. I will never forget combing my hair and Mother's with my fingers, because our supplies had been packed. When she and I appeared downstairs, Father summoned the family and house servants, all of whom were going, into the parlor for a lengthy prayer for blessings on the excursion and for a quick word on what we might expect. Maureen was not with us, for she was away in Richmond, staying with the governor's children, enjoying a course of study in "all things feminine" at Miss Sylvester's acclaimed summer training school for "Little Ladies of Aristocratic Promise."

I thought he might warn against pickpockets, as was usual before any outing, but instead he said we "would do well to consider the path of sin that led those murderers to this end. You should examine yourselves to see if such impulse lurks, and if so, repair to the North, where they tolerate shame against their women that Southern gentlemen abhor." I almost giggled, as did Clarice, over his invitation for his Negroes to leave. "Those men deserve to die, and you will see them do so. I will make sure we are in front."

Mother sat down in a slipper chair and closed her eyes. Father made a few remarks on comportment, and then had the children and Negroes and me line up so he could present coins for us to spend at the circus. The boys were made to give their coins back because they had no pockets. They did not want to relinquish the money, but Father assured them that he would keep it at ready dispense. He had not allowed Whately pockets in his pants until he was twelve, for pockets, Father held, made boys look roguish.

I was to ride with Mother, Clarice, and John. Although Father had removed the children's asafoedita bags for fear we would appear unfinished, John still stank. Clarice stopped the procession before we reached the end of the cedar lane and put John in another carriage. Mother was not ready for heavy odors. She rode the entire way with her head on my shoulder and would not take the corn dodger Clarice offered her. I read from *The Lives of the Saints*, which I had taken along as a strengthening tonic for what

I would witness. I was not afraid, but revulsed. The child that lived within me wanted to see a lady walk across a rope, and I wanted to see the wild animals. Oh, and Too-Whit-Too-Woo! Whately used to fall about on the floor laughing at his weekly poems. I had taken as my own Whately's imagined picture of him: a small, effete man with thin purple lips and a beak of a nose. Whately and I could not reconcile Father's love of words with his appreciation for a hack, as Whately referred to all Southern poets save Mr. Timrod. As we bumped along in the carriage, I stroked Mother's hair the way she had Whately's, for it had soothed him verily. At times such as these, when my brother came to mind, I tried to think only pleasant thoughts of him. I distracted myself by telling Mother and Clarice of Saint Friand, who by incessant prayer drove waves of wasps from the fields of those who had persecuted him.

"Why," Clarice asked, "would he want to do that?"

"Because he was a saint," Mother answered.

Clarice said that the world could use more saints. I told some other stories, their favorite being that of Gertrude, who is beseeched by those in fear of rats and mice and by those needing respite from dreams of the recently dead.

For all the stopping it took for the drivers to lay down boards against the mud, we were near supper getting to the Edwardses'. Father always stayed there when on business in Williamsburg, and so I did not harbor fear that his behavior would make the ladies weep. What I did fear was the young man I was supposed to charm. Not that I was averse to meeting someone. I had avoided associations with young men because I did not want someone who needed use of my mind only as a device that would give him praise, give him encouragement, give him esteem. Several girls on the James had already drifted into easy marriages in which no thinking was necessary. I saw my mother as a lady who could have enjoyed developing her mind and might have found the same pleasure in using it that she did in reading light magazines and chatting at sewing circles with her friends, but her survival took the place of whatever mind-work she might have accomplished.

And here came Too-Whit-Too-Woo, hopping around, directing his Negroes where to take bags, clapping his hands to see these "pretty, pretty children!" I stretched myself, out of Father's notice, and observed this man. He was exactly as Whately had envisioned. Father beamed, proud to be able to present such healthy offspring and Negroes.

"And where is my handsome Alice?" Father asked us all.

Clarice helped her out of the carriage, where she had stayed until made to get out. There was no telling of discomfiture in the way she sprang into ladylike action, presented her cheeks to Mr. Edwards, and praised the beauty of the house.

"We have a splendid view of the square," he told us. "You may notice that the gallows are already established. The rabble from everywhere, everywhere, has already started to gather. I'll have to keep a Negro on the porch all night to make them stay off my daylilies."

Father said, "Damn, damn, damn. I promised the children I would have them up front."

Mr. Edwards told Father not to worry. He was a man of some worth in town, and the officials would make sure we were satisfied. I looked at Clarice. I thought, as she must have, Outstanding— another man of means, another man of some worth, by God. She and I stood by the edge of the yard and looked into the square, where gangs of small boys were playing chase while the girls and older people milled about.

"Oh, this is something, a-Lordy," Clarice murmured. I agreed. "He ought not to have brought the boys here," she said.

All three of the boys had been crazed since Father had read the newspaper account. Clarice had several times had to yank them off their feet for playing pretend that their asafoedita bags were the girl's ear.

We went inside to meet this small family, but I could gather no real impression of them until supper, which was virtually thrown at us by servants. Clarice would later tell me that the help was disgruntled because they wanted to go to the "ceremonies," as Mr. Edwards called them, and could attend neither those nor the circus because one of the James's finest families was alighting and they were needed to wait on us. I was seated across from the young man, William, by Father, who thumped the base of my neck, not enough to hurt me, but perhaps enough to make me pay attention to the glorious youth and fall madly in love with him and marry him and take up lovely housekeeping on the Tidewater so that Father could be proud of me. William, it appeared, had been trying to raise a mustache, and when it had not occurred in time for meeting me, he had sought the aid of art. I had noticed that his little sister had used the same charcoal stick to dot freckles on her cheeks. They are now called goo-goo eyes, what he began making at me at once. I worked at not looking at him.

Mrs. Edwards seemed exceptionally peevish and hard to please, sending her plate back again and again because the asparagus was not properly peeled or the chutney was too warm. She did not ask any of us if we needed a thing, and she did not engage Mother in chat. No, Mother, as did I, had to listen to Mr. Edwards and Father pick up their conversation where they had left it at Father's last visit. Jews. Father reported that Austria had been nasty with them. Mr. Edwards was privy to knowledge, which he would share only with us, that the mayor of New York City was planning to squeeze all the Jews, like "juice from an orange, into the lower portion of the city, where they will soon taint the water and poison themselves, one by one by one." Father surveyed my face for a treacherous grin and, finding none, returned to Mr. Edwards and continued with how Jews made themselves pests wherever they migrated and so forth. I ceased to listen and followed Mother's lead in shielding my senses and smiling. All the while, though I dared not look, I felt the Edwards boy's beady eyes on me.

And then, Bing! Mother and I sat bolt upright, wide awake

now to hear Mr. Edwards chiming his fork on the crystal. "I am," he told us, "about to declaim."

William, to his credit, rolled those beady eyes. Mrs. Edwards shocked Mother by offering her some of the snuff she had balled up in her handkerchief, and when Mother jumped back, Father rushed to say that although Mother was an aristocrat, the powders made her dizzy. He then hurried Mr. Edwards along, but he had to wait for the poet's wife to brace herself. When she was ready, Mr. Edwards stood.

"Upon greeting the specter of the gallows across the square," he began, "I felt moved to pen an epitaph." He cleared his throat, patted his mouth, looked to the ceiling:

> "This monument proclaims this solemn truth.
> Beauty is fading, frail the bloom of youth;
> Life is short, a dream, an empty show,
> And all is fleeting vanity below,
> Careless spectator! Learn from hence to die;
> Prepare, prepare for immortality."

Father had before checked my face for treachery, and now I checked his for the same. Would he tell Too-Whit-Too-Woo that his epitaph was written in the 1750s by Samuel Davies, whose volume of verse lay on our library table? Father did well. He gave away nothing. His heart must have been pounding, but he pronounced it yet another fine poem, like the many he had been honored to hear at this same table on other nights of splendid, warm hospitality. When dessert was served, Mr. Edwards invited William and me to take ours out onto the porch. He snapped his fingers, and a sullen Negro woman followed us out to chaperone. I looked to Mother for comfort but—finding none—left with William.

The Edwardses had a double swing. William sat across from me and pretended to finger his mustache. Something came over me, and I could not help saying to this silly boy, "I know it's not real. You can't make it real by touching it."

He stopped what he was doing, studied my face, leaned forward out of the swing, and asked me if I realized how very flattened the bridge of my nose was. I had noticed, when I made thorough inspections of myself before a tall mirror, the way all young ladies do, but I was appalled to think he had seen. "It makes you look"—he sneered—"rather Negroid."

I composed myself and told him that Father had said many times that I was turning Negro. William did not let go his game. He asked if that bothered me, and I said it did not, for I loved the race. There, I thought.

"Then sit out here with a big, black greasy one," he said with a snarl before he went inside and slammed the door. To keep myself from rehearsing the ways Father would curse me when he found that I had spurned his chosen mate—this boy did not have courage to tell anyone the entire reason why—I went straightaway in the side door to the servants' pantry, where I told Clarice what had happened. With a chee-chee-chee, she sent me to bed.

I had been put in a room with Mother, who was up half the night with the whistles and catcalls issuing from across the street. Perplexed at such salacious-sounding noises, I went to the window to see, in the moonlight, girls going up the gallows steps and prancing across the platform as though they were on a Paris stage. It was one of the most incredible sights I had ever witnessed.

There were more the next day. But Mother and I got a late start. I stayed inside with her while Father led everyone else across the street for Methodist mutton chops. Mrs. Edwards's ancient spinster sister, who had refused supper with company the night before, kept knocking on our door to rouse us. "This house wakes up at five o'clock, and it's six o'clock now. It was five-forty-five when I came to this door last time." Mother and I would scooch together and try to ignore her, but this was a family hard to ignore. I had a rod in pickle for every one of them, including the little girl who had sneaked into our room during supper and broken my tortoiseshell combs so they would fit her head.

Mother and I arrived at the square in time to hear the English gentlemen make pleas for money to take home to the chimneysweeps. I had my circus coins, which I had intended to spend on frivolities, but these men made the situation sound dreadful. I asked Mother what I should do, and she had me keep my money. When the hat was passed, she put in two dollars, which a grimy-faced boy went to lift. "Pickpocket!" she screamed at him, shaking his arm until he dropped the money and ran away. Though alarmed at such a vehement display from such a vision of femininity, the English gentlemen thanked her greatly and moved to the next clump of ladies. I was astounded myself, and oh, Mother and I had a fine laugh over a lemonade. We wanted to move to the front, where Father, Clarice, and the boys would be, but we were forever in getting there. We had to wind our way in and out of a nightsweat-smelly crowd of poor and loafering whites, and I kept tapping Mother on the shoulder to tell her that she did not belong there.

She insisted that she stay, to be with the boys, but I knew they could have been cared for by Clarice, who had come out early for that purpose. "They must know I will not leave them to such as this," Mother said as she gestured toward the gallows, where, true to his promise, Mr. Edwards had collected everyone. Right as we found them, a man who introduced himself as a Baptist preacher of some renown asked Clarice, for he was, he said, inquiring of all the sons and daughters of Ham who were on hand, if she would like to purchase a letter from Jesus Christ for ten cents. She told him she would not, for she was Episcopalian and therefore had a whole wad of them at home, which He had written her for free. Father told the man to "leave my niggers alone," for he had already tried Lazy and Bertha, whom Father had to stop from paying out their circus money.

Filled with the same holiday sensation that infused the rabble, Father actually kissed Mother good morning and did not seem to mind that we had missed the breakfast. When she asked Mr. Edwards how his poem had been received, he said disdainfully that he had been brought up onto the platform before the

Englishmen, who felt that he and Harold the Baptist might prepare the crowd for mercy unstrained, but he had been harassed off by the over-anxious mob, whose ears were deaf to the art of poesy. The preacher had been likewise shouted down.

In a whoosh, William came from nowhere, breathed, "Saved your hide—said nothing," into my ear, and vanished into the throng. Mr. Edwards told us that his wife's supper had not agreed with her and so she would, regrettably, have to forgo the event. Father remarked what a shame that was, for as he had told his dear Alice and the children, "You will always mark this day in memory." About then a boy with a highly asymmetrical head asked Father if he would give him a quarter-dollar for being deformed, and no sooner had he been paid to leave than a girl about my age with a terrible welt on her face asked Father what he would give her for having crawled in the ashes as a baby. He fished around for a coin, paid her, letting Mr. Edwards, who, I noticed, did not pay either person, think that he was always such a big spender on what he called freaks and other foolishness. "After all," Father said, "this is for the children. If you pay these imbeciles, you see how they will march around a bit. Nothing harmed by a little lost change."

By the swelling of noise and by the way we were all of a sudden jostled about, I could tell that the crowd was impatient for noon. They wanted the hanging, the circus, ice cream. They wanted to go home drunk and pretend to their sons that they remembered more than they did. This was Virginia's first double execution since the British. And it was starting. The gate next to the courthouse was pulled open, to deafening cheers. Father and Mr. Edwards, being representatives of the Quality, remained composed. But I made study of them. Inside they were jumping up and down. Father had Mintus, Bertha, and Lazy put the boys on their backs, for the children were skittering around on the ground like frog legs on hot grease. Mother sighed in relief, for she had been afraid they would be trampled if the crowd got away from itself, which it threatened to do as the cart with Barrett and Pratt drove forward. I held Mother tightly at the waist. When I pointed to her head, asking if she was getting sick, she pointed in turn to the boys. They would remember that their mother stayed.

I do not recall much of the faces of the two men as they were unloaded. I remember only that they looked hard, and very much too wise. The noise that I thought was as loud as it could be became an incessant ringing from a fire wagon as the men walked up the steps. Mother began blinking. I gave her my handkerchief. She was in white organdy that day, the only spot of beauty there. Father had left her with me to watch this sight, and I could protect her only by shielding her eyes with my hand. She was not meant for something this menacing. She moved my hand away, but she did look quickly at her feet when the sheriff calmed the crowd to say, "Pink, Lycurgus, you two got any last thing to say?"

Everyone stayed hushed, a true triumph of will for most of them. Pink and Lycurgus shouted in unison a chorus that they must have devised over their dainty food of the week previous:

"Ashes to ashes and dust to dust. If it won't for the bunghole, the belly would bust!" The crowd stomped and hooted its approval. Still with her eyes on her feet, Mother shook her head. I put my hand on her back. You miserable, you sorry, miserable man, I thought as Father made sure the boys could see what was happening. Then came the stillness again. The door was set, the nooses tightened. I saw nothing else. When the crowd roared again, telling me that it was over, Mother and I were holding each other greedily. Clarice backed into us, and I told her to stay right in that one place with Mother while I told Father I was taking her back to the house. She needed to be put to bed. I had to chase him to where he, the servants, the boys, and Mr. Edwards were already waiting to see the men cut down and declared dead. A partition had been built along the bottom of the platform, where the two men dangled, and only special guests were allowed behind it. Father made me wait to speak to him, and in those moments I saw the bodies cut down like cured meats, and I saw mirrors put to their mouths and gas-blisters brought to their faces with live matches. I averted my eyes when the match was lit, for I knew from tales of murder what was happening. As was the custom, the judge who had sentenced the condemned men presided over this scientific evidence-gathering so that death could be made known to the crowd that was already milling away from the gallows, waiting for the circus caravan to be brought out. When the judge lugubriously took out his watch and nodded over the time, I kicked at Father to get his attention.

He wanted to know what the devil I was doing. I told him I

was taking Mother back to her room, that Clarice needed to go as well. He said he supposed that was very well, for Mother had looked puny for a week and he wanted Clarice off his back, "which she has been clawing at since I woke up this morning."

When we returned to the Edwardses', Clarice and I put Mother to bed, had luncheon thrown our way, and seated ourselves in the double swing. As we talked over the horror of it all and watched from across the street the circus that I had lost my desire to enjoy, the boys came running to the house, the three of them screaming. It was not until they were on the porch that I realized they were not playing wild Indians. They were terribly distraught. We took them on the swing. Clarice tried teasing them: "Y'all see mens hanging from the throat, and now y'all running from a caged lion?"

Henry, being the boldest, spoke his brothers' parts. "There won't no damn lion. It was a big cat. There won't no damn nigger frying pancakes out of a hat. He had a fire and a skillet and this little toy cap wrapped around the handle. One man had this doll on his lap he was going to make tell jokes, and when the doll's mouth opened he moved his at the same time. And that girl that was supposed to walk on the rope? Well, she fell off."

Randolph whined, "And she didn't even get hurt!" and then buried his face in Clarice's bosom. John cried silently into my sleeve, wiping his nose on it again and again. Clarice asked Henry what else didn't happen. He kicked one shoe to the other and said, "Nothing. Not a Goddamn thing. But they did have this one nigger. He could squeal like a pig, but it won't much fun."

Father had given Henry language to suit his small needs, but Clarice and I were too amused to scold him. We let the boys rest. And then here came another uproar. Father was hounding Mr. Edwards across the street. When they reached the porch, Father popped his friend on the shoulder, a hard lick for such a delicate man to absorb, and asked him to take a look at the boys.

"Look a-there," Father shouted. "See?"

Mr. Edwards explained that they were mere children and that no child should expect to see feats of the sort marveled about in the newspaper. Father would not budge. He wanted to know why his boys had been let down.

Mr. Edwards twisted his already gnarled frame and said, "No boy really expects to see a lion or a tiger. Nobody expects to see pancakes fried in a hat. And as for the lady who fell, that was an accident. I saw her practicing just yesterday when I was out strolling."

"Forget your Goddamn stroll, Too-Whit, and apologize to my boys."

Mr. Edwards refused to apologize to "mere children."

"But they are *my* Goddamn mere children," Father shouted. "Apologize."

The poet did so in a most cursory fashion, which only infuriated Father even more. While Clarice and I held them, while they snuffled in thanks, I understood that Father was the boy who had wanted to see a pancake fried in a hat. He had wanted to see the ventriloquist. He wanted the magic. He was the one. And the fact that his boys had been disappointed reminded him that he was once a child who lived days connected in his mind only by his father and Clarice and a thorough and unrelenting lack of magic.

We left very rapidly. Very rapidly. But Father did take the time to speak on the way out the door. "Mr. Too-Whit," he said, "I ought to kill you, but I'm going to let you live so I can enjoy more of your beauteous and highly original poetry."

Mr. Edwards replied weakly, "I thought you were Quality."

"I am!" Father shouted from the yard. "Samuel P. Tate. That is my Quality."

seven

We had Eden. Quincy and I turned inward on our household, making a joyful life that I can now thread my way back to along a golden river of years that coursed fast and sure by my door until the day in 1859 that Mintus brought the news of Seven Oaks. Until then, I arose each morning with the singular intent of making a beautiful day for Quincy and the three baby girls, who came in three successive years. I was glad to have the children so close upon one another, for I wanted them to be playmates. I wanted them to be jolly together. And they were. Mary, Leslie, and Louise were all good babies, healthy at their births, which were attended by Quincy and Clarice. As I lay resting with each new one beside me, I would have Clarice write to Mother the same message: "We have had a blessing." Soon thereafter, Mother would send a baptismal gown embroidered by her own delicate hands, an engraved silver cup, and a silver comb and brush. From Father would come a gold coin with his assumed family motto, *Perge*, stamped upon it. And Mother would send prayers and all good wishes for the baby's long and happy life, while Father could manage only his *Perge*, the exhortation to proceed.

During those years before Mintus appeared on Blount Street, the days had a soothing sameness that was remarkably different from the explosive interruptions I had endured in my childhood that forced me to often contemplate what ordinary families were like. At the Carters' and Throckmortons' I gained glimpses into worlds that were not presided over by tyrannical fathers. I envied children whose affections were not manipulated, children who were allowed to grow in an orderly progression from innocence to experience without troubles being thrust upon them before they were properly hardened, as a flower's shoot is nurtured indoors before being subjected to harsh sun and hard rain. I was determined, having borne the premature heartaches of my youth, to raise the girls in the shelter of a love that Quincy and I nourished, for the maintenance of our shared, life-joined spirit was as necessary as taking breath.

The way Quincy conducted his home life showed how fortunate he felt, perpetually thankful to be alive. So different was he from my father, who carried on the most quotidian affairs of his days as though he were bracing himself, protecting his prosperity, against the hour that his past would rise up and jerk him back to the terror in the woods. The past both tortured and tempted him, made him both howl and lock himself in the library with his banker to scrutinize interest statements. At suppers with that banker he could announce his worth today as opposed to yesterday and chide the banker into declaring his relative status on the James. So many times I heard him damn Landon Carter for having a fortune that seemed to be "fed from some Goddamn subterranean stream of smelted bullion."

The contrast between my childhood and the peaceful days on Blount Street was evident almost everywhere I looked in our home, whose mahogany-paneled walls imposed a quietude on all the rooms. Unlike Father, Quincy had not built our house as a temple to Mammon, as a showplace, a symbol of accomplishment, a signal to others of what he had become. Seven Oaks was sepulchral by comparison. It was devoid of spirit, save when Mother and Clarice managed to cast off their traces and endow the environs with a certain beauty. As the Blount Street house had been designed in the English style, with a half-timbered and stuccoed façade and a terraced garden that led to a high gate at the street, Quincy wondered if I might like to follow British inclination and name it. In London we had enjoyed collecting the names of homes we strolled past, Felicity Cottage, The Gables, Chauncey's Folly, and thus such. But I had lived in a house with a name, and the posting of "Seven Oaks" on a bronze plaque at the river pier and at the end of the cedar lane did not make the place a home. I was tired of the accoutrements of high-toned existence. I wanted truth, authenticity. I wanted people to walk into our house and know by sheer feeling, know the moment Charlie took their wraps and umbrellas, that they had entered a home.

We furnished the house slowly, first placing the beautiful and useful pieces sent by the Lowells from Boston. There arrived in one of the earliest loads a pie safe, which we put to immediate use. Mr. Thomas Day, a free Negro whom Quincy commissioned to finish the library and complete the nurseries, had not yet made adequate space for all of our books, so we kept pastries and cold meats in the top of the safe and Quincy's medical journals and my books in the bottom. So many times Mother would write that she wished she could send the armoire and vanity from my old room, but Father would not let anything but my clothes leave the house. To smuggle out the books, Mother and I had packed them in chests with my dresses and pantaloons and stockings. When the house was as finished as it could be—not counting the endless ways a lady will spend her time arranging bric-a-brac, until one day she falls asleep in a room replete with evidence of a life fully lived and does not awaken and is discovered there amongst her treasures—I would sometimes walk from room to room saying to myself, "I am finally at home." Even the smallest objects brought me joy, if only for their intrinsic beauty and the glad association I had of Quincy's constant gift-giving. I know a lady who marked all her porcelain so that there could be no dispute upon her death about which Meissen figurine was destined for which niece, but my daughters are not vultures. My only wish is that they do not put anything up to public auction.

I see now the way the afternoon light, dying into darkness, casts a yellow glow on this library, and I abhor the thought of looking down with Quincy to view items unceremoniously carted out by curiosity-seekers. We decided years ago that this house would belong to all three girls and that they could make use of it as they desired, as long as they kept it free of swallowing vines and choking ivy. Lately, I have been approached by Peace College, that it might be used as a dormitory for its students, but I loathe the thought of strangers in a home that was, and still is, sacred to me. Although I was eighteen when we moved in, it was here that I finally acquired my maturity. I became a lady of my own, beyond Father's reach. This house was a sanctuary, and I want it left intact as a museum of delight, a place where the girls can bring their families on holidays and pass on to their children the joy we all had here. My worst fear is of strangers, walking through and complaining that the house does not suit their modern needs, that the hydraulic plumbing, the wide oak floors, the maid's pantry must be ripped out. Quincy and I would be dejected to see the soul of our home, the library fireplace, become the dominion of a family deaf to the memories that the blaze speaks.

When the late sunlight slants across the floor, when the carriages bringing men downtown from their jobs have ceased rattling by my window, I stop whatever I am engaged in to hear Quincy's carriage again come into the drive, the horses stayed by Charlie's "Whoa here. Whoa here, now." And then Quincy is through the door, calling for me, saying we should celebrate his being home at a regular hour. There was a sweetness in the way that he stepped into all the rooms and called out, usually finding me getting the girls up from their naps. During those first few years, I rarely saw him before midnight, but as time passed he hired men he could trust so that he could take some suppers at home. He worked on Saturdays, but he kept Sundays to the family, taking the girls and me for long walks to Lovejoy Park, where he would sit for hours with us beneath the plentiful and fructifying sun. Some days the park was full of families on outings, and oftentimes common folk who had walked over from the flats would seek out Quincy, who diagnosed kidney colic, hernias, and foot fungus on the spot.

I will never forget the time he took a man to the stream, washed his feet, and scraped off hideous instances of plantar warts with the encased scalpel he kept in his pocket in place of an ordinary pocketknife. It is not without symbolism that the man's complaint was "spots" on his feet, for the consequence of knowing him would be the solitary blemish on those halcyon years. I can see the time so well. Quincy tore off part of my petticoat to bind the man's feet and had him sit with us and enjoy tea until he felt ready to move. When he did leave, it was upon the back of Quincy's horse, where he rode with his legs in the air like oars uplifted from a boat. The next day his daughter, dusty and weary from having walked five miles with a load of green apples in her apron, appeared at our side door and told Clarice, "This is all we've got to give. I ate some, made my stomach hurt, but if you put enough soda in the pie, you won't spew." I remember exactly what I was doing at the moment she appeared. I was reading Dickens's thirty defenses of the phenomenon of spontaneous human combustion in preparation to hearing Quincy's rebuttal at the next meeting of The Dialectical Society in Chapel Hill.

Clarice walked the girl through the house, and I followed them as silently as I could to observe the careful way she tiptoed along the perimeters of the needlepoint runner. She took pains as well not to let her soiled sleeves touch the walls, and when I called out to her with a simple, "How do you do?" she turned to me and said, "I done apologized for the apples, but Papa ain't been to work on account of his feet, so there won't nothing else to give, and these is wormy." In the kitchen, she dumped them onto the kneading board and beheld the beauty of the girls, five, four, and three then, who were playing tea party at a marvelous play table with all sorts of hidden drawers and compartments that Mr. Day had made as a gift to them. She was so slight of frame, in that malnourished way, as to appear unreal. She touched the girls as if they were delicate dolls, saying she was the only girl in a family of five boys. She expressed interest in a tin of cocoa on the table, asking whether that was where we kept our money. Clarice fixed her a cup of chocolate, then another, and she began asking questions about our lives that caused me to detect in her that quick-marrow, that quest for avid living, that ignores lines of class hierarchy and race, that does not depend on one's ability to read oneself into curiosity. Quick-marrow is a natural state of being, enjoyed by those who love this life and want more from it than food and shelter and sleep. That earnest quest for peace of mind and heart, mingled with the desire for the titillations, the intrigues of romance, the questioning of why we are on this Earth and how we got here, the drive to know why crazy uncles are locked in the attic, the need to know why maple leaves turn scarlet before oak—these varying levels of desire have been readily discernible in people I have known. By the time the girl lit on her third question, why I kept books in the safe where "stovepots belong to be," I knew I would help her.

The girl was named Lavinia Ella Mae Dawes. She was fifteen. Her mother was a washerwoman, and her father shoveled coal, thus the reason his feet had put him out of commission. I sent Charlie to her home with a cartload of supplies from the larder, which I asked her to choose. She was unfamiliar with some of the more fancy foods, pickled okra, pickled beets, stewed tomatoes. The last, which she called "love apples" as did the old folk, scared her, she said. "Mama would only let us eat them if we were starving, which we are, so in that case, can I have two jars?" she said quietly. When Charlie asked her if she was ready to go along home, she looked to Clarice and me, her hazel eyes wondering whether she might stay with us. She offered to mind the girls while I tended to my business, but I had no business right then but her. We sat at the table with Mary while she cut drawings out of magazines, and when the girls were ready for a nap, Lavinia asked if she might go upstairs with us so she could see the "whole big house." She peeked in each room as we passed, and when we reached the guest room, which she loved for its wallpapering of trailing irises, I asked if she would like to stay there a few days. I promised to send Martha each morning to help her mother care for her brothers and the household.

Clarice and Mavis and I made Lavinia over. Quincy was so very kind to her. At the supper table, where she was desperate to show proper manners, he calmed her by introducing her to the orchids I used as a somewhat unorthodox centerpiece, but she needed no introduction. She astounded us by touching the leaves of each plant and naming cattleya, vanda, dendrobium, oncidium. When he praised her splendid knowledge, with the implied question of how she had learned what she knew, she explained that her grandmother worshipped orchids, that the daily struggle to keep the stubborn things abloom kept her alive even as shingles gripped her so badly that she crawled on her hands and knees to nurse them. People from all over Raleigh brought ailing plants to the woman and paid her a penny a day to bring them back to life. Quincy asked Lavinia what she liked to do best of all, a query he frequently put to strangers so that, as though by miracle, he could anonymously make their wishes materialize— a new fishing pole, a brass cricket box, a voucher for a suit of clothes from his Atlanta tailor, a nursing apprenticeship at the hospital, a subscription to *The Progressive Farmer,* dental plates, gravestones. He was a magical filler of desires, big or small, that people he treated—tradesmen who lingered at his door, maids who shared Sunday supper in our kitchen, boys who served us at the Yarborough House when Clarice and other cooks from the downtown neighborhoods enjoyed their Sunday night off— might sheerly breathe a wisp of longing for; he would act as a quartermaster of the soul. And now he wanted to know what Lavinia needed.

She was with us three days before he discerned her inner need, and in that time Clarice tamed her wild red hair with hot linseed oil, I soaked her hands in pressed olives and softened calluses that should not have marked the hands of a girl of fifteen, Mavis sewed skirts and blouses for her and Charlie measured her for shoes, and the girls accompanied her on walks in Mordecai Woods, where she taught them nomenclature by the shapes of fallen leaves, and they in return taught her how to drink imaginary tea from their tiny cups. She was shyly grateful at every act made in her behalf, and when Quincy and I took her with us to see a production of *Macbeth*, she met our other company, the Haywoods, with ease, introducing herself as "just Lavinia Dawes, up visiting from the flats." When we took our seats and perused the program, Quincy realized what should have been obvious to us all along. Without a hint of shame, self-pity, or neediness, she expressed a desire to "read along with the show, what little of the words I can make out," so she could steady herself for anything unexpected. "I don't want something to alarm up at me," she whispered to Quincy.

The next day he went to her home in the flats, gave her father a pair of sturdy-soled shoes that would allow him to return to work, and asked permission to enroll Lavinia in the introductory program at Saint Mary's School, where a girl could receive, he told her parents, a good and thorough education. Lavinia had explained to us that her family was Primitive Baptist, and this sect, founded on paranoia and the certainty of an imminent, clamorous rapture, was adequate reason for her to suspect that surprises lurked behind stage curtains, reason for her to ask reassurance from Quincy, who recited the sequence of events aloud to her to ease her worries. Quincy knew she needed to read herself into a world that was more predictable than what she endured in the flats. She required enough education to make her see that days can be lined out, planned, anticipated. She had to know that she need not fear stepping off the edge of a flat world.

And so she was enrolled in day school. Charlie took noon dinner to her every day. At first, she would send a dogwood blossom or a rose stolen from the chaplain's garden as thanks. Then the notes began, growing from "Thank" to "Luv to Mst Qinc" to "I Thank Yu" to "Thank you, thank you." On some Sunday nights, with everyone but Charlie off work, Quincy and I would ask her to sit with the girls while we enjoyed a quiet dinner at the Yarborough. Without fail, when Quincy was taking her home, I would find my jewelry slightly rearranged in the drawer, nothing missing, but everything touched. Powder would be flaked on the bureau, and the children's Limoges figurines of storybook characters turned awry from the tableaus of their usual arrangement. I kept a Fabergé egg, a wedding gift from Quincy, wrapped in cotton batting in a box that his father had sent from Egypt, and sometimes after Lavinia left, the wrapping was loose at the edges. Even when the wrapping was not loosened, I could sense that she had held the egg, in the same way a child knows another has ridden her cart even though the seat has not been moved, in the same way Clarice could lay hand on the copper bowl bought for her at a dear price in Paris and know by feel, by the supernatural touch shared by women and children, that an unauthorized user had whipped cream in it. I do not recount Lavinia's ramblings in our household with any animus or ill intent toward her memory. I remembered the way that I had caressed my mother's diamond brooches, her ruby and sapphire rings, her engraved sterling bracelets, how it felt to hold things so dear.

Quincy maintained her through two years at Saint Mary's, and he saw that her brothers received what tutoring their father would allow. Charlie would take them to the Lovejoy School of a morning, dressed and shod courtesy of Quincy and Burke Haywood, and in the afternoons they rode the coal cart with their father. Clarice kept the family in vegetables, for Mrs. Dawes was brought down by dropsy and could not keep a garden. When Lavinia graduated from school, second in her class, poised now and quite eloquent, she wore a white eyelet dress sent by Mother. Through letters to Seven Oaks I had let her know of my "project," as Quincy called Lavinia. A small society of our own making—the Haywoods, Judge and Mrs. Hugh Bailey, the Governor and Mrs. Reid, and the Bishop and Mrs. Cheshire—attended her graduation, and I arranged a supper for her at Milburnie Lodge, the latter causing a stink among mothers who had wanted to reserve the river lodge for their "more deserving" daughters. Lavinia's parents would not come, despite my going to the flats and making a spirited plea, describing the governor as a good and ordinary man, accessible and genuine of heart. They had the clothing, sent weeks before by Quincy, but they were intimidated, so very afraid. They were grateful for the education given their children, but they would stay at home on Lavinia's fine day. "My glory," Mrs. Dawes said, "will be the light on Lavinia's face when she tells of it, all the doings of a party." Sad to say, she concluded, "And you see, the worst of it is, we would feel queer having fun. We won't raised to jump around."

The party was indeed grand, picnic hampers open and overflowing with hams and cheeses, Negroes filling champagne, and best of all, the sight of Lavinia conversing with Governor Reid with a confidence that belied the fact that she had spent her childhood breaking aloe on wasp stings acquired at a tilting outhouse, and a head-thrown-back laughter that proved a thorough farewell to the dour pessimism of her hard-rock religion. Quincy spoke my thoughts for me as we stood with the Haywoods watching Lavinia enjoy her day: "What a little learning will do to ward off the boog-bears of this world." I had let her borrow a gold necklace with a filigree heart to set off the scalloped bodice of the eyelet gown, and that evening, when Quincy and I were faced with the sad reality of returning her to the flats, to that unpainted shack that sat as lopsided as its outhouse, I entreated her to keep the necklace. She cried her thanks and admitted what I already knew: "I have touched it so many times."

The next week, she took a position, for which Quincy had recommended her, at Warren Academy. I loved the notion that she would be where Whately had been. He would have made a lively mentor for her. The girls sent her pressed flowers, and when an orchid was waning, I would place the blooms between the pages of a book and send it to Warren and feature Lavinia's pleasure.

When *Leaves of Grass* was so popular with the young people, I mailed her a copy, advising her to keep it hidden from the old masters who had punished Whately for owning books of similar vigor. Instead, she read aloud from it to a first-form class, who complained that the poems did not have a rhyme they could go along with. With the insight of a Boston Brahmin, not a flats girl, she wrote to me: "As I was afraid at *Macbeth*, the boys could not predict the next stanzas and sat frozen in fear that something might jump out at them. They need the regularity of rhyme. They need Longfellow, but did you not, Mrs. Lowell, send me the future?" Her pay was cut as punishment for teaching out of the canon, but Quincy made up the difference.

At eighteen, Lavinia married, taking as her groom a circuit-riding lawyer whom she had met at a Warren alumni gathering. "He has a leonine mane and deep, sea-green eyes," she wrote me. "He holds me in the highest regard. I think often of the way Dr. Lowell gazed at you, and I pinch myself to be so lucky. Thank you both for showing me this life. I want to have children soon, three girls just like yours. Give them kisses and please take this bit of money, all I have left this week, and have Charlie take them to buy toffee from the German." She asked me to have Clarice, on her next vegetable-bearing trip to her parents' house, dig up a profusion of peonies, the only flowers that blossomed in the weedy yard, to take to the governor, in honor of his reelection. I took the flowers to the mansion myself, and he remembered so fondly the "chin-up young girl from the flats."

Her luck in love did not hold. Her letters ceased, and after I sent a worried note to the headmaster at the Academy, he returned news of her death with childbed fever. I had not even known she was expecting. I was sick with grief. When I went to commiserate with her parents, they blamed me for her demise. I reminded them of the gratitude they had rained down on Quincy, of the boys' schooling, of the vegetables. Still they saw nothing but a daughter snatched out of her place. Her father sneered and said, "You ought to heard them tell, all these niggers that come up and by here, how she danced with the governor with her shoes in her hands, danced like she was somebody."

"Well," I told them, "she was indeed somebody. And these boys will be somebody, too. My husband and I will sponsor them at Warren Academy, and you will have only yourselves to feed, and that will be minus my pickles and vegetables."

The old man said I could take the boys, for their brains were already rotted for decent labor, and I could tell "that uppity nigger woman what you send with the collards and carrots to stay away from here." I wished my "uppity nigger" had been with me at that moment, not at home preparing Quincy to go to Warrenton to see after Lavinia's affairs.

When Quincy arrived in Warrenton, he found Lavinia's husband in custody on a charge of trafficking in stolen goods. He had tried to sell the jewelry that I had sent Lavinia at intervals, each piece engraved with my initials, nothing of high value, but all recognizable to a clever jeweler as being far beyond the purse of a country lawyer, whose dubious legal practices had already marked him for suspicion. Quincy cleared the matter, reclaimed the jewelry, and was asked by the widower, who spoke his grief rather than showed it, that he be granted a loan that would set him up in practice in Louisburg, away from "all these bumpkin goober-grabbers." When Quincy told him that our relationship had been with Lavinia and that he looked to be quite capable of earning a living, the man said, with the nonchalance of someone commenting on balmy weather, "Well, I reckon she was your whore." Quincy had the constable lock the man up again, this time on the charge of defamation of character. He made an arrangement with a magistrate and paid the man's way for thirty days in jail. The court was glad for the money.

Quincy went to the academy and spoke with the chambermaid who had attended the fatal birth and seen to the burial of both mother and child. While Lavinia was sick, the woman tended to her gently, for her beauty and grace and care of her pupils, she said, warranted somebody's taking a concern to her. Lavinia's home was within walking distance of the campus, and after Quincy retrieved my letters from the house, he hired the woman to close the place and then found the landlord and quitted the lease. He negotiated with the headmaster to receive Lavinia's brothers, and went on to visit her grave in the Congregationalist funeral yard. I remembered her writing to me that she had chosen that church because it allowed her mind to wander. So far had she come from the simple, halted notes of thanks, the wonder at my copper bathing tub. Only my pride in her journey assuaged the grief.

And then a year or so later—I remember reading the letter when Louise, at eight, was laughing over finally being able to skip a stone across our goldfish pond—one of Lavinia's pupils wrote to me after finding my calling card in *Leaves of Grass*. He had stolen the book from her and felt so guilty over the act, especially after her death, that he dared not open it for a long time. And when he did, he wrote:

Dear Mrs. Lowell—

I thought you'd better know. I thought you would understand and know what to do about him—Miss Lavinia's husband. See, I was much enamored of her. I thought myself grown at sixteen, a silly thought, I know, for a boy. But one night I went to see her with some fetched-forth question about an assignment. I went when I knew he was there, so she would not get a name for having one of her pupils showing up. Well, the truth I thought you should know—the door was cracked and I could see in. She was on the floor, whimpering. Her hands and arms were over her face. He had a sack of oranges—I knew it was oranges because I could smell them. Smelled like Christmas. Anyway, Mrs. Lowell, he was beating her with the sack of oranges. I am sick to say, but I ran. I ran back to my rooms and did not

tell anybody and did not get help for her. I know that
your husband installed the infirmary at the Academy. He must be a powerful man of some means. If
he gives me the word, I will hunt down her husband
and shoot him like a cur dog. Just let me know.

Sincerely, I am

Septimus Wrenn

Quincy was terrifically well connected all over the states, and
it did not take but a matter of months to find Lavinia's husband.
He was doing menial title work up North. Quincy's uncle Barton,
a member of the Massachusetts State Court of Appeals, was
more than happy to help his nephew smooth any legal problems
that might arise from having the fellow disbarred. And when
that was accomplished, he was humiliated into making the ardu-
ous journey to south Texas, where, in those days, men were ru-
mored to disappear into the big, broiling, unforgiving sky.

To help my spirits, Quincy bought the girls and me a mule.
She would eat sugar out of Clarice's hand, but to me she exhib-
ited only a sour, resentful, pessimistic outlook. I was not ready,
my heart was not ready, to train another creature to enjoy this
life, and so I had Charlie trade her for a crate of rabbits. The girls
and I delighted in them, and after they multiplied, we set the
grown ones loose in Mordecai Park. They returned the certain
rhythm to our lives, the way they grew in a season, to be let free.
Lavinia's sad story was the only blight on those years, and for
that I am grateful in knowing that it is extraordinary to have

such a span of time marked by happy births, sunrises, sunsets, holiday dinners with crown roasts and stuffed hams, pleasant walks with girls playing chase about my legs, and the sweet footfall of an adoring man, coming through the door, loving me, loving me, loving me. Loving Quincy. Not long now. And it will be my feet he hears coming one night, all the way from North Carolina, just to find him.

eight

Clarice had taught Martha, Mavis, and Charlie the rudiments of reading and writing, and by 1858, after nine years of kitchen-table tutoring, mainly from *Murray's Grammar*, they were able to follow along in the Prayer Book, copy down messages left by Negroes from around the neighborhood who needed Quincy to attend to them on his weekends, and read with the girls. Mary, Leslie, and Louise spent their early-morning hours in study. After they finished their lessons with me, they would often find the servants and share tales from Irving's *History of the Life and Voyages of Columbus* or their favorite, Peter Parley's *Winter Evening Tales*. Mothers on Blount Street were sending their children, by eight, to the Lovejoy School, but I could not bear to part with mine, even for them to spend days only the three miles away.

With Whately's books, Quincy's anatomies, and those texts I ordered from various concerns, I was able to bring the girls along to a knowledge and understanding comparable to that of any boys their ages. As I struggled through Herodotus with them, my mind drifted back to Father's nightly consumption of Greek texts, his exhorting loudly from his chambers, to emerge after having triumphed over a conundrum, swiping his mouth like a starved man who had just devoured a hot buttered loaf. Language comes easily for young children, as the mind is fertile and ripe for acquisition, not cluttered with the anxieties and emotional obstacles of adulthood, and so I would regard, with regret in my heart, how my father, had he not threatened and disowned me, might have visited Raleigh, arranged the girls about his feet, and imparted to them the purity of Greek grammar.

But the ideal was impossible. They regarded Dr. Lowell as their only true grandfather. He wrote letters regularly and sent exquisite gifts from Paris, where he lived for a time to instruct at medical school. Whenever the girls asked after my father, I would deflect their inquiries, say in a hundred different ways that he was a very, very busy man who did not like to write letters; but I doubt that he even knew the names of his granddaughters. Truth told, he carried on a vehement correspondence with every pro-Negro newspaper editor in the South.

I filled the girls' minds with pictures of their grandmother, who did write sweet letters to them. And as a way of absenting my own mind of its grief over Lavinia, I completed my first artwork in a long while, a charcoal drawing of Mother. I had not attempted any artistic project since I had, at ten, made a watercolor study of a Negro child washing her arms at the horse trough. But the tutor Father had arranged for me derided this subject as pedestrian. He was a most arrogant and pedantic man: "Aristocrats paint aristocrats," he insisted. He did, however, teach me the fundamentals of style, how to appraise the collection at Seven Oaks, and the lessons helped me, on my honeymoon visit to the Louvre, better appreciate the glory of the Galerie Médicis, the compounding of the Baroque, reality, and fantasy. Had it been proper, I would have lain in the middle of the floor to absorb the room in its entirety, as my girls did of evenings when Quincy spread a coverlet on the lawn, reclined with them and told the stories that sparkled in the constellations of the clear night sky.

One of my greatest admirations for my husband was his eagerness to explain the world around him. At the Louvre, he interpreted the allegories of Marie de' Medici to Clarice, who remarked upon seeing and hearing how Henry IV entrusted his government to the queen when he left for war in Germany, "I like to see Mr. Tate let Miss Alice run the house when he goes off to agitate." She referred to Father's grandiose intentions of going to Richmond and converting peace-lovers and compromisers to "throw off the shackles of invidious Federals by organizing a militia of power and purpose not seen since the days of Julius Caesar." When he sent his proposition to the governor, with a similar offer posted to Virginia newspapers, he received a formal but polite note that his abilities would be kept in store. He made his fury over the rejection known in another round of letters, a blaze of words that would one day be repeated to him in General McClellan's pronouncement of his doom.

My mind so easily strays to Father, perhaps because on these afternoons the window by my table frames low-hanging white oak limbs, on which are suspended feeders for sparrows, the only birds my father refused to shoot—"His eye is on the sparrow." I must close the shutters and light the lamp so that I can see beyond him to her, to Mother. Leslie now has the sketch that I made of Mother. I gave it to her upon the birth of her first baby, so lovely a child, because Leslie grew into a resplendent image of her grandmother, not just in the face but in the easy elegance of her every move, her grace, her quiet intelligence, her compassion. I composed Mother's picture from memory, bringing a diffuse halo about her in chiaroscuro, as I had recalled sunlight used in Vermeer's *Astronomer* and Rembrandt's *The Archangel Gabriel Quitting Tobias and His Family*. Quincy and I made copious notes in the museum, but whenever my memory faltered and I craved visual memory, all I needed to do was consult Clarice, describe a bit of picture, and she might say, as with the Rembrandt, "Oh, that one where the light sucked up the angel." Vivid as were her memories of the paintings, Clarice had been transfixed by the mummies and the brilliant funerary gold of the Egyptians.

Quincy thought my sketch of Mother an accomplishment of some worth and urged me to buy paints and easels for the girls and teach them what I could. The other little girls in the neighborhood took lessons from a man not unlike the tutor of my youth. In fact, Saturday-morning sessions with him at the home of Colonel Andrews, three houses from us, were *de rigueur*, but after interviewing the instructor, I realized that the girls would be enjoined only to paint flowers, the façades of their homes, the ducks at Lovejoy Lake, and one another. I do not mean to imply that I alienated the girls from the society about us. They played daily with the Andrews children, helped Josiah Bailey paint his front door red for Christmas—a grand decorative sacrilege—sang in the Cherub Choir at Christ Church, and chased the governor's children through the woods, and at the children's celebration before the 1858 June German, the social event of the high season, Mary was crowned the Queen of Love and Beauty.

As I painted with the girls, I detected their personalities in their individual styles. Louise's landscapes of our back gardens were almost defiant—birch trunks were black, leaves swirled as though contorted in agony against a wind always personified as fingers thrust from the corner of the paper, the water of the goldfish pond was perpetually in a tempest. She did not have an unsettled or disruptive soul, but she was the one of the three girls who would most strongly assert her considerable will. Quincy gave each of the girls a weekly allowance to spend as they pleased, and Louise was the sister invariably elected to campaign for an increase. When he refused, she would say, "Well, you think about it, Father. I'll be back."

Leslie, who possessed an otherworldly visage, was frequently transported into the sphere of imagination, into the lands we encountered in Whately's old geographies; she inserted into her landscapes fountains, fairies, dragons, leprechauns, fictions of all classes. When she meant to show wind, an instruction I gave in hopes of teaching them about force and motion, she painted a nose at the top of the paper. As for Mary, her paintings were stylized views of the gardens, her palette as true as she could figure it, the great white cat that sometimes slept underneath the grape arbor just as in life. She could convey the animal's comfort and serenity. She was also the child most tender and true, softest, easiest to tears, the one who left butterscotch on her father's pillow when he was to be home late of an evening. I could not have asked for girls more singular in spirit yet so kindred in their capacity for affection and respect. Many times, I rolled their paintings and sent them to Mother, who pinned them to the curtains of her room, which more and more, she said, needed closing against the glare of her western light. "Bertha has made me several poke-bonnets," she wrote, "and I pull them half over my face to work the roses. The sun pierces me, but I am managing rather comfortably, going about my affairs when clouds come. I drove myself in the phaeton to the Carters' for a quilting. So I am really quite capable. You must stop your worry. Keep your mind on the girls and their lessons. They sound so smart!"

Oh, they truly were. Quincy helped me with their Latin. As a treat for a well-received lesson, a thoughtful translation, the girls would take parts reading the Roman myths. Louise always demanded to be Diana, even if the goddess had no scheduled appearance in a tableau. Charlie had made her a bow and arrow, and she lived to pose with it. We wanted their minds trained. We wanted them to know excellence, for that is the essence of virtue. As we studied together, when my thoughts fell back to my father, I cursed him for locking himself in his chambers with Mintus as his only listener, hoarding language, excluding me, curious as he knew I was, in his journeys to Carthage, to Rome, to his favorite place and time, Athens in her golden age.

I would think—and I remember the words as they first entered my head as it rested on Quincy's knee—I could have been Father's girl, except that my heart's mission did not match my sister's. It was clear to me so early in my life that we harbored different hopes. Maureen conformed like a well-fitted satin glove to Father's vision of resplendent young ladyhood. She asked nothing of him, but received a bounty solely because, as said, she was all he could have wished for. She did not make trouble; did not want to read anything besides his religious assignments and the red-back romance thrillers he bought her from the Norfolk concern he traded with; did not linger in the kitchen; did not touch a Negro save when she was being dressed, undressed, or bathed. And she sang. He liked the idea of a daughter singing by the grand piano that his lovely wife played while James society sat about in Hepplewhite chairs with teacups on their knees and listened with rapt attention, each no doubt whispering to the other, "She is an angel." Father outfitted her for her destiny by teaching her salon French, enrolling her for comportment classes at Miss Sylvester's School, and, after her sixteenth birthday, making an exception to his mandate against

Northern schools and sending her to study voice at Miss Carpentier's in Philadelphia. She trained with the great Parelli, who was so impressed by her abilities that he arranged for her to open a performance for Gay Gazzaniga. Mother did not feel well enough to escort her to Philadelphia, so Father broke another of his rules, leaving Seven Oaks to a hired man, and took her himself.

John and the twins had moved to Columbia, South Carolina, where Father had arranged for them to learn the business of cotton exporting. His end was for them to secure positions in London and, according to Mother, "influence trade on behalf of the Tidewater and return to run Seven Oaks into what your father is calling the pinnacle of prosperity." Mother wrote that seeing Maureen, who was, I concede, a gorgeous creation, on the stage was "the highlight of Samuel's life. He is sure that Maureen can marry a senator now, or even a duke or an earl. He plans to take her to England with your brothers and make the rounds with her. He has requested a reception at the Court of St. James's, but no word yet."

Do not think that I hated my sister or writhed with jealousy. No, she had what she wanted, and I had satisfactions in the same degrees, but of inherently different aspirations. I would read letters about Maureen's doings and then turn to my family, to minding my soul, while my sister minded the ephemeral, her beauty and talent, and sought a match based on physical, financial, and social fitness. Mother said so many times that young men sent roses by the dozen to the house, and at the Christmas of

Maureen's sixteenth year, right after her triumph in Philadelphia, young Landon Carter festooned the front door with mistletoe and camped on the veranda. When I wrote to Mother, having to state the obvious, perhaps out of a snip of justifiable envy, that I had never been so harassed by callers, she replied, "My dear girl, you know it to be true, for you are wise, that gentlemen are always talking about clever young ladies, saying this and that about how much they enjoy their company, but in the end, they make the biggest stirs, create the deepest tragedies, over the comeliest ones. You have your heart's fortune in Quincy. How glad I am that you made a love match." Still, when Maureen wrote to me of a tally of proposals, all declined by Father, I could not help warning her that a person of beauty within never publishes her trail of suitors as though they were competitors in a horse derby.

Clarice often remarked on my girls' beauty, hoping it would not get in the way. She meant that she did not want their loveliness to impede a thoughtful life. Quincy, Clarice, and I were determined that the girls feel, as we did, the joy that follows a task met head-on and conquered. Although Clarice did not study Latin with us, she did read poetry to the girls, all the time with a dictionary on the kitchen table. And when the girls completed the first readings, guided by Quincy, of the same lessons being learned by boys their age, Clarice bought them, with her own money, a mechanical organ grinder and monkey that all three of them had been clamoring for. They had done well. While at times Louise, being a bit too young, flounced off to play with her dollhouse, Mary and Leslie listened to original and translated readings, questioning all the way the odes of Horace, Cicero's orations against Catiline, Virgil's *Bucolics*, a small part of Sallust, and Caesar's *Commentaries*.

The plan was that as the girls grew, they would return to these basic texts and understand them more fully, examine etymologies and contemplate deeper meaning. They never balked, for I leavened the classical studies with plenty of open-air play, with music, with Lazy's old scary nursery tale "The Indian with the Froze Arm." Clarice broiled pig tails, brought from the Mordecai plantation, in the fireplace, as she had at Seven Oaks. She made ash cakes and raisin scones. She played what they called "Ancient Maid" when she washed them with perfumed soaps in the copper tub. Again and again, Clarice would say to me, "Happy mother, happy children." When Quincy took time away from the hospital, he read to them from a book Mr. Bronson Alcott had read to him as a boy, light morality stories. Quincy and the girls would be in this same room I am in now, but with the full light of the sun streaming in, the girls on the needlepoint footstools Martha had made for them, and Quincy would tell of Slovenly Peter, Rocking Phillip, and Greedy Jacob. So many of these scenes were of a Sunday, and after the stories, we would say good-bye to Clarice and then go to the Yarborough and have turtle soup and sourdough crackers. Always, for dessert there was a nice trifle.

People always mingled amongst the tables on those Sunday nights, and I can remember precisely that it was August 21,

1859, when little Armistead Neely, about ten or so then, appeared breathless at our table. He had just gotten a report from one of the waiters, who was "in tight" with the newsprinter's devils across the street, and it seemed that the same Frenchman who had already walked across Niagara Falls on a tightrope while blindfolded and pushing a wheelbarrow had now crossed with a man on his back. The girls were all a-flutter, having seen numerous renderings of the Falls and also having been promised a trip there one day. I had to think of the execution carnival, with its hapless tightrope walker, which I had related to Quincy early in our marriage, in one of our night-owl talks..

The girls were hard to put to bed that night, but when they were finally snug, Quincy and I took glasses of Madeira out onto the veranda. As was the soothing ritual, he unpinned my hair. He asked if I had a letter for him to post to Mother the next morning. I did. I had not heard from her in two weeks, and I was full of concern. In that last letter she briefly mentioned an increased tightness in her temples, but spent much time on Father's failure to gain admittance into the Society of the Cincinnati, the hallmark of Southern nobility. He assuaged himself by purchasing a new Arabian horse, a satin riding coat, and an Hermès riding saddle "ordered on dire rush from Paris. He rushes, you well know, so very much."

Maureen had sent Leslie a birthday letter three weeks prior and, in a rare note to me, reported that Mother had not been feeling well, but not to worry. Father had called upon a doctor to come take up house at Seven Oaks and see if he could divine the origins of Mother's constant head-miseries. Quincy, I remember, told me that she had not written probably because of some prescribed geographical or rest cure, perhaps had not had time. "Any doctor worth anything would send her to a spring. She needs the lithium in the waters," he told me. I knew that was true, for when he had arranged for her to take the waters and to follow a course of deep-sleep therapy over the past ten years, her condition had improved. Father had, surprisingly, asked Mrs. Carter to accompany Mother to Shocco Springs for a duration when he was in planting or harvesting seasons. Until now, he had never summoned a doctor for her, which made no sense to me, since he nurtured the image of himself as the sort of man who liked to get to the bottom of things. He specialized in conquest. Perhaps he discounted her pain as a mental aberration, a phenomenon best treated by a resort's traditional offerings, water, rest, and pleasant conversation. Quincy wished Maureen had given the doctor's name or something of his credentials. As he had said so often of Mother's head troubles, "Her problem is extreme tension, and the tension is with your father."

I told Quincy that she also needed Clarice, that we were so very overdue in taking her back to Seven Oaks and bringing Mother to Raleigh. During the years I had said these words so often that they had begun to lack true will and intent. Mother's letters never sounded any crisis. If anyone seemed to have misery, it was Father. His gout sometimes put him on crutches, although nobody saw him hobble in public. And his morale must have been taking a beating—his calls to raise a militia scoffed at, the rejection by the Society of the Cincinnati, his certain realization that his eldest son's end was common knowledge. Sally Willcox saw Mother at Bruton Parish and at gatherings of the Episcopal Church Ladies and often wrote to me of how beautiful she was, how affectionately she spoke of her granddaughters.

The trip to Seven Oaks from Raleigh took three or four days, depending on the weather. There was no train on which I could travel at top speed back to Virginia. And I was so in love with my life that I could not take leave of it, had to settle this, had to settle that, had to find a time when Quincy could go with me. Twelve years. Mother was fifty-one now. She no doubt went to sleep wondering of the reality, the clear features, of the drawings I had rendered of the girls and sent to her. She must have wanted to touch the softness of the skin that was muddled by those ambrotypes I sent on her birthdays. I had no right to stay away. And now a doctor was with her.

That Sunday evening of the girls' sleep-robbing excitement, I worried aloud to Quincy until he put his fingers to my lips and said, "Soon, we will go very soon."

I recall that we stayed on the sleeping porch rather than in our bedroom. I listened to crickets and cicadas and napped in snatches, got so little rest for thinking. When I thought forward, I saw war. When I regarded the present, I saw perfect peace. My considerations were all of the past, and of Mother. Mother with her head buried in a pillow of down feathers. A doctor sent for to cure her, finally. That was good. Or was it?

Father tended toward the old ways of healing. After a discussion of Quincy's training, during his first dinner at Seven Oaks, Father had looked stricken when Quincy said that what he called "robbing the body of its energy"——he meant bleeding, but could not say it at the table——was antithetical to all common sense of sound medical judgment. After dinner, when Father claimed that he was "much lately affected by the bilious temperament" and needed a course of cold-sheeting to restore his "balance," Quincy countered that the notion of humors was a quaint fiction, useful in the dark times to explain the unseen, indecipherable mechanics of the brain and body, but not taken seriously by any modern school.

Father left the table and returned to show Quincy his medical Bible, the manual of Dr. John C. Gunn of Knoxville, on which he solely depended to keep the elements in check. "Earth and fire and wind and water. All we need we have in nature."

Quincy said that he knew Dr. Gunn's reputation well, that while he was in school in Philadelphia he had attended one of the famous doctor's lectures, an inspired talk on the classification of medicines and the preservation of roots, herbs, and barks.

Instead of expressing any pleasure that Quincy had found something to praise in his trusted medical reliance, Father said nothing. But later that night, I heard him shout to Mother, "He wasn't agreeing with me. He was condescending to me, the Goddamn ninnyhacker."

As Quincy arose to go to the hospital in the morning, I was tortured with fatigue. I had remembered so completely his first dinner with Father, had realized, just as the first lavender light of day broke, that Father, who had spent his life insisting on the best of everything, had hired for Mother his version of the best doctor money could buy. I was sure Dr. Gunn had been summoned to Seven Oaks. As I tossed and turned toward that ragged sleep that avails itself to guilt-ridden worriers at ravaged dawns, I prayed that he was a sound doctor. I had lived the last twelve years justifying daily, hourly sometimes, my distance from my mother. And all my life now, I have punished myself for reprehensible neglect, for profound dereliction of duty. Although I am seventy next week, I still do not feel adequately chastised. And then Quincy speaks again, as he did of Whately. *Tell. Say it this time without flinching. Say it dry-eyed, and when you are finished let it be over. So go. Walk out in the rain. Again. I watch you from the window.*

She had died ten days after her last letter.

The girls were at Ellen Mordecai's home viewing her son's pet alligator. I am terrified of reptiles, so I stayed home. Clarice and the servants, eager to see such an oddity, went with the children across Lovejoy Park to Ellen's grounds. I was reading—I clearly recall—a newspaper article about an elevator that had been installed at the Fifth Avenue Hotel, where Quincy, Clarice, and I had stayed the night before our honeymoon sail to Europe. When I heard the gate at the street creak and then the knock, I did not jump to open the door, for I was so seldom without Charlie to meet company. In fact, I was irritated that it might be the old lady who peddled stale pies. It was about her due time to come around. But then I heard familiar voices. "This be the house? He say this be the house. You reckon this be the house? You don't know nothing." Mintus and Ezekiel in dispute. As I have always done in my life when hit with a bolt of sudden recognition, the prescience of disaster and death, I vomited, into a wicker planter, and then held on to one piece of furniture and another to reach the foyer.

I opened the door and told Mintus to shut up. That plainly. Ezekiel took off his cap, nodded to me, and asked if he might sleep in the yard. I knew how far they had come, the complexities of the passage—ferry, steamer, cart—how they must have worn soggy the notes of permission and credit Father had given them. Mintus, who was too old for such a journey, looked pitiful, but I despised him anyway. His alliance. His loyalty. The sheer association that he evoked when he began the sentence "Your mother . . ." made me scream again the words "Shut up!" I slammed the door on him, and on my way to the library, I looked out the window to see him stretching out beneath the trees, where Ezekiel was resting with his head on his folded hat.

I do not know how long I lay on the floor, which seemed the only appropriate place to be. I cried until my eyes were nothing, strangling from hatred and unfathomable loneliness. With misplaced anger—the true object of my wrath was our procrastination in returning to Virginia—I silently cursed Quincy for being at the hospital, away from me when I needed him, perhaps coaxing a patient to eat a cracker, maybe out in the flats on a quarantine mission, possibly suturing a sawmill injury, or, worst to my skewed vision, calming a daughter who had just lost her mother to a ruptured appendix. I wanted him home with me, and I had no way of retrieving him that did not involve the sleeping Negroes or myself, and I could not move. And those of my household were off viewing an alligator. Abandoned. That is what I was. My mother was gone, and there was no one to help me. I had never felt so desperate for somebody from somewhere to come and make things right for me. I wanted an apology. Somebody had to say, "I am so sorry."

Mother had taught me how to be an adult, and now, at this moment, I revoked my own privilege to be one. I wanted to be a child, and I cried like one. When I managed a thought, the first to come was that Mintus had given me no note from Father, who had not had the decency to write the words "My dear Emma Garnet." Neither had Maureen. She was twenty-three, an antique virgin. Father had turned away countless suitors because their stations and prospects were inadequate. He had put my sister off too long. Her friends were happily married. She remained at home, waiting, waiting. My brothers, busily engaged in their work in South Carolina, were excused, but by little. Although they had grown up without me, and thus I did not know the intricacies of their characters, I knew that they were of mind enough to have helped Mother. Somebody could have saved her. That much I knew. And with that realization came the next, the inevitable: It should have been me.

And then thoughts raced and fell upon one another in heaps that I tried to sort into some logical order. I arrived at my surmise: She had died in her bed, at least there was that. Father,

God for it to be true, must have gone outside himself and shown her some tenderness. Her friends were called, and they came right away and did all the proper necessaries. They made sure she was beautiful. And she was given a small service, for Father, I could feel it, had been too ashamed by the manner of her untimely departure to call attention to it and himself. For the first time since he was the boy in the scrawny woods with the rifle kicking his back, he did not want people to gather witness. People of the James adored my mother and only tolerated him. He would not want a congregation of those wise faces seeing him make a spectacle of the end of a life that had been more gentle and true than he deserved, more forgiving, faultless, generous. I trusted that the bishop had made a simple, lovely service, and that Mother had been carried from the church by men whom Father envied, men who had shown her more appreciation in instances of their visits than he had in a run of years.

I gave little thought to Maureen, for I did not believe she had the capacity for grief of the extraordinary kind that daughters will have when they reach their arms out like the lost blind, to find nothing where something, someone, by virtue of that irrevocable bond of birth, should be. But Maureen was his now. Away with the roses and proposals and the play-acting damsel she was. She would be Father's. He would not squire her about the Court of St. James's. Not another thing as planned. He surely knew Clarice would never return now. He was a dependent soul, as are most people of this world who shout the loudest, "I am, I am, I am!" Maureen was stuck. And I wondered, in a perverse moment of inappropriate and utterly profane satisfaction, when and how she would realize her predicament. The bride of Seven Oaks.

And then again the thought, Mother is gone. She suffered, and she died in pain. Moment by moment, I became convinced of it. Where had the doctor been? What had he been doing? I recall setting up a growl. I was dry of tears. There was the bit of laudanum that Quincy kept in the house to subdue Martha during her vile moontimes, but I thought better of it.

I went to the backyard, past the rabbit hutch, past the stable and chicken coop, all the way out to the edge of the property, and began screaming for Clarice to get home. I had two miles to yell over, but I felt that the rage in my voice might power the distance and bring her and the children home instantly. One of the Andrews boys was playing a few backyards away. I heard him chanting: "Nigger, nigger, black as tar. Stuck his head in a jelly jar." I took off my crinoline, crawled over one fence, then another, and went straight to him and smacked him. I dared him to say "nigger" another time. "I'm going to tell my mother," he cried, and I told him I would tell her myself. She was a decent lady, harried with too many civic duties of no effect that I could discern, but she was at home, in the kitchen. She surveyed my dress first, and my hair, which must have looked as though the witches had ridden me. I gave her no time to speak. I had no time to offer.

"These two Negroes," I burst out, "are asleep in my yard.

They came to tell me my mother has died. I want you to send for Quincy."

She made a business of scurrying about for the proper servant to harness a carriage, and on and on she seemed to go, indefinitely, and I had to bang my fists on the table and shout, "Now go get my husband. I want him now."

She sent her maid to fetch the butler to find the driver, and I thought I would throttle her before she finished making the proper arrangements. And then she offered me tea. I did not want any, but in the time it took me to consider sitting there and trying to act sane and drink a nice cup of tea, I calmed somewhat. She expressed genuine sorrow, and I felt ashamed for having slapped her child, who would indeed tell her, I supposed, after which, having allowed me a decent interval for grief, her husband would come and talk to Quincy about the incident. On my way back across her yard, I saw the boy, playing with a stick in the mud. I told him that my girls had a fortress of lead soldiers. They would never know if one was missing. He could come in a few days. He drew me over to him, motioning with the stick, and said, "I heard. I bet you had a nice mama. Mine don't like me to say 'nigger,' either." In a confluence of circumstances, he grew to raise the money for the Southern Railroad, which would have taken me home to my mother in the time needed to enjoy luncheon from a small hamper, nap, and chat with fellow passengers about the miracle of a simplified journey.

Clarice, the children, the other servants, and Quincy all arrived about the same time. Quincy held me tightly for a long while. He smelled of chloroform. He had the servants take the children to the German chocolatier's, and together we told Clarice. She pressed her chin onto her chest, heaved enormously, but did not cry. Without looking at me, she said, "I am so sorry. So, so sorry." Mintus and Ezekiel were in the kitchen now. Quincy had let them in. Clarice told me she would go find out what she could from Mintus, and then she wanted to rest her head. Mintus knew nothing or would tell nothing, out of innocence, obstinacy, and fealty. Father had never told him anything that was not designed to make him more in awe, more obedient, more pliable and serviceable.

Quincy arranged for Mintus and Ezekiel to stay at the livery stable and for the girls to spend the night at the Haywoods'. I promised to tell them on the morrow why I was so blue, and they left agreeably. Sweet girls. Always sweet girls. Clarice, Quincy, and I had a cold supper that none of us wanted to eat, but the hour called for eating. I felt an intense need to obey the decrees of the clock. Quincy and I read from eight until ten, as we always did nights when he was home. And at eleven, after he washed my face and held the cloth for me to cry into, for tears had begun again, we sat together on the lounger on the sleeping porch. A thousand times, he heard me ask, "Why?" He promised to find out soon, as soon as possible, what had taken her. I did not want him to ask Father. I had already heard a plethora of his lies, all of those lies he had held out to me as truth, and, filled with his mendacity, I had stared at my hands and asked, "What is it, truly? What is this I am being asked to believe?" I have said that Mintus knew nothing, but that is not quite right. He knew that Dr. Gunn had been at the house. That was all Clarice could wrangle from him.

Quincy located the doctor at his highly trafficked office in Knoxville and wrote him. I read the letter of inquiry and signed underneath Quincy's name. A letter came from Maureen while I was waiting for Dr. Gunn's response. She knew I was "indeed sad at the dreadful news." She was "holding up fairly well." Father, too, was managing. But then, reading on, I felt the first sorrow I had felt for her. Even at my brother's urging to pay mind to "the way she will have to go through this world," I had diminished her as an intellectual cripple, supported wholly and extravagantly by the alms of my father. Now, reading her words, I was faced with the fault in my assumption of folly in the center workings of a soul that I had cast aside when she was still sitting on the kitchen floor, eating cornmeal, blissfully removed, I thought, from the hard reality of life in that household. I had sealed her off, secluded her in a cocoon of ignorance, when she was actually as capable of human want and feeling as anyone could be. She wrote:

> But the worst part is, I have had to write Mother's
> family in Savannah, and I am not versed in telling
> someone that Mother has died. You will want to

know about the end, but there is not much I can say, because she would see no one, except when Father would go in a little bit. I last saw her the day before she passed, and she was too groggy to make sight of me. I held her hand for you. The doctor tried every trick to save her, but he said she "went the way of Byron." I do not know exactly what he meant, and he is not the kind you ask questions of. I know you hate me. You think I did not love her. That I love Father more. I did love her, but there you always were.

I am sorry for your pain, for I know in my heart that it is greater than mine. I truly miss her pretty face and sweetness. Her painting on the wall scares me. I long to marry and live here, so that I can have a nice husband and care for Father as well. But time is gone. He made so many nice, handsome young men go away. They will not return.

Father wants us to divide Mother's jewelry. He would not let me see her body and I do not know why. He would not let anyone, save the bishop. Father was always so jealous over her. I know which pieces of the jewelry you like best because I used to peek when she let you try them on. I know you think I don't miss Whately either, but I do. I remember when he and I walked in the thicket and he bade me be quiet so we could watch a mother wren feed a baby from her beak. "The simple passage of life to life," he said to me. I just did not know how to make over it when he died, and so I kept to myself.

If you can bring yourself to, please write Father, or have Clarice. He is about to start a war before the Secesh crowd can get around to it. He wears mourning garb but struts to hide what is signified.

All of this to say I miss you, and I am sorry. Wasn't she good to us? I know you are such a fine mother. I can tell all the way from Virginia. I want to be friends with the girls.

Your loving sister, I am,

Maureen

I wrote back immediately and tried to make myself understood, tried to tell her that I finally appreciated the fact that she deserved Mother's company as much as I had. If my earlier thoughts of her molting in that house with Father as her only lasting company had been physical things, not horrid notions, I would have burned them in the basin and been rid of them. But I had the thoughts to live with. And she would have dashed hopes of a pretty life, and there is no sin or evil or shame in having that if that is what you want. Was I not having my own pretty life? Yes, and I was enjoying it splendidly. Since Maureen's debut, she had fielded courtiers, had seen them pass one by one, for want of Father's approval. And now that was it. That was all. I knew in my heart that gloominess would soon overtake her, that Father's lifetime romance with her would turn against her as he became more and more lonesome for Mother, angry over Clarice, bitter over me, madder and madder that a war of secession was not starting on his lawn so that he could direct the troop movements. The only lucky ones, to my view, were Henry, Randolph, and John. Father was running their lives from a distance, but it was a safe distance.

On Friday, Charlie brought the mail from the depot as usual, and as was my habit, I opened letters on the veranda. I never opened letters addressed to Quincy, but I certainly did when I saw one from Dr. John C. Gunn. Today has been long, many days recalled, and I am out of the umpth to say exactly what class of feeling passed into my heart when I read the letter. I am especially weakened today, but I will say this: Memory, it seems, is my old mortality, again and again, dying and coming back, going again, coming. If I am over-preoccupied with death, it is because it dominates my memory. Have I not seen nearly all whom I have loved die? Is it not then my right to speak of that which I most intimately know? I believe with all my heart that it is God's most gracious blessing to mankind that we are able, with various degrees of fortitude and stamina, to triumph over the pity and grief that we endure in our losses, to fight to achieve an accumulation of days well lived in honor of those we commit to God and His ground. On many days, this one in particular, I feel that I have pushed death away from my door because I do not wish to leave my children. The girls pull against the door for me, but now the moment builds to give in, to concede, and to rest. Soon, I can feel it, I will go gladly beyond memory.

The doctor's letter read:

Dr. Quincy Lowell:

Received your inquiry pursuant to my "involvement" in the unfortunate death of your wife's mother. Let it be known that I am involved not in death but in the perpetuation of life, always and forevermore. Also, on a more personal note, I am a great admirer of your father's work in gastrology, and I read with keen interest your monograph on arterial ligation.

As pertains to Mrs. Tate: I was called to her home by her husband after she had complained of an unrelenting, excruciating headache for nearly two weeks. Mr. Tate described her to me as "half-wild, half-comatose." His letter came by advance courier. He quite demanded that I come. I knew of him as a man of formidable reputation, but do not think I cater my practice to the wealthy. On the contrary, he knew of my household manual for the poorer classes, and he had enjoined the aid of a local man of no name in treating her according to my strictures, but these had not been performed fearlessly, as her condition begged. Mr. Tate reported that his wife had suffered pain of similar nature for many years but never to the magnitude he conveyed to me. Following my guides in *Domestic Medicine,* he had seen that she was properly ventilated, sedated, et cetera, but her stomach would not bear any opiate. When she began bleeding copiously from her nostrils, he called for me. He arranged for no fewer than six different conveyances along the route, a healthy Negro and horse at each avail. Quite a man.

I found the patient insensible, yanking her head from side to side, and at the instant I approached her, my rapid diagnosis, let me say, did not rule out rabies. Her husband and daughter, however, convinced me of the impossibility, and I began my examination. Both family members, I made them to understand, needed to realize that Draconian measures were warranted. The daughter seemed overwhelmed by my equipage, the leeches and such, but after her father shook her by the shoulders, she proved an able nurse, until I thought it best to keep them both from the sickroom. Your wife's sister is not of substantial constitution, so I spared your family another possible calamity—female hysterics. The Negroes took instruction well and should be commended upon their duties. Let me say, it was one of the loveliest homes I have ever had the privilege of practicing in. So very highly European. The Titian was impressive.

Her course:

You may know that in the case of Lord Byron, the brain, without its membranes, weighed exactly six pounds. From all aspects of examination, I expect that the brain of Mrs. Tate weighed no less. I suggest an over-fullness of blood on that organ was the primary condition of her demise. Remarkably, she did not present the characteristic fever, but that absence of condition is dispensable with regard to the other classic presentations—red eyes, the aforementioned bleeding from the nostrils, failing memory, refusal to speak or take nourishment save simple liquids, dry tongue, hard, quickened pulse. Dr. Lowell, need I delineate the obvious? She must have been a lady of severe emotion and intense study, for such trauma of mind was evident in her drawn face. Her husband would not answer questions regarding her mood, save to merit her as a cheerful, pleasant lady. Families will hold their secrets, and we defer to the authority of the household, even when the body tells its story.

But I wander. I began bleeding her at once, a bold brachial stream. When the pain was not subdued, as evidenced by her obvious agony, I shaved her hair, cupped and scarified her all over the head and down along the medulla oblongata, using differing sizes of cups for increased suction. She had a most delicate neck, and to apply the cups took some heat, which, in the next hours, did arouse substantial blisters. Afterward, I applied a cold-toweling, with water of the utmost purity supplied to me by Mr. Tate, who, if I may say, did not take the usual route to drunkenness generally characteristic of distressed husbands. He read Plato and paced a great deal. I waited for the courses of the first instant to renew her vigor to the degree that she might recognize her surroundings, but when she became worse, I began immediate purging—twenty grains of calomel and twenty of jalap. No effect. We were now into the second day. I composed a clyster of thin gruel and a tartar emetic, and in the effort to prevent as much as possible any continued flow of blood to the brain, I propped her bolt upright, as you well know she need have been. To further draw off the determination of blood from the head, I kept the feet wrapped in pounded mustard and cantharides. While I was bathing her feet for a second, thorough medication, she died. As my witness, the cause of death was Inflammation of the Brain owing to over-exertion of an organ not constructed by our Maker for life other than that of quiet domesticity.

By your inquiry, I detect something of an implication that I might not have done all within my power to spare this poor lady's life. By the above outline, you will see proven that I did all I was asserted in this high calling to perform as an administrator of His will. I wish your wife peace in her grieving, for

unless a boundless grief is soon reined in and miti-
gated by prayer, rest, and proper doses of laudanum
at assigned intervals, the mourner may soon join the
mourned.

> Your servant, I am,
> John C. Gunn

Quincy wrote to the bishop, who had seen Mother's body. He asked specifically about any lines of distinct discoloration from her many wounds. We waited for an answer. Meantime, I wrote a short letter to Father: "You monster. Send me Maureen. Now." When Quincy received the bishop's reply, he sat me down in our quiet place, the corner of his study, where two armchairs faced each other. "You read Gunn's letter, and you did not fall apart. If you need to now, I will catch you," he said. He took both my hands. "My dear Emma Garnet, there was no inflammation of the brain. I knew she was prone to those headaches, but as I have said so many times, she lived with her heart in a grip. Your mother died of direct blood-poisoning. The cupping wounds he made on her neck—foolish, stupid—mortified. Feel right now the top of your head, sweetheart. Feel how there is not adequate tissue for substantial veins there? Had he kept the cupping and scarification to her crown, things might have turned out differ-ently. The neck is our certain vulnerability. You may say that he treated her to death. He should have let her be. *Primum non nocere.* There is nothing that we can do now. Let me hold you to dreams of sleep."

I let him hold me like a baby, all that night and into hundreds of mornings, coming forward now into the years with those dreadful dawns that bled me into wakefulness, and I would see those soldiers, see Jacob, see Whately, see Lavinia, see Mother, see life and death mingle in what I sometimes, in the strain of fatigue, felt might be the deliberate intent to cause me confusion. But I know good from bad, life from death. Clear now. Here always.

nine

Today is my birthday. Upon awakening, I made count of my teeth, which is not so queer an enterprise, for lately I seem to be losing them during the nights, swallowing over the past five years two molars, an incisor, and a canine. I am to be grateful that age has been more benign than violent in its assumption of my system—no broken hips, no attacks by malingering youths when I walk out downtown, no seizures of palsy, no fits of rage against time. When the hall clock sounds the hours, I merely stop my writing or thinking or reading and say, *There passes another hour I shall never have again. Here comes another one. Let me do all I can with it.* But as slowly as I move, there is not very much I can accomplish in the span of an hour. I can take the streetcar to Mr. Gardner's shop and see the new arrivals of hats that my granddaughters might enjoy. That gives me pleasure. I can follow the same line to the depot, see what sort of people embark and alight, and arouse my imagination to stories of why this one or the other has come to Raleigh. An old man alone—a longed-for reunion with an old flame he dreamed of even as his crippled wife lay dying of consumption, and now he is here to woo her once more. A handsome, laughing couple—here to take home the newborn orphaned baby from the infant establishment, the child they know they will love as their own, the one they believed they would never have when the wife heard the news that she was barren. A Negro woman and her well-tuckered baby—returned from Chicago to visit her family, who would not budge from the South during the starving times, days when this woman, as a child, looked at a chicken neck on a cracked plate and pledged to live one day where a Negro is paid money sufficient to buy a drumstick, a thigh, a breast even.

Already of this morning, I have received gifts and letters from my daughters and their families. I put all their pictures underneath the glass of the sofa table, and I can stare at them in one vision and wish them here. Do not think them cruel to stay away on my birthday. They come when they can. A joy is that they grew with such affection for one another that they arranged their lives to settle in close community, in New Haven, where their husbands teach in the medical, law, and architecture schools. They met their husbands in one clot, all three of them, at a social when they were at Mount Holyoke. My grandchildren sent me today months' worth of outlandish obituaries from their various towns, knowing that I never tire of seeing what bizarre snippets surviving relatives will publish, in some misguided frenzy to characterize the existences of loved ones who were known for an avidity for juggling large fruits, treasured for the record set in holding a certain plenitude of marbles in the mouth, famous for the number of lip-smacks set on the Blarney stone, much to be missed at Church of the Good Shepherd bridge parties. They know I had rather have these columns than dusting powders or toilet water. There is so little I need now.

In fact, last month I canceled my newspaper subscriptions down to one, kept Mr. Pope's paper not just out of friendship but because of the florid paid obituaries. When I wrote my notes to the others, I sent along checks to the editors for rolls of paper I would not be using and asked that they be sent over to the mental hospital. The patients are so of a want for goods of all classes. Of my experience amongst them, I noted in many patients a heightened propensity for drawing. In fact, when one achieved sanity, enough clarity to go and do his days, Quincy's money paid for him to enroll at the artists' colony in Asheville, and he was among the muralists chosen to decorate one of the rooms at Mr. Vanderbilt's estate. Miss Dorothea Dix had written him up nicely in an article that appeared in *Harper's*, and in the interview he made mention of the scholarship donation in a way that Quincy would have appreciated. Quincy's cousin Amy, a poet, who finds time to visit me on her annual trips to Sarasota, was so enthused by the man's use of art to "tame his soul" that she campaigned her compatriots to finance drawing lessons at the School for the Blind here. Those children flail about in true darkness, but, when put before paper with charcoal in hand, they create swirls and flourishes that impressed me, and I collected some of the drawings and sent them to Amy, as livable chaos. That is what so much of this world is anyway, livable chaos.

Amy lives now with her brother, a curator at the museum in Boston. He regularly sends me plates of pictures under his consideration. We have no art here for me to pass time with, and both Amy and her brother write brilliant descriptions of technique and form, calling my eyes to astonishments they find. I have been most grateful for the one sent of a mother caressing a child, a specialty of Miss Cassatt's. I saw adoration in it and felt a sudden need to hold a baby. When I next visited the mental hospital—the women's ward established by Miss Dix in 1886 as a place a woman might have her child brought to her of a Sunday, when all over everywhere else ladies not so mightily afflicted are holding their children's hands in church, glad for the day—a woman so dejected that she had not taken solid food since her admittance let me hold the baby girl her husband had brought in. The child was dirty, so I bathed her. She was hungry, so I found a pastry bag in the kitchen and fed her mashed potatoes from the end of the nib.

When Amy's brother sent me a sheaf of Mr. Brady's photographs that were to be hung on the twenty-fifth anniversary of the commencement of the War, I looked at each of them carefully, looked a long time, took them to the tall window so I could better see into darkened corners, used Quincy's magnifying glass and read labels on kegs of powder, peered at matted whiskers. I surveyed them all for the better part of a day, and when I was finished, I felt nothing. You may say I felt the "Yes now, so what of it?" that I do when the man tells me my furnace is due for a cleaning, the same absence of meaning I find when I read a day's posting of the baseball scorings. If Monet or Manet or Toulouse-Lautrec had performed the scenes of battle, I might have been urged toward emotion, for the horror would have quivered on the surface of the page and beckoned my mind to follow attendant sensations deeper and deeper to the core, down into the true, wasted, stupid, futile blasphemy of that conflict.

Instead, I saw torn-up fields and torn-up bodies, flattened into geometric patterns of light and dark. Despite the blank eyes of death and the stacked corpses, grim by any estimation, I was able to put the photographs aside and eat a turkey sandwich immediately thereafter. In Mr. Brady's pictures of leaders and of women, I did attain a reckoning of acquaintance with the subjects' souls, but in the battle scenes, nothing. And my numbness was not owing to the truth, as I have asserted of a day previous: Humankind cannot bear very much reality. Neither is my lack of feeling proper evidence that ladies, understood as we are to be inherently flawed in our comprehension of the rules of engagement, cannot grasp the grotesque. I was not so hardened by the many deaths of loved ones that I had little anxiety left over to feel for boys I did not know. To contrast—what an artist of an impressionistic bent would have done is allowed room for my heart to tear itself down again, spread out in my chest and bleed, make me heave for the next beat, the next breath, as Clarice had done the moment we told her of Mother.

The photographs said everything, gave me no room to say, "I

still hurt." I want those years with my girls back. I want Quincy back. And I want Clarice. The four years of war were snatched by men who thought the maintenance of the peculiar institution more important than ruined homes. And the gall, the gall, to pour blood over fields that women were keeping, over smoke-house floors where the farm poor boiled salt out of the dirt and tried to preserve measly hanks of meat for their children, over kitchen tables that were scrubbed by women who toiled when there was no need because there was nothing to spend the after-noon cooking. I still hold that it was a conflict perpetrated by rich men and fought by poor boys against hungry women and babies. Now that my mind has transformed those photographic plates into stippled paintings that crystallize in my memory and im-press upon me pure amazement that we spent so much time killing one another, I feel more overwrought than I want to on a birthday that has seen the postman bring—I counted the letters as I did my teeth—forty-six missives. That tally does not include those from my own family and Quincy's, and Miss Fannie Farmer, who sent a new receipt for pumpkin bread, and the sad, sad brother of Colonel Shaw, who prayed over a Thanksgiving dinner in Boston, I think the year was 1868, and said to his God, "You will remember, my Lord, that I buried my brother in a ditch." The other letters? They are from the boys and from the mothers and sisters and wives of boys whom I had the honor of knowing. The boys themselves had something more remarkable than that—the honor of having lived through it all.

One death reported. A man name of Chutney Jones, called so

by his mother because she birthed him in her pantry and kept her eyes on the rows of preserves to focus her mind during her laboring. In late 1864, when our home was full of the overflow from the Fair Grounds Hospital, Quincy performed surgery on Chutney on the lid of our grand piano. He was neither the first nor the last to lie on that piano. One boy even lay there in recuperation while Leslie entertained the others, who rested on every available surface in the house, with quiet melodies that would not vibrate his tender, broken ribs. When the African Zionist church, which housed the Negro wounded, asked Raleigh citizens to open their homes to those soldiers, Quincy, Burke Haywood, and Alliance Maupin did so, gladly and promptly. No sooner were the Negroes installed than an anonymous note appeared in the letter column of the Raleigh *Register*:

> For those who have colored men in their homes, I think it immoral and liken it even to miscegenation to have little white girls running around when they should be boarded for the duration at Saint Mary's School, which is open to protect the young ladies of the South. If General Lee sees fit for his daughter to attend there, where her eyes might be averted from sin, then surely should not a gentleman who declined rank do the same for his daughters, who are known to tear wild anyway?
>
> I am yours,
>
> DISGUSTED

I did have the girls at Saint Mary's, but only for the day academy. I was gone, for the majority of the four years, about sixteen hours a day, save when I nursed men at home. I wanted Mary, Leslie, and Louise at home, demanded it. We all had to be available to one another's hearts every minute we could, and of the scorn I have remaining for the War, I rue most the time I missed from them, the time they missed from their father. Before the War, the school enjoyed the reputation of lavishing care on its charges. But from the onset, if Charlie had not taken Mildred Lee, General Lee's daughter, meals three times a day, she would have had to subsist on the same short rations all the other girls subsisted on. Mrs. Lee, a friend of my mother's, had written me to ask that I see to Mildred whenever I could. Dr. Smedes, Saint Mary's administrator during the War, had such a difficulty collecting tuitions—the school was so very embarrassed in its pecuniary affairs—that he was forced to make constant pleas for money. Quincy's father, who gave the girls their educations as gifts outright because he lacked the nearness of them and cared deeply that their minds be seen to, replenished the coffers at the school when it was struggling. The Lowells were and remain without prejudice—no rancor, no differentiating between a certain brand of person and another.

Quincy's upbringing was one of the reasons he could remark, as he did at that dinner at the governor's palace, "Everyone is my own kind." When South Carolina seceded, on December 20, 1860, just in time to destroy Christmases all over the country,

Quincy was asked to take a commission and to assume command
of a military hospital already under construction on the edge of
town, across from a railroad siding, where men might be loaded
off cars and brought quickly to care. Oh, so many arrangements
and considerations, such as the placement of the hospital relative
to the train tracks, were under way long before Sumter, even
though North Carolina did not hasten to secede. Quincy refused
the commission but gladly accepted responsibility for the hospital. His own, the Mary Elizabeth, was not of adequate space to
take in masses, and so it was given over to the concerns of women
and children. Quincy was, as I think I have failed to mention,
darkly handsome, smooth, and extremely self-confident. Of instant nature, people gave him their trust, and so it was not extraordinary that little mention was made that a Yankee, and one of
the famous Lowell family at that, was to head the Fair Grounds
Hospital. We did have one brief message posted to us: "Let one
of us die you Yankee and I'll get you." Quincy, Clarice, and I had
a snicker over the note. When his first patient did die, Clarice
stuck the note in Quincy's lunch pail and told him he had best
nail it to his office wall for inspiration. And he did. But their
blood ran in bucketfuls anyway.

At the end of that December of 1860, I received my brothers'
address in England, where they were, as Father had directed,
essaying to convince the British government that the empire
would cease to function without the continued trade of Southern
cotton. Because I had left Seven Oaks when the boys were so

young and had had such little correspondence with them, I hardly knew how to make my wishes known to them. I could not credit the fact that they were grown now. They were suspended in time for me, halted in growth on the day they cried on the Williamsburg porch after the botched circus. As well, they were babies I had employed to buffer my mother from Father's harangues on all those nights of the make-believe fevers. True, they were doing my father's self-serving bidding, yet I did not fault them. I complained frequently to Quincy that they had not communicated when Mother died, for I felt sure my letters had reached them. But the only matter of it was that they simply did not know me well enough to broach commiseration. To them, I was as a cousin twice removed. Never had I shared my love of books with them, although I did read many stories to them on my lap. Literature was the province of Whately and me, our place. I chose to treat my brothers as I would my children, for that felt most natural. I had to tell them to stay in England, so strong was my urge to mother them:

Dear Henry, Randolph, and John,

Hard for me to believe you all are grown enough to be taking care of yourselves in a foreign country. You know Quincy and I, with Clarice, took part of our honeymoon in London. Clarice ate herself to death on boiled sweets. The National Gallery is one of the most astounding places I have ever been. Also, the Church of St. Martin-in-the-Fields—adjacent to the gallery—gave me goose shivers, so beautiful. Please attend a service there if you have not already. I remember how loudly you three used to sing at Bruton Parish. I remember how you, Henry, thought "A Mighty Fortress" proceeded as "a bull worth never flailing." This may be of presumption, but I do believe that I still feature enough of all three of you to assume almost a certain righteousness, as one who loved to hear you sing and who hid from Clarice her cherished hummingbirds that you snagged in the fishnet—you never knew I did that, did you?— in saying what I must. Memory may furnish me, you may think, scant evidence to cite my authority in telling you how to run your lives, but what I do recall of you three, I cherish. Now:

Stay in England. Do not under any circumstances come home. If you do return, Father will see to it that you are soon among the chivalric dead. He will live through you, and you know it. Stay there, please. Do not give a thought to Seven Oaks. With South Carolina's secession, other states will quickly follow suit. Quincy is a very wise man, and although you know him scarcely, trust when he says that the war will be fought in Virginia because it is the destiny of that place, a beautiful country for killing. He is right. Believe me. By the time you get home, there will be no Seven Oaks to tend. Father has shouted too brazenly for too long. Maureen writes that he is

mean with gout and still is able enough to drill militia in the clearing past Shirley Plantation. You will
not be avoiding the fight, and do not pay mind to
any letter from Father telling you that you have
done enough business and now owe him and his glorious Commonwealth, his glorious James, the duty
of service. Think of yourselves half dead in a field
where you once rode to hounds, a bullet hole in your
cheek, in your stomach, and feel the sun come up
and the gnats and blowflies at you. Remember how
we would take the way across that far pasture walking over to the Throckmortons' property? Where the
cows grazed? Just think of the times lightning would
strike one of them, and it would be days before one
of us walked through the pasture and found a cow.
Exploded. See? This is coming. I listen to Quincy.
You listen to me.

Find the company of ladies who remind you of
Mother. Marry them and have children. When this
trouble is over, bring them home. Clarice and I will
take care of everything. Maureen says that Father is
still livid that I tricked him into the loan of Clarice,
and now with Mother gone, I see no reason to send
her back to him. He has a raw place where she abandoned him, but, as she says, "I suckled that one long
enough." Clarice wishes she could have helped
Mother, but you know she is of spirit unparalleled
and wanted, again in her words, to "have some life

out from under" Father. I suspect that is also why you all left home, but you do not need to explain anything to me, not ever. Life is full of difficult choices, is it not? Just remember that Clarice is here forever and would be a comfort to you. She often speaks of missing her boys. You may not remember her birthday, but she was sixty last week. You know she is built like a lead stovepipe and twice as durable. Quincy says she has the workings of a woman of forty. I bet you all would love one of her garlic hens for your supper. I often say to Quincy that Clarice is the only reason that Seven Oaks did not go the way of the Seven Gables.

And now—if you are wondering why I say all this about Clarice—I simply want you to understand that if you come home and need direction, she is the one to guide you. This home is open to you. Three floors, ten bedrooms, and Philadelphia plumbing! I have money to sustain you. Do not let money woes ever concern you. Enclosed is a check that may be cashed at any of Thomas Cook's concerns. Use it to go to the opera. Quincy fears for Father's finances. He has outfitted a regiment and invested a fortune in munitions. Maureen knows some things and tells me. But do not ever worry about money. Do not fret over any threat of being disinherited. Remember how Father used to say that he hated Landon Carter and his subterranean stream of capital? The Lowells are a major tributary. We will always help you. Write.

I am, your eldest sister,

Emma Garnet

On New Year's Day, eager to be the first-footer, Charlie left the house and returned with best wishes at the front door. In those times we regarded a tall Negro man's early-morning appearance at the new year to be a sign of coming good fortune. We had a merry crowd over for nog and oysters. I recall getting one so large in my mouth that I had to hide behind the Japanese screen to eat it. The company chatted awhile of Christmas gifts given and received—Frances Haywood displayed a diamond-encrusted watchclock on her blouse—boys popped crackers and lit rockets in the yard, people spoke of family members gathered around their holiday tables, how sad they were to see carriages leave for distant counties. And then voices deepened, parents glanced at their girls to see if they were listening, and war talk overtook joy.

We wondered aloud, "When?" We remarked over having seen boys by the Capitol, marching around with red cockades on their hats. Rumors, some vague report that a special legislative session would be called. Who of these men would be elected to represent Wake County? The downstairs rooms were filled with political men, and after a time, they went with Quincy into his study, and the door was closed. I was left to the ladies and children, and we minded our cares with talk of varying methods that we would use to protect our little ones. We were scared. I spoke of my brothers in England, and the ladies I had grown to admire over the years thought me right in having told them to stay in Europe. I did not hear a single lady around my maturity, rather young for the staid mansions of Blount Street, wish aloud that her son were old enough to fight for state sovereignty. Older ladies who had sons of appropriate age said very little. But I could surmise the workings of their minds. Medical deferment. Poor eyesight. Partial deafness. A mission to the Continent. Yes, somewhere abroad.

By the time Mavis wheeled in the coffee service, a remarkable event had played out in my parlor: The younger ladies, I observed, had surrounded the older ones, the ones with the worries, whose minds had drifted to where, how, when, and why their sons might escape the conflict. Nobody was quoting soaring passages from *Ivanhoe.* There was in that room the unspoken agreement that martyrdom was for dead saints. Three ladies who had, all totaled, nine sons, whose fathers were now in Quincy's study reckoning the fate of the county, sat as though pulled together by a magnet on the piano bench. Mothers smell blood before the wound is given. We see the rent place on the child's arm before the arrow strikes. We gathered around those ladies, who were so still. We were circling, as females are bound to do, around their children and the future. Within a year, four of the nine sons were dead. A sniper at Bethel. A charge at First Manassas. Dysentery at Camp Holmes. A skirmish in a wood.

Henry, Randolph, and John remained in London. Quincy

opened the hospital. In the first six weeks, six hundred seventy-five men were treated. Quincy asked me to help him, and I did. On the second day I was there, he showed me how to perform a tracheotomy, and then, in an emergency, left me to complete the procedure on my own. And so began my mind's collection of photographs, tinted with shades of crimson. I have those images, and I am angry to this day that I did not, for four years, have the sanctity of my home. We let the place out to war. You know it to be true, we deserved a happy home. After my childhood. After Old Virginia. *I did not mean to kill the nigger! Did not mean to kill him! He had a name and it was Jacob. How in the pluperfect Hell did you raise a son who brings me nothing but torment and faro debt? Samuel, you know Emma Garnet loves you. He bit her ear off and hung it around his neck for good luck. Mother? Yes, Louise? Why did you cry on the sleeping porch last night and call your papa a bastard? What's a bastard?*

ten

If somehow you curried favor with a hawk that could take you on wing up and over the campus of the Fair Grounds Hospital, you would have thought yourself contemplating the attitude of a splayed horse. You would have found me at the horse's tail, supervising the critical patients. The ceilings were low, the rooms long and narrow. Although serviceable, the hospital was no monument to medical science, as was the facility in Boston where Quincy's father treated the Union wounded while his feeble wife lay fading into enviable oblivion. There was no glass available for windows in the wards, save those in the operating theaters, only stretched canvas, thickly painted to keep out the cold. When the first casualties arrived from Bethel and Manassas, both highly trumpeted Confederate victories, the old men and Negroes had not completed furnishing the wards with bed frames, so men were nursed on straw patches on the floor. The pharmaceutical factory in Lincolnton was not yet in full production, so Quincy had to send runners to Wilmington to stock the apothecary with the basic supplies—opium, morphine, quinine, sulfuric ether, silver chloride, and the like. On several returns, the boys refused to make another trip, for they had had to brawl on the ships' docks for the crates, fighting other runners from the state's twenty-one hospitals. When, at Clarice's suggestion, we sent an orderly to comb the saloons for volunteers who would gladly take a whipping for whiskey money, Quincy was able to have enough medicines to get him through those horrible battles of 1861 and the spring of 1862.

On one of the trips, the fellows, having requisitioned corn liquor from a farmer along the route, drove their laden cart into a ditch, and a sheriff sent a deputy the rest of the way to Raleigh with the medicines that were not wasted. That incident was the only hindrance in Quincy's hiring of drunkards, but it gathered notice in the newspapers:

> Drink-addled roustabouts sent by Dr. Quincy Lowell
> to harass the Wilmington ports for medical supplies,
> jailed after overturning cargo, sobered up, went back
> to the Fair Grounds Hospital, only to be sent by the
> determined doctor for another run. They broke both
> arms of another runner, sent by the Durham Hospi-
> tal, wresting away a carton of dissecting supplies,
> which they tore open on the pier, and threatening
> other purveyors with the scalpels and scissors found

within. Dr. Lowell has been censured by the state
surgeon but vows to use whatever means necessary
to outfit his facility.

Although I had never lived a charmed life—thanks to deaths
and my father—I had never, not ever, felt desperate. But the first
time bearers brought huge numbers of men across the road from
the railroad shack, where volunteer ladies of the Aid Society as-
sessed the priorities of the wounded and sent word to me that
distinctions could not be adequately made—"Everybody needs
everything"—I lost my wind. My ward, which Quincy had assigned to me because nobody else wanted charge of the worst-
maimed, was already at capacity when, after a string of battles
in western Virginia, the bearers gave me four dozen men at once.
The Society's apology over not being able to order the severity
of the injuries was scribbled on a wooden slat lying on the chest
of the first man brought through the door. Frances Haywood, as
committed to the hospital's work as was her husband, who ran
the operations in the west wings, nailed the slat to Quincy's wall
next to the directive not to kill any Southern boy. She was with
me when these were brought in, and, seeing my distress, she assumed a general's mien and relieved me of some of the worst
cases. She took them to her measles rooms and sent the conta-
gious outside to stay in tented areas that had been used by the
ambulatory for matins and vespers.

As my men were placed on the floor, close alongside one another, in a manner not unlike that of slaves packed belowdecks in drawings by abolitionists of the day, I ran to Quincy's principal theater, unable to breathe. He pulled up his apron and tried to clean blood from the only available stretcher, but when he saw my face go white he stopped and laid me down. He fanned me with a triangular saw, saying all the while, "Please go home, please go." I recall thinking, incapable of speech: But they will die. I had been awake forty hours, a span of wild alertness cranked to the extreme. Quincy had been conditioned from the days of his young apprenticeship to withstand the brutality of fatigue on the senses; but I had not. As my breathing became more and more regular, he sat me up and gave me cold coffee he kept in a nearby gallon jar. I craved sleep, yet I heard the boys screaming.

Quincy's patient, attended now by another doctor, was slit open from his waist to his breastbone. Although abdominal injuries were usually fatal, Quincy was always trying novel approaches to rescue the hopeless. I stared at the boy, my skin prickling with the heat that accompanies panic. I took off my stockings. They seemed to be crawling all over me. I was stripped as much as modesty would allow; I removed my over-blouse anyway. Again, Quincy beseeched me to go home. My ward's primary assistant appeared in the doorway and told me that Julian Opie, a snaggle-toothed boy I had nursed for a week, was calling for me. "And they are piling up in there," he added.

Defying Quincy's orders, I walked back to the ward. Bodies were everywhere. I slipped in blood and fell headlong onto a young man. When I landed, blood pumped from his mouth. I lay as though in intimacy with him, stunned with the fear that I might have killed him. His blue eyes bulged and then closed. The man who lay beside him, whose arm was wrapped with a torn pant leg, spoke gently to me: "He was due to die. You didn't do it. Give me some morphine if you want to be doing something. I hurt. . . . You got hair on your legs like a man. I never seen so high up on a lady's leg. . . . I like it. . . . Give me some morphine, please. I hurt."

He lisped. His front teeth were missing, a common injury, caused by repeated ripping of the paper from bullets on the firing lines. I called a nurse, and he gave the needy boy his morphine. The nurses were male then, save those few hardy young women of the middling classes approved for service by the chief surgeon. Quincy recruited them heavily from the flats; he did not allow young unmarried ladies of the better families to work in the hospitals. I threw my shoes into a corner of the ward and stepped barefooted across the other bodies, calculating their needs as I went along, calling to orderlies and nurses. Tourniquet here. Rosin there. Dead, please take him out.

Julian Opie was not bleeding out of his bandages, not in physical agony. He was simply mad. "I don't like them all in here," he told me.

I shoved his legs aside and sat down. He was on sheets that had been on Louise's bed a month before. Out of necessity, I had asked Martha to empty the linen presses of all but one change of sheets for each bed. Martha had not wanted to surrender any of her personal linens or towels, but Clarice shamed her so successfully that from that night on she slept atop a bare mattress and dried herself with one of Charlie's ragged shirts. Sitting there with Julian, I knew that he would cause trouble in the ward if he was not subdued quickly. The first day after his surgery, he hectored another patient, whose dire wounds were being set with maggots, until the other boy vomited and would have aspirated had a nurse not turned him over on his stomach. From three cots away, Julian had asked the boy again and again, "How you like them things crawling all over you? Can't you feel them eating? I'd rot before I'd let a maggot bore into my belly. I bet you taste good. You suppose they can get them all out of you?" He carried on until I left a patient with post-operative pneumonia who was unwillingly eating mashed snakeroot and hickory leaves from my hand, and went to his cot and boxed his ears, screaming as I slapped him for someone to tend to the vomiting boy.

Julian, now as before angry over the crowding, asked me what I was going to do about the infesting rabble that was stinking up the ward. He had suffered shots to his right shoulder, and one of Quincy's assistants had made a fair mess of things extracting the balls. He would never enjoy use of his arm, but he could walk and talk, court and marry, work at some suitable task, survive to see his mother smile at his eventual arrival home. All along, he knew he would be sent back to his regiment to do "nigger work," and he was embarrassed—a state of mind that easily mutates itself into a venomous spite over one's situation and surroundings. Although I knew his heart, I could give him no quarter. He had been due that morning to be moved out of the critical ward, and now we had been overrun. I sat there for the few minutes it took to rebuke him so harshly that he reared himself up, sore, mangled shoulder notwithstanding, and spit in my face. Wordlessly, he lay back down and closed his eyes.

As I wiped my face, taking trouble not to seem nonplussed, he said, "Nobody talks to me like that. I ain't evil. I know about you. You crawl in bed of a night with a nigger-lover. I got a ulcer in my mouth. You might get the clap. Clap spit. Nobody calls me 'common.' Give me something. I want to sleep, and can't nobody rest for the stink. Give me something."

I leaned on him, hard, my palm pressing on his bandage. He kept his eyes closed, but his mouth tightened when my face drew near to his. "You whore," he said. "Get off me."

I whispered, "Your shoulder is what stinks. It's putrefying. Here come the maggots."

He did not reply. Leon, the Negro man who kept care of the maggots as though they were his entertainment, was outside the window, where the things were stored in tin buckets. He fed them on wheat meal, and he was sprinkling meal into a bucket when I lifted the canvas and told him he had a project. Julian truly required their application, but he did not need to hear me say to Leon, "They really must root down hard in him. Hurry."

I had been taught the efficacy of a well-placed blow to a person's hateful spirit by nursing boys who were by nature cruel, those who, I suspected, had joined the fighting because they despised their miserable lives. They also denigrated Negroes, whom they were too poor to own but loathed out of the human tendency, its downward trope, to find someone lower on Mr. Darwin's ladder to disparage. And most of all, they vilified Northerners, who were held in contempt for meddling in the South's affairs. Boys who had never met a Northerner until Quincy calmed them before surgery nonetheless detested anyone above the Mason-Dixon line for choking the cotton trade with a tariff that kept their families in muslin and them breaking their backs chopping tobacco while all the Yankees, the most ignorant of them believed, went to college in flowing silken gowns. Only among the wounded officers did I hear the words "honor" and "glory," and by the time they reached the hospital, some of them would tell how they had enlisted to defend their homes, hoping for a chance at that elusive honor and glory, and say dejectedly, "Look where it got me." But the others had fought fueled by free-ranging hatred, which was oftentimes mingled with boredom and a desire to get out of their native counties, off clay dirt, for the first, and possibly only, time in their lives.

Much was said, especially in 1861 and 1862, when the Confederacy won most battles in the east, about a poor Southern boy's natural propensity for fighting, his ability on horseback, his sureness of aim, his knowledge of the woods. It seemed that we had produced an army of Natty Bumppos, though without the integrity and quick intelligence. But brains were not needed in the ranks, not wanted. "It don't take no learning," one pockmarked boy told me after Manassas, "to shoot somebody between the eyes." Of that lot, I generally detected no ambition to rise above private, no drive to be among the officers, who had uniforms and state-issued shoes, until those luxuries were depleted and available only to the men whose families had them made at highly inflated prices.

There was no supreme calling, but an almost fanatical grasping into the vast unknown, perhaps, and that enterprise takes a certain courage, which was confused with chivalry by some newspaper writers, who sat behind the safety of desks and edited accounts of battle, making readers believe that a banner truly shimmered in the sun as it was carried over a knoll, that a boy found shot by a sniper had—and I read this—"a look of quiet repose on his face. He had performed well, followed commands. No doubt he died in regard of his Cause." No doubt he died wishing he was home, thinking Yankees and Negroes might not be worth the exquisite pain in his side, wondering if he would go to Heaven or Hell, trying to rush some class of prayer to Jesus.

After I left Julian to Leon's skilled ministrations, I turned to the new arrivals, who cried, moaned, cursed, whined. They made every sound available to them in an effort to draw attention to their conditions, to be among the first sedated and sewn. Somehow, these fellows who could not write their names on the admission forms that we presented when they were cognizant of their whereabouts, who were not able to name their parents or to say where they were from—a fact many did not know except to answer, "Over yonder near Pikeville"—knew exactly what to call for the minute I bent over them. They wanted morphine. When the blockade choked its supply and I had to say, "I'm sorry, there is no morphine," they knew what to beg for even then—sulfuric ether.

During that huge crush, I administered both morphine and opiates to those I felt could best survive a decelerated heart rate, and the room quieted enough for me to concentrate worry on two great urgencies, the lack of operating theaters and the shortage of surgeons. The few surgeons we did have were weary with fatigue, irritable, and sometimes haphazard. When I brought one out of his theater, took him to a patient I had just checked, and asked why he looked to have been stitched with baling twine, he barked that he took orders from my husband, that he had been on his feet for three days, had amputated five legs, three arms, had cut out enough intestine to stretch to Washington, and the day previous had extracted a bird—feet, beak, and feathers—from a boy's stomach.

As livid as I was sickened, I said, "Tell that to Quincy. Show him that boy's stitches. Then come back out here and take at least four of the worst of these into your theater and work on them."

He looked around and suggested that they all appeared too far gone, even if he were to take his direction from a woman.

I had never traded on having been raised in the acquaintance of the War's great men, but I looked hard at him and said, "My kitchen feeds General Lee's daughter every meal she eats. Wade Hampton's men were clothed by my father. Varina Davis writes me weekly letters. I take for granted knowing people who could devour you."

My voice was raised louder than I thought, for Quincy

emerged and interceded. He told the surgeon to do as I asked. "Exactly, to the letter, to the dot," he said.

Quincy let the surgeon finish out the day and then arranged his transfer to a field hospital in Tennessee. Of my faults, the tendency I have to wallow in the satisfaction of vengeance is probably my worst. But no matter that the surgeon took what I felt to be his quota of men off the floor; there were plenty more. I worked until dark, when the tension in the ward abated into the cool night, and Leon lifted all the canvases, letting in the breeze. I slept ill that night on a stretcher in a supply closet, but on the next morning relief came. The rector at Christ Church had announced at service that the train had brought in new men, and called an intermission so that the worshippers who wanted to could depart to help with the wounded. I was rarely so glad to see people arrive through those doors. Some, who were there for the first time, turned away and did not come back. Others stayed. Quincy and I went home. Clarice made us a bath, and we ate with the children, tried to have a normal conversation with them. But those were abnormal times. And the years stacked upon one another like those wounded souls, like transported slaves in their hold.

We needed rest, but we needed more to hear our girls in the Cherub Choir that evening. As they sang "That Sheep May Safely Graze," Quincy pulled down the velvet bench, took to his knees, and cried into his hands. I had never seen him weep. I knelt beside him and held him in blessed return for all the tender days and nights that he had let me love him ceaselessly. Before leaving the church, he told the rector that a larger brass plate should be engraved and fitted into the end of our pew. "We will add the name of Emma Garnet's mother, and we will also add the names of those who have died beneath my hands. Leave room," he said, "for there will be more. Many, many more."

eleven

On a rare Sunday home together, Quincy asked me to come into his study, where I was to sit, close my eyes, and hold my up-turned hands in my lap. My birthday was due, and I told him not to spoil a surprise, for those of the good variety had become all too scarce. He came over and pressed a small wrapped box into my hands.

I opened my eyes, and there was his face, so close upon mine that I could feel his breath when he spoke. Odd to think, but as I listened, I made note to have Charlie cut his hair later in the day. He was bushy. As he folded my fingers around the gift, he said softly, "Emma Garnet, you deserve an early birthday. You have come so far from the night I found you and your cramped feet. You were destined to be a lady of refinement but have become instead my heroine. A lady of refinement would not go to that hospital every day. But you could go to work in my place tomor-row, so much have you learned, and so quickly. And this"—he put his hand on my bosom—"is not the heart of a frail lady. You might vomit, but you will not faint. I am proud of you."

I will never forget those words.

I smiled when I finished taking apart the wrapping, which he had done himself. He always said, "It doesn't count as much if a stranger does it." For someone so skillful with the delicacies of surgery, he could mangle a wrapping. But I do not think he realized it. Clarice, the girls, and I pledged never to tease him, even as many times as Clarice whispered in my ear, a gift from Quincy in her hands, "It looks like they wrapped it over to the blind school."

Just now, I have pinned to my blouse the brooch he gave me. It is sterling, circular, and below my initials is the date, 1861.

Not wanting to ask right away about the date, not wanting even to contemplate the notion that he might have lost his reason and given me a piece of jewelry with which to commemorate the War, I hugged him in thanks. I did ask where he had found sterling, whether one of the fellows he sent to Wilmington might have "requisitioned" it.

He laughed, giggled actually, and made me take three guesses, none of which I recall. Who could? For my dear husband clasped the brooch on my dress and said, "The silver? Well, sweetheart, Burke called me into his theater a while back to show me the most outstanding dental work he had ever seen in anyone's mouth, rich or poor. And while we had the patient's mouth open, he died. I thought nothing of it, of the dental work, except that it was very fine, until the Negro man attending

Burke said, 'If it was me and I wouldn't get strung up, I'd snatch it out.' "

"You didn't," I said.

"No, Burke and I had to go to a meeting, so we let the Negro do it. He melted it, hammered it, everything. Burke and I each gave him a dollar for his time and his forgetfulness. Burke asked me if I wanted the silver, knowing I always give you jewelry for your birthday, and with the shops closed down except to repair clocks, I thought it a gift from God."

"And the engraving?" I asked.

He beamed and reported to have done that himself, with the tool he used to amputate fingers, the curvatures of *E* and *G* being perfect shapes for the blades. He asked me not to look too closely at the date, though, for that, he said, "was the devil."

I told him it was the most gruesome gift ever made to me, and I loved it. "But what of this date?"

"Oh, Emma Garnet," he said, "it is the year I hereby graduate you from medical school."

I was glad Quincy educated me, for by late spring of 1862, I was over-cropped, my load so heavy that when I came in of an evening, Clarice, who always waited for me in the front room, would catch me in her arms and half carry me to bed. Had 1861 been deceptively easy, had my ability to endure longer and longer hours on my feet not, of God's will, expanded to meet the growing demand, the amount of work would have made me croak, as Clarice often said Quincy and I looked ready to do. Times Quincy did make me go home and when Clarice made me stay there, the girls would lie in bed with me and read while I rested. When rest would not come and I felt like Mary's new kitten, which ate herself insane on catnip and stood rigid as though stuffed, and meowed until Quincy let her lick a dab of laudanum off his finger, I had the girls massage my head and neck. Louise, who herself often seemed to have eaten catnip, was the gentlest of all.

I recall awakening from fitful rest one hot afternoon when I simply could not get myself going, could not motivate myself. I have never tended toward drink, but I felt on that day and on a great many others during the War the way I featured those did who overindulged. I knew it would take an hour or two until the fatigue that a sweaty afternoon nap seems to augment more than diminish left my system. I felt as if I had been raised from the dead, and the only way to wash off my rotted shroud was with coffee. But there was none to be had. I stumbled to the kitchen and asked Clarice for a cup of okra. That is what then passed for coffee——burnt okra seeds. As I choked down the liquid, Clarice said, "Will yourself for it to be coffee, and it might do you some good." I replied that she was the only person I knew capable of transmogrification. "You could turn water to wine," I told her, "but all I have is okra."

Because of our priority with the quartermaster, we fared better than most families, those unfortunate ones who were forced to eat the cat, the dog. We sent Charlie to team with the other butlers-cum-drivers on Blount Street and hunt rabbits and squirrels, which fed the women and children adopted by Christ

Church. One time when Clarice took the rabbit-and-squirrel stew to a family, she saw little girls gathering stray bits of corn left uneaten by horses. She returned home shaken, and that night I overheard her prayers: "God, come end these starving times. They have done nothing against you. Come now, please. Hurry."

Green vegetables and potatoes were easier to come by than beef and poultry. Charlie kept a garden for us in the back, and when seeds were scarce, Ellen Mordecai let us have a generosity of hers. We repaid her in candles, one of the rare exceptions Quincy made to his rule of not bringing supplies home from the hospital. When lard candles flared into a fire that scorched the dining room table—and would have burned the house down had the linen cloth been on the table instead of under a patient— Clarice fashioned serviceable ones out of sweet potatoes. By those lights, I would write to Maureen and to the parents of deceased boys, sometimes sending families letters with the hope that they might be located by an address only of the variety "Over yonder near Pikeville." The letters from Maureen sounded increasingly dejected but amazingly calm as the fighting drew closer to Seven Oaks. She did not, as did Father, think the place invincible. She had reconciled herself to a ruined life, and if they were blazed out of house and home, that was simply more of the same:

> Father says nothing can happen, but I don't care. If
> they take the Negroes, and he says they will, I shall

see if they will let us keep just a couple so we can make do. Father won't admit it, but his purse is rather thin. What you had been sending me I had been saving for a rainy day, and the skies might pour down before long. Poor people come begging and I give them everything I can before Father catches me. A few stragglers came by, Bertha and Lazy had been off fishing and I didn't know the difference, so I let those boys have something to eat. Father interviewed them, and when they did not know what was what, he had Mintus lock them in the smokehouse while Ezekiel went for some honorable soldiers. They got taken away and Father spoke sharply to me and threw out the plates they had eaten on. Do not have a stroke of the heart. It was not the Spode.

Mintus is coughing up blood. Can you ask Quincy what to do about it? Father pitched his medical book into the fire, you know, and won't let me think about calling him a doctor. And there is a nice young one, I hear, in Williamsburg now. But what would he think of me? I look at myself in the mirror.

We hear nothing from Henry and Randolph and John. Have you? Father has disowned them. I think I told you that the last time he did it. He changes his will about as often as I did my shoes before most of them walked off Seven Oaks on the feet of a roving family I had let camp in our wood. Father went out and came back angry over somebody cutting down

some trees. Anything they might have used for a fire
could not have been larger than a sapling. Do you
think he has made count of all his trees? I reckon.

With love, I am,

Your sister

I had heard nothing from our brothers, and although I was
saddened, I was not worried for them. When I wrote back to
Maureen with Quincy's suggestion of hot vapor baths for
Mintus, I received a letter from her before mine had had time to
reach her: He was dead. Father had gone to awaken him, and he
was cold. Maureen said Father would not cry, although she could
tell he considered it:

Father saw me looking at him, and right then
stanched his tears way down so deep where they
dwell. Then he said, "I suppose you'll be the next
one to leave me." With the current state of his gout
and the infirmity in his hips, pain makes him ramble so. He dilates on who has abandoned him. I can't
think of anybody who calculated to hurt him.
Mother and Mintus, all they did was die, no intention of harm in their departures. And he was the one
who arranged for the boys to go to England. He
sometimes says that they belong to be in Virginia,
that they should be crucified. I try to herd all his bad
thoughts and lay them to peace. The boys did not
send him as much trade as they had anticipated. I

read in the newspaper of how England is not eager to get involved with the Cause. Father blames the delegates sent overseas for failing the South. And you know he thinks he himself is the South.

He sometimes names you as one of the culprits, you and Clarice. I tell him that you simply got married and needed Clarice's help. You can see his mind roaming parts of his world I am unfamiliar with. Then he rants about the "bluegum in the barn" and things that make no clear sense to me. I know he killed the man. Maybe it finally bothers him. He tells me I'm losing my looks and my figure, and that stings me. He'll talk out of his head when the pain worsens, but although we have opiates in the house, he will not open his mouth when I come with a dropper. I hear him in the nights. He made me move into the room next to his. He dreams. "I can't do it. I will not do it. Please don't make me," he will cry out in the wee hours.

When he alarms himself into a fit, I attend to him. At times I find that he has gone to bed wearing his day clothes. Some mornings, I greet dawn by singing to him. His constant longing is to hear "Dixie." He has me sing it slowly. He says he has to hear all the words. One day you will have to sit me down and tell me what in the world is happening, for you know so much. Just never, ever write me any mention of him in a letter. If he finds it, he will flay me. Remember when I could do no wrong in his eyes? Remember?

Give love to the children for me. Thank you for the ambrotypes. The girls have your wise face. They will surely grow up to be handsome young ladies, forever lovely. Today I turned my mirror to the wall. I no longer relish birthdays. Father gave me a Confederate bond for my last one. I thank you for the china rose.

In hope, I am,

Your sister

Maureen's sadness concerned me, and her confusion at Father's midnight ramblings led me to consult Quincy. "Should I tell my sister what little I know of his impoverished childhood?" In Father's history Maureen might divine some clue as to why he lived for money, why he was obsessed with his status on the James.

Quincy told me to wait. "Your sister has enough on her mind," he said, "enough woe." He said the time would come when I would learn everything about Father, when all the gaps would be filled. "Then Maureen and you can heal wounds. But for now, her situation in that house with your father argues against figuring him out." Quincy sighed and continued: "And the War. God knows that is enough business for now. You have to fight who can guess how many battles before you engage in a flanking maneuver against your father. Let him be. We have work aplenty at the hospital."

I said, "I know, Quincy. Oh Lord, I do know."

And indeed, the work seemed to increase like the loaves and fishes. In May of 1862, after the Confederates retreated from Yorktown, we were in church when the rector was handed a note, which he read silently. Then he announced the imminent arrival of trains. He added, "We were forced to retreat. The papers may not tell you that, but this church will." Although most reluctantly, he had been made by the diocese to drop Lincoln's name from the rolls of leaders prayed for, and to include Davis. After the announcement of the retreat, a Negro in the balcony forgot himself and let up a small whoop. As most of the congregation gathered itself for either the hospital or home, to change clothes and take whatever food and linens they could, the rector shouted, "The young man who hurrahed will not walk home alone. He goes under my protection."

In the siege we endured over the next few weeks, I maintained a sleepless vigil at the bedsides of howling boys. My previous account of Julian Opie's great ire is not full testament of the soldiers I saw, for in that May batch, as we euphemistically termed the clots of wounded who were sent from the railroad cars, I met so many sweet, needy boys. By nature of the Yorktown retreat, many of them were shot through their backs. Shells exploded like infernal firecrackers, and I spent long hours by Quincy's side at surgery, picking out shrapnel with tweezers. Too often, I would hear Quincy say, "Emma Garnet, you can stop now. He's gone."

Picturing to myself the action at the battleground, I saw

wrath in the eyes of Union soldiers as they took aim at scared boys who were already running, already admitting defeat, heading for home. I would say to those boys, who wondered why someone would target them when the threat had ceased, "You did not deserve this. Think of clouds. Think of your mother rocking you to sleep when you were little. Think of combing your horse's mane. Think only of good things, and let me break these aloe leaves onto your back. It will feel so nice."

"Yes ma'am, it does," they would say. "Keep doing it, please." They suffered from what Quincy called battle weariness—the sole nostalgia of the heart.

Most of the boys asked me my name. Did I have children? Did I have a pretty house? Would I please bring some more chicken soup? Did I make the last I fed them? I told the boys that a very kind woman named Clarice arose at dawn and made the soup. They always laughed when I said, "The only thing I have ever cooked that did not taste like poison is popcorn."

And then would come tumbling memories of the food their mothers cooked—salted ham and cabbage, collards, suet cake, black-eyed peas. For months, they had subsisted primarily on hardtack that tasted like the mildewed leather pouches they carried it in. I wanted to heal them and take them home to Clarice's table. I wanted them to know how it felt to be served, as I had been at every meal in my life. Over my left shoulder had always appeared a china platter piled with portions of tender meats already sliced, and vegetables were spooned onto my plate until I said, "Thank you, please." I knew that these boys had spent meals reaching into the center of a table for some tough, charred pork chop, frantic to pierce the best-looking piece before another one of ten or twelve other children got to it first. In my world, the last piece of chicken was always left. But I imagined in theirs a brother or sister or callous father triumphantly devouring the last thigh while the others knew that their stomachs would growl all night long.

What these boys wanted to eat most of all was eggs fried in lard. I wanted to accommodate them, but eggs had become scarce. Hens did not have time to lay before their necks were wrung. The vendor was charging, by the second year of the War, a dollar a dozen, which was beyond people's purse. A common soldier was paid only eleven dollars per month. Every commodity was high as Haman's gallows. But when I had heard, "An egg. I could really eat an egg," enough times, I told Clarice to spare the lives of some hens so that they might produce. "That might make good sense," she said. "I been meaning to tell you, but the children have been asking for cake, and I've had to satisfy them with a cracker." Clarice had explained to them, "Everybody wants an egg. I am very sorry." This lack was the only shortage Clarice allowed herself to admit. And when the hens would not nest because of the frequent report of rifle salutes at the nearby Oakwood Cemetery, she had Charlie build cubbies inside the kitchen, and she wrapped the hens with blankets to comfort them from the noise. After a while, the boys had eggs now and then. You would have thought the yolks were made of gold. Their gratitude was unending.

When, in June of 1862, I read that McClellan had com-
menced his Peninsular Campaign, I saw horror at Seven Oaks.
"At least," Quincy reassured me, "the man is known to be a gentleman. He was at West Point with my cousin. He is doing his
job. Please do not worry."

In the middle of the month came a letter from Maureen:

> Oh, Emma Garnet:
>
> We are coming. We have nowhere else to go. The
> staff officers want the house. They give us three
> days to move and allow us one large wagon. When
> they arrived, Father met them with a pistol in hand.
> A soldier knocked him to the ground. Some are out-
> side now, making sport of riding about the grounds,
> whipping the heads off the chickens and dear geese
> with their swords. I hear them laughing.
>
> We will be there I do not know when. They have
> Father under guard. I have to go now, so he can tell
> me what to pack. I knew it would happen sometime.
> But now? Just look out for us. Bertha and Lazy are
> being made to stay and keep house and cook for the
> officers. Most of the Negroes, including Ezekiel, left
> in a great "hegira," Father calls it, to follow troops
> down the river road to Williamsburg. They left with
> only the clothes on their backs. I have no time to
> hide anything. Father's money will be taken, what
> there is left of it.
>
> Please prepare Quincy for Father's coming. I will

have to reveal to Father our destination when he is
in the wagon. I don't even know the way. It is a far
piece. That much I know. Just look out your window
and we will be there. Please don't let this shake you
too much. Who knows but what this letter won't be
there after we arrive. Now *that* would rattle you. I
am so sorry, Emma Garnet.

> Your loving sister,
> Maureen

The following day, I was in the ward when Clarice appeared
at the door. I knew why she was there. She walked over to me,
laid both hands on my shoulders, and said, "Your father, he is
over to the house. He says for you to get there." As I left with her,
I was gripped with the stern reality that I was walking toward
doom.

twelve

By the time Clarice and I arrived home, Father had overseen the removal of Quincy's Hogarths from the wall of the front room. Up went the Titian, the Copley, the Gainsborough, and the Sully painting of Mother. Father was berating Charlie for generalized incompetence when I walked in.

"And there you are," he told me. "Broad in the beam, if I may say. But never mind that. You can work the fat off by toting for me." He reclined on the sofa and continued: "For I am here now, to be waited on. My spirit calls for it. You owe me care."

Clarice dismissed Charlie and pushed past me—I was standing in the archway that was perpetually hung with a sprig of mistletoe that gave Quincy, always, an excuse to kiss me—and marched to the sofa, snatched my angora blanket from Father, and said, "She don't owe you nothing for nothing."

He tugged at the angora. I could see, despite his dirty trousers, that his legs were swollen. He meant to comfort himself and hide his legs from me at the same time. "Nigger," he said to Clarice, "give that back to me. Then go make me a Sally Lunn. And not a Goddamn Confederate cake. I want to feel the sugar crunch in it."

I watched. She wrapped the blanket into her chest and said, "You ain't learned nothing. You ain't learned that a white nigger beats a real one any day. You ain't followed the statutes of His judgment. I have waited on you all your life, and you call me the bad name. I worried over you when the world whipped you. And there ain't enough sugar in this house for a rat to crunch. What there is of it is marked for Miss Emma Garnet's children and the patients."

He looked past Clarice to me. I had been fighting for words to hurl at him, but they would not come. All I could do was stare at this massive man who had installed himself and his treasures in my house. I knew he would convert this room into a roost, and from it he would try to run our lives to suit himself. But Quincy, Clarice, and I would not allow him to assume possession of our home. He asked where the girls were. He had seen their pictures when he had been forced to ransack Maureen's room to "get some idea of what in the Hell she was conspiring against me over." He said that my girls were "pinch-faced," as if they didn't get enough air to breathe.

"You have not changed, have you?" I said.

He reared up, supporting himself on arms that looked to be as full of excess fluid as his legs, and said, "This world has changed, all right. My niggers left in a Goddamn orchestrated hegira. McClellan's bandits are at this moment stripping Seven Oaks to the ground. He came himself as we were leaving and said if it weren't for your husband's reputation he would have burned it and set up shop at Carter's place."

"That has to be of some consolation."

"The Hell it is. The only consolation I have in regard to the famous Dr. Lowell is that if he hadn't taken you, nobody else would've. There you'd have been, all these years, snooping, criticizing, deceitful, blaming me every time you stubbed your God-damn toe."

"And now," I said, "my husband saved your home, and you come to mine, like this? Wanting to be catered to and doted on?"

He told me what he had told McClellan: "I said to the son-ofabitch, 'Take it. You have ruined my life. Take everything I have. Take it.' "

All civility abandoned me. "Well, Father, it seems that you have set afire your bridges." He maneuvered to make himself more comfortable. When he was settled, I asked, "What of the money? Did they take from you what was left?"

Clarice shouted out loud, "Ha! The money? I reckon he aims to borrow off you! What he ain't wasted in Confederate bonds, I bet he sent the most of it to Mr. Davis. He wouldn't keep nothing green. Didn't credit that it would ever be worth anything again."

Glancing at Father, I could tell by his aspect that Clarice was absolutely on the mark. I was furious. "Do you realize," I screamed, "what the Confederate dollar will count for when this is all over?"

He would not answer. His entire life he had worshipped money, and now he had thrown away a fortune. I could see his mind, even without an answer. He had been one of the richest men in Virginia, and his misplaced trust in the ascendancy of the Confederacy, his Machiavellian calculation that investments made to Richmond would one day be repaid with interest, would come to nothing, and he must have known it. Like a common refugee, he had traveled the long route from Seven Oaks to Blount Street, wondering if his self-exiled daughter and her "nigger-loving" husband might give him room, board, and perhaps even adequate seed money for the regeneration of his postwar existence.

· "I don't give a damn what Seven Oaks will be worth," he said. "What have you all been living on? Pieces of eight?"

Indeed we had. Bottoms of potato baskets in the cellar were lined with gold that Quincy had acquired slowly, quietly, long before war came. He sent deposits to his father. He invested in the new rail line. We had his salary for daily expenses. I wasn't dreaming when I told my brothers that I would look after their finances. But my father?

I told him that we were making do.

"We're grabblin'," Clarice added.

"Well, I intend to be grabblin' with you until I can get back home," he said.

I could not help saying, "To the home that is being spared thanks to my husband."

"Spared, yes," he replied. "But when McClellan noticed the

marble in the foyer, the Goddamn Italian marble, he called one of his thugs and told him to mark it. He said he had need of the stone to make a fortification."

Father began to ramble about other things McClellan highlighted for removal as he surveyed the house—velvet draperies for saddle blankets; corded wood for laying by against winter fighting; carpets to protect tented troops from wet ground by the riverbanks; lanterns, chickens, cows, horses, pigs. "And the chickens his bummers lopped the heads off, what they didn't traipse over, they meant to feast on. And the niggers, well, McClellan didn't want them following him, but they were gone by then. He wanted my books, and I said, 'By God, you shall not have them.' And he said he would. One of his force had knocked me down when they first got there, and he said if I fought him over the books, he'd have me to my knees again. The sonofabitch." He started again on his list of atrocities, but I stopped listening when Charlie tapped my shoulder.

"Your sister," he said, "she's calling. I was by your room, and I think she must have heard you come in."

Clarice rushed past me, muttering that she had left Maureen to wrinkle in the bath. I had not given thought to her. Of course, she was there. I had been absorbed with Father.

"Go on to the girl," he told me. "She's as full of mouth as you are. Tell that nigger in yonder to bring me something to eat. I want some Goddamn cake."

As I left, I said, "We have ash cake. You may have that. And the children are due home anytime now. They will not become your prey. You will not entertain for one second the idea of filling their minds with any of your crazed ideas. They are curious, as Whately and I were. But take no perverse pleasure in that fact, and do not take advantage of their innocence to intrude upon their spirits. I will not give you the chance to change them. They will move about this house as though you were not here, if one might ever be able to ignore the presence of a mad elephant in an otherwise peaceful home."

He grumbled and rooted into the sofa.

Maureen was soaking in the copper tub. To say that her appearance stunned me is an underestimation, but I have not the language to tell it. Nowhere have I read words adequate to convey my feelings. In approach, I can say only that she was not a great beauty anymore. Worry had wrecked her beauty. As she smiled in weak, tender greeting and rose to take the towel Clarice gave her, I saw that her body, the one she had, even as a girl, petted and groomed, was losing in toil against gravity.

"I'm awful, aren't I?" she said. "Vanity. I'm shot of it. You look wonderful. Come kiss me."

Clarice dried her body with the slow, loving care of a mare cleaning her foal of the gore of birth. She seemed to be trying, in her exertions, to massage years of woe from my sister.

Wordlessly, I helped Maureen step from the high tub so that her legs and feet could be dried, and I took the towel from Clarice. She excused herself to fetch Maureen some chamomile tea. Through tears that came when I saw her bruised calves, I said, "Oh God, Maureen. What has he done to you?"

She wrapped herself in the robe I held out, and whispered, "It wasn't him. I had to drive the distance, and several times the horses slipped their traces and I had to fight them back into their buggy harnesses, and my legs bumped against the buggy. Father was of no help. Hold me, Emma Garnet, I have the blues."

I held on to her tightly and took her to my bed. When she dropped the robe, I saw on her back racked lines of bruises that made her look as though her body had been pressed in medieval torture. I asked her, in as calm a tone as I could arrange, what had happened. My fear was that he had beaten her, and, as if reading my thoughts, she said, "No, he did not. Please, no worry."

She could not stand the weight of the counterpane. She rested beneath the sheet, praising it for being crisply clean, mercifully cooling.

I sat beside her, wishing I could provide her something other than rest and the time needed for healing. That much she would have with me, time and rest. But I had to know.

She lay on her stomach, like those soldiers hit in their retreat, and explained what had happened. "We stopped several times along the way, for food and sleep. The people who took us in, they were so poor, so very, very poor. They let Father in, though. They were kind enough to let him in. He was hobbling."

"Were they good to you? Did someone assault you?"

"I didn't have the chance for them to be good or to be bad. But they brought me food and cover. They had children bring me some cornmeal. That was all I wanted. You know, I still do love it."

I asked her what she meant. Why had she had cause for someone to bring her food and cover? Where had she been?

"In the wagon," she said. "He made me guard the paintings. The first night, he caught me laid out on the Titian—I needed a cushion. We hadn't brought much clothing, not enough to fashion any class of comfort. He spit fury at me. You know how he is. The next night and the next, I slept on the bare rough boards. There was no going in a stable, either. I had to stay there. The boards pained me. I can't see my back, but it hurts. Do you have anything?"

He had denied her minimum comfort to protect pictures that the host families would not have been able to distinguish from torn-out scenes they found in tattered copies of *Harper's* or *Godey's Lady's Book* and might have had nailed to their walls for some hope of adornment. They might have wondered, as did the provincial legislator, how the squirrel sat so still, but that would have been the end of their concern. When Clarice brought the tea, I asked her to send Mavis or Martha up with some aloe leaves.

I broke the leaves onto her bruises and rubbed as gingerly as possible. Clarice sat by the window and watched for the children. She pointed to the floor, to the room where Father lay, and mouthed, "Sleep." I soon had my sister asleep, too.

The girls were playing chase on the way home. Through the open window, I could hear everything that went on near the center of town, even the cries of mothers who gathered at the Capitol each morning, when the reports of fatalities were read on the steps. I could hear coffins being hurriedly nailed together at the livery down the street. Sounds of death drifted in my windows even when I came home from the hospital in hopes of some respite from incessant encounters with it. But then I would hear the day students at Saint Mary's let out, those girls running for their homes, for welcome. Clarice and I raced downstairs to intercept the children before they awakened Father and met God knows what. We were too late.

"Goddamnit to Hell," he cried. "What is this banging in the door like a bunch of savages?"

The girls threw their satchels on the hall bench, and as we reached the end of the staircase, they were peeking around the archway. Clarice and I stood behind the children, who drew back in one knot at the sight of Father fighting to come to his feet. I have never seen manatees, but I have read of them, and that is how I see him, a manatee struggling out of the surf to find a foothold on the shore and not being very successful at it. Mary reached back until she found my hand. Louise whispered sotto voce, "Mother, is it the bastard?"

Clarice tipped her finger on Louise's head. Leslie, true to her nature, giggled. For good, Father did not hear her. Leslie took note of the paintings on the wall and shrugged away when I tried to keep her from entering the room. My mind wandered back: Father eats people. I worried that he would grab her, that he would lunge forward and take her into his sweating, swollen self. But she avoided him. She walked around the edge of the carpet and went to Mother's portrait. To no one but herself, she said, "Oh, she is beautiful."

Father told her, "Come here. I've got something for you in my pocket. Which one are you?"

She turned from Mother's picture. "I am the one who is Leslie. You are Samuel P. Tate."

He reached for her. Again, "Come here."

Leaving Mary and Louise with Clarice, I went and stood in the center of the room and told him that none of the girls would be coming to him. "Do not try to lure them," I warned.

"Or what?"

"Or I will choke you," Clarice told him.

He ignored her and said I could at least do him the honor of introducing his grandchildren to him.

I reminded him that he had laid a curse on them the day I left Seven Oaks. I stared him into memory, and then decided he should know their names and that would be the most of it.

Clarice, at my unspoken direction, brought the children to me. I held them by the shoulders, presented them as though they were bolts of fabric being put forward for perusal, and when I had introduced them by their names only, not with the attributes I would have listed had my mother been sitting there in his stead, he said, "I shall look forward to knowing them better."

"No you won't," Clarice said. "They will treat you like you got the itch."

When he expressed an anticipation of knowing them, I heard, if not a tenderness in his voice, then something on the edge of genuine desire. But I could not traffic in his imaginings, for I knew we would all regret an excursion into his world, his darkness. I would keep the children away from him. They would come and go through the back door. He could set up his house in my front room, surrounded by his treasures—and when I looked closely at the bookcases around me, I saw that they were crowded with his Wedgwood and Revere—and he could call out to the servants, "Bring me some water! Bring me some pie!" and he could stay there until the War ended or until he died of the heart ailment that brought about the swelling in his limbs.

I dismissed the girls, telling them to fetch Charlie.

"That slow nigger?" Father asked. "I thought he'd never get those cheap Hogarths down. Running on about how Dr. Lowell wouldn't like it."

"Dr. Lowell," I told him, "certainly will not like it."

"He can live with it."

"And this"—I kicked at the stool upon which he had propped his gouty feet—"is how I plan to live with you." He wanted to say something, but I would not hear his commentary. I said, "You may stay here. Even if I wanted you upstairs, you would not stand the effort. But I ought to have slow Charlie drag you so slowly up the steps, up that hard oak, the way my sister endured nights on the jagged board of that damn wagon. I will have a curtain hung in the archway to afford you some privacy. Martha and Mavis—they have names, you will not call them 'nigger'—will see to your feeding. Clarice does not, will not, help you. Charlie will help you in whatever ablutions you have need of, and will see to them right away, for you carry an odor."

He declared himself of proper toilet, denying the plain fact that if he were, at that moment, assassinated with whatever class of perfumery I had hoarded in my bath cabinet, he would still smell as sour as any soldier I had sponged clean of fetid matter that seemed to have taken hold of his skin as algae on a wet rock.

"My house smells pretty," I told him, "and it will stay that way."

He said he noticed when he arrived that I had copied the flying staircase from Seven Oaks in some latent longing for home.

"Actually," I said, "a Yankee made this house. I had no hand in it. And now here you are. Do not try to distract me. Quincy will be home shortly. He had a rather brief surgical agenda. You will not assault him. You will not call him 'nigger-lover.' You will respect my husband and our children and this house, or you will be gone."

He laughed in my face.

I told him that my husband had saved more lives than he could imagine, and that, unlike Quincy, he would not be able to bear the strain of one day at the hospital.

"And what do you do, pray tell, when you go there?" he asked. According to him, I knew how to do only two things: read and lurk.

I did not have to justify myself before him. "Believe what you will. You no longer rattle me. In fact, once the novelty of having a dying man in my parlor wears off, I might even be bored."

"A dying man in your parlor?"

"Your heart will choke you before Clarice has time to. You will be dead in a month."

I closed my eyes and turned toward the archway. I did not want to see if he mocked me, if he was incredulous, if he was worried, if he despised me. He said nothing; thus was I spared the burden of making adequate response. To his mind, perhaps, I had inherited his penchant for lying. Perhaps I had been endowed with his capacity for torture. When I reached the hall, I did say over my shoulder, "I will send to the hospital to have Quincy bring something home for you. Take it and be grateful. And do not bother him for an instant when he comes in this house. He has been helping others, and he is the only one who can help you. So take it. Take his help."

"Why can I not stay in one of the other rooms down here? Your niggers room in the house. I understand that Clarice has large quarters." He was full of complaint.

As parting word, before I went to look for the children so that I could instruct them on their new comings and goings, I told him, "Those rooms are occupied. You will stay put. You will be made comfortable, as befits such a man of means."

I found the girls in my bedroom. Maureen, they assured me, had been awake when they entered. She seemed delighted with them, tired still, but pleased. Her feet were out from under the sheet. Louise was examining them, for her way was to inspect any sight put before her. "You have such pretty toes," she said, "each one only as long as it's supposed to be. I study Father's anatomies."

Maureen said sadly, "Yes, I do have my feet."

Mary wanted to paint her aunt's nails, feet and hands, with my lacquer. Maureen agreed to the feet but would not allow the hands. I suspected that they were blistered from holding reins and she did not want the girls to see them. Martha brought her a tray, and as she drank her broth, she told my daughters pleasant tales of how curious I had been as a girl. I sat in the slipper chair and listened to her mount evidence that she had watched me as we grew, that she had loved me enough to remember, for telling, the times I had given baby John sugar teats to quiet him when Mother was resting. She remembered that I had offered my Christmas candy canes to the children in the trash gang while she had hidden hers in her armoire.

"Were you greedy?" Mary asked.

I answered for my sister. "She was not greedy, merely building a store against the future." What I did not say was this: "For so much has now been taken from her. God knows she deserves a stick of candy." As it was painful for her to lie on her back, when her toenails were dry, hastened along by the girls' blowing on them, she turned over and asked if she might rest. We closed the door and went to the sleeping porch—night was falling—and read funny tales by Artemus Ward.

The girls heard their father before I did. They notified me

when they detected the singular creaking of his carriage wheels. I asked them to go prepare their lessons for the morrow. They wanted to know when I would be available to help them, when their father and I would be able to tell them stories and lay them to sleep like in the olden times. Here they were, ten, eleven, and twelve, and they could already evoke longing for "olden times."

I nearly tripped down the steps when I heard Father greet Quincy. "She's got me set up in here like a Goddamn poor relation. I have you to thank, let me say first in the spirit of our new enterprise, the promise of a protracted visitation, for saving my home from the torch so that Yankee officers might establish their camp-following whores in the bedchamber where my wife suffered her last breath. Goddamn, come in here and let me shake your hand. Or is it bloody?"

Quincy rolled his head on his neck, as he often did in strained circumstances, and went into the parlor. He did shake Father's outstretched hand. He stood there, a true gentleman, and said, "Welcome, Mr. Tate, to our home. I must say, though, that you do not look well."

I walked in and told Quincy that I had sent word of Father's decrepitude to the hospital; the message must not have reached him. "No," he said, "but let me see you, sir."

I lit all the sweet-potato candles in the room, hardly light by which to make an examination, yet Quincy managed. I suppose Father allowed him because my intimation of his end had frightened him. Quincy said that he would be fine through the night, that deep rest was in order, and that in the morning he should start a strict diet of hot fluids, as hot as he could make himself swallow.

Father did not thank Quincy; he said he would follow his instructions only because they seemed benign. "I do not want anything done to me that will infiltrate my system," he said.

"Yes, a restoration of balance is needed," Quincy replied. "You will have your cherished humors balanced. Either that or your heart will seize you one of these nights, and I will have to split you open and squeeze life back into you with my bare hands."

"Good God," Father sputtered. "Have a nigger bring me some boiled water, now."

"You will have your water," Quincy said, "and I see that Charlie has made our parlor into an infirmary, and that is fine. It is also fine that those paintings are on the wall. But you will not, under any circumstances, use the word 'nigger' to call for collection of any of the servants. You will not abuse language around our children. And you will not agitate Clarice. She is slowing down herself. Slightly. You will keep to yourself your feelings about her leaving Seven Oaks. And you will not, in any manner, interrupt the rhythms of this household. The War has seen to enough of that already."

"Where's something I can read?" Father asked him.

"I will bring you my Shakespeare and several of my Greek tragedies. You can occupy yourself with those and with pushing the fluids out of your system. Any accommodations of a personal nature will be brought to you. And I want to say finally, Mr. Tate, that your daughter is my wife now, and the mother of three children whom she has raised without benefit of your authority. She ligated an intestine yesterday when a surgeon showed up too drunk to perform his duty. She is, in short, a grown woman. She is no longer yours to berate."

Father nestled his head into a pillow. "I have not berated anybody."

"You may not have," Quincy said. "But I know you. It is merely a question of time. Go to sleep."

Quincy blew out the lights, and as we took the stairs, I whispered that we would be on the porch that evening, or in one of the spare rooms. "Maureen needs our bed," I told him. So tired that he kept himself steady by touching the wall, he still had the love in him to ask if he needed to tend to her. I told him no. I had taken care of her, and would.

Father endured. Each time I left the house for the hospital, he asked where I was going, if Clarice was going to look after him this day better than she had the day previous, if Maureen was going to stop whatever she was doing up there where I had her hidden and come down and sit with him. Maureen was reading, always, all day. For a refreshment, she would walk to Saint Mary's and help the highly appreciative music teacher with his piano and voice students. I would not let her work at the hospital. She had done her part. Clarice was running the house. She and Father took passing snipes at each other, but she would not touch him. As for my departures to the hospital, I began simply naming the reasons I was collecting my bag and bonnet to go gather the reapings of battles he read about in the newspapers that piled by his sofa: Malvern Hill. Cedar Mountain. Groveton. Second Manassas. Chantilly. And, oh my God, Antietam. September 17, 1862.

Blood poured. I would come home with my clothes soaked crimson, and Father would say, "Who've you got on you?"

He heckled Quincy and me from the throne that he established for himself, propped by my best pillows, bolstered against all reality by newspaper accounts that diminished truth with such decorous conclusions as: "Confederate forces were pushed back. Wake County guards performed admirably. Some were lost." After Antietam, I would have thought he might in some fashion begin to reconcile himself to the fact that the War had turned, that "we" were now fighting in futility. Quincy began to lecture Father on the horror of it all, his initial sentence usually, "Mr. Tate, do you know what I saw today?"

"No, Quincy. I have been chasing the furies today. Just tell me."

Quincy would sit on the stool by Father's sofa and say, "I gave aid to a boy with his jaw completely blown off. I do not see how he made the journey alive. He wished himself dead. I know it. Emma Garnet gave him some milk through a pipe she inserted into his nostril, what there was left of that."

Father would say, invariably, "If you intend to shock me, you have not. If you intend to make me feel guilty that I am not a young man and cannot be in the fighting, you have likewise failed. If you chide me for wanting a severance of the Union, I despise you."

And then, late in the month, when General Lee had retreated into Virginia, Quincy came home to find Father writing a letter threatening a newspaper editor whom he thought a mite too pro-Negro: "Some news of true worth, my sir: That you may find yourself with your head turned around backward, crumpled at the bottom of your stairs, with your wife and children crying over you and wishing you had not been such a pluperfect nigger-lover. Your commander has been forced to fall back, and you, sir, think it 'perhaps for the best.' You think it may quicken the end. Reckon now with your end."

Quincy tore up the letter and shouted at Father. "You will never, ever write such missives from our home. You will lie there and be the sick, bloodthirsty, impotent braggart you are."

Quincy was enraged. His sleeves were stained with the commingled blood of perhaps ten or twenty boys. He shoved his arm to Father's nose and said, "Smell it. Smell it, I tell you. You like blood. You want this bloodletting to keep on? Smell this for a few years."

Father raised a swollen arm and tried to push Quincy aside. He told him to back away. Quincy did not want to, and the two of them were terrifying me. I wanted this time to stop. Father said, "I have been here since June. That is now nigh four months that you have treated me like a Goddamn leper. I finally got Clarice, and I can't have her. I see those girls, and they run. The nigger women bring me my food and that Goddamn ever-loving hot water and leave it here like you'd feed a rabid dog. Scared because you've made them scared. That nigger Charlie, he complains about how he needs to be off shooting squirrels. I can't get up for hardly anything. I have to beg somebody to keep me in something to read. I have to read your Goddamn glossed Horace and see you get it all wrong. Schoolboy scrutiny. And you have the temerity to tell me what to say in a letter. My own affairs."

"If you send that letter from this house and there is an occupation, do you realize what destruction will be rained down upon your daughter?"

I was at Quincy's side. I told him to never mind me. "Mind the children," I said.

Father uncapped the bottle of ink and poured the contents on the rug. We had bought that rug in Paris. I was stunned. Quincy retrieved another bottle from the parlor desk, opened it, and doused the Titian. "Look," Quincy told him. "If that were blood, it would come out. But it's gone. A thing of beauty, gone."

Quincy was out of his mind. He appeared calm, but in a quietude that afflicts only the most dire of the afflicted, the maddest of the mad. He took a seat and motioned for me to sit beside him.

Father tried to come to his feet, but Quincy moved forward and pushed him back onto the sofa. "You bastard," Father said. "Do you know what that picture cost me?"

"Do you, Mr. Tate, know what my wife's childhood with you cost her?"

"It cost her the price of fine dresses and kid shoes."

"It cost her peace," Quincy said. "And I want to know which

is worth more to you, the Titian or her solace. Do you want me to count for you the nights she has cried incessantly for her brother and her mother? The nightmares?"

I asked Quincy please to stop. If he did not, I would have to leave the room. Quincy would not allow me to leave until Father apologized. "First, Mr. Tate, you will apologize for praying for the continuation of bloodshed about which you know absolutely nothing save what you read in the newspapers and what you see of the lines in your daughter's face when she comes in from having nursed the casualties of battles you lie here salivating over. And then you will tell my wife you're sorry. If you refuse to do either, you are out of my home. I have had all I can stand of you. How were you going to manage throwing the editor down a flight of steps? Tell me. I'm interested."

"You listen to me, you son-of-a-nigger-loving-bitch. I have more power in this country than your crowd can dream of. I know people."

"And yes, Mr. Tate, I have become acquainted with several people you know. Wade Hampton thinks you a fool. Landon Carter thinks you a bumptious misfit. Henry Hammond thinks you an overreacher. Braxton Bragg regrets having known you."

"You know nothing," Father said.

"Men are most sorry about the amount of time they have had to spend disassociating themselves from you. You were convenient to a great many people. I will credit you that. And now look at you, not even a credit to your own family."

Father told Quincy to go to Hell.

"For one who has read and critiqued my Horace, that is hardly an imaginative response," Quincy said, "but never mind. What I need to know is, how many of those types of missives might you already have penned in my home?"

"Very easy. Atlanta. Vicksburg. New Orleans. Knoxville. Nashville. You care for me to continue?"

"Oh Father, you surely did not," I said.

"I surely did. And I told each of them that I was trapped in a house with a Yankee and his compatriot and their spiteful children. I told them who love the nigger to come one, come all, to this house of merriment. I told them you are a Lowell, a name I detest. Always. Always, Alice saying to people at church and here and there and yonder, 'My daughter, she married a Lowell. They are very fine people.' I would say, 'What is wrong with us? Why do you place my family in such an unfavorable light?' She would say, 'But you have no family.' Lowell. Uppity bitch of a mother, looking down her nose at me. And the grand Dr. Lowell, sneering, being better."

"You hate that, don't you, Mr. Tate? You hate it that in your scheme your daughter married one of your betters?"

"This is what I think." Father reached for the cane I had not seen him to have, and struck Quincy across the face.

I jumped to help my husband. Father sat with the cane still raised, brandishing it as he had the bloody knife that had killed Jacob. I grabbed it. It was mine. Quincy told me to put it down. I said, "Goddamn, Father. Antietam, your end. You write letters from here meant to harm. Enough are harmed. Haven't you done enough? Are you not satisfied? And you worry about society like a possessed matron? Have you no pride?"

Quincy took the cane from me, calmed my arms, and had me sit. But he would not sit. He once again shoved his bloody sleeve into Father's face. "That is the blood of boys I know. Emma Garnet and I can call the names for this blood. Smell it, Tate. I'm going to make you drink it. Some sprayed into my face today when I popped open an artery. Surprised me. But I'm used to the taste. It is rather like an overripe port. Come on, Emma Garnet."

He left by telling Father that he was putting him out of the house the next day. "Do it," Father told him. "Some woman will take me in. If I had not rescued Emma Garnet's mother from Savannah, her next turn would have been taking in wayfarers. You just have your nigger set me out on the other side of town. That's where Alice's family was living when I found her. On the other side of town. But my God, did they nourish what bit of aristocracy they had left in them. Your mother had on starched bloomers the night I took her."

I thought I would lose my reason. My father either had lost his or was spewing the most vicious lies he had ever told. But in a corner of my heart I wondered if there might exist in his diatribe a terrible kernel of truth. As Quincy walked me upstairs, I said, "I want to kill him."

Quincy held me close around my waist and said, "No, nothing. Do nothing whatsoever. He wants to fight. I've already done too much. I threw the ink. My God, I'm a rational man."

And then half into the night, more than that, for I could hear the next morning's departing troops gathering at the governor's palace, I was still asking Quincy, "Is he lying? Why did he say those things about my mother? Was my dear mother forced to live with a man who believed he had bought her at a fire sale? He used to trade on her background. She knew the Rhetts of Charleston. She was so good! Why, Quincy? Why did he say those things?" I begged for laudanum. I wanted again to fall beneath the river of memory and lie there, with time flowing over me.

Quincy got out of bed. He said, "It's your father. I hear him moaning."

I had heard nothing. I followed Quincy. He lit one of the few tapers in the house, found his medical bag, and went downstairs. Light was just crackling outside. You can hear dawn's coming when the house is so still for listening.

"Your father's in heart failure," he said as we moved into the foyer. "I can feel it."

"Then do something, I suppose," I whispered.

"I am."

He knelt by the sleeping man on the sofa. I was accustomed to seeing the dying show some evidence of distress. My father showed none. But Quincy knew things. From a vial, he shook some powder onto a paper, folded it, and sighed. Then he parted Father's lips, lifted his head, and shook the powder into Father's mouth.

I tugged at Quincy's sleeve. "What is it?" I asked.

"Digitalis."

"Dear Jesus," I said. "How much?" I knew the drug to be dangerous, unstable, unpredictable.

"Enough," Quincy told me. "In a minute, he will taste blood. It won't wake him, but he will have tasted it. Go now. Go to the steps and wait."

I did not leave. I saw Father gurgle. His lips foamed. Quincy listened to his chest, pulled the blanket over his eyes, and said, "Now, now you will have some peace. Do not ever speak of what transpired here. Not until I am dead and beyond the reach of shame. Then you may unburden yourself. But for now, no speaking. Go to bed."

To report, I did not lie awake for long. I pretended my mother alive, happily with us. Quincy had ransomed her from my father, who had made veteran hostages of us all.

thirteen

Nobody wept for Father. Maureen stood over his body until noon, while Quincy tried to make some arrangements, and said with great equanimity, "If he had to go, I suppose better now than after Mr. Lincoln calls for freedom. Father would have swallowed poison." A voice inside me said, "But he did. He did!"

Clarice had hurried the children out with Martha and Mavis before they knew what had transpired, and then she knelt by him and whispered, "Here he lays. He wanted to be a great man. And a good mighty many did look up to him. But he led them the wrong way. I know most people thought he was out of his place. I just hope he didn't die knowing the worst of it. They say you see the truth on yourself when you die. He had come so far, and he must have been tired. That's all I've got to feel sorry over him for. I gave and gave and gave, and he lets his children down and calls me 'nigger.'" She touched his toes, as I had seen her instruct those Negroes to touch Jacob all those many years ago in the barn. "You know what I'm doing," she said. "You do it, too." I wanted to take no chance of his assaulting me in my nightmares, so I touched him.

Maureen looked baffled. "It's tradition," I told her. "Father's Guinea Negroes thought that touching the toes of the dead would keep evil from dreams. You were too young when I saw Clarice make them touch Jacob, and his ghost assaulted no one except Father."

"Then by all means," she said, and touched him.

Quincy returned with a list for Maureen and Clarice—the coffin, a train for Williamsburg, burial at the Bruton Parish cemetery, even a girl to sing "Dixie."

Maureen volunteered to sing Father's tired anthem instead of a stranger. But Quincy said, "No. We need to get all this finished with as little emotional expense as possible. Go get Charlie. Tell him to find some help. We can put your father in my carriage."

As Charlie and Quincy were taking Father's body out the front door, Quincy caused the load to be rested over the threshold while he called out to me, "Sweetheart, some things I forgot. Start with the sofa. I want it burned. I want you to have some of these people who pass by here wanting a job to clear a place in back and set fire to it. They can take the wood of it home for their stoves. And the Titian. Throw that on top of it. And the angora blanket. He held on to that too much to suit me. I'll buy you another sofa and blanket when I can. And my Hogarths— Martha and Mavis can rehang them. Leave your mother, though.

She looks beautiful there. I can live with the others if you have Charlie move them to the back library when we return. I'm not in there much. But please leave your mother in the front room. I like the way she looks at us all."

Maureen marveled at his efficiency. But she was just as capable of managing an abundance of necessities as he was. When we took the overflow of soldiers into our home after Gettysburg, she played her part with courage. She comforted boys by singing, they often remarked, like something sent from Heaven. She would sing arias, her specialty, while the girls took turns playing the piano. At her urging, we let her change some bandages, but she gagged and had to take a fainting break in her room. Again, at her pleading, I allowed her to rinse bloody sheets, but Clarice found her sick in the yard. "Hang them on the line, if you got to be doing something you're not any good at. No more blood for this one."

Clarice was not well herself, but she would not rest. She cooked around the clock, sleeping on a cot in the kitchen after insisting that her room be given to soldiers, and I could hear her up with Charlie, washing kettles for another meal when midnight chimed. She blamed her slowed gait, which she fought to hide when I was around, on a summer cold, but at a Fourth of July celebration, which our family enjoyed quietly for fear of being chastised in the newspaper for Unionist tendencies, she began coughing into a little paper flag one of the girls had made, and could not stop.

I made her go to my room and lie on my bed. All the way she

protested, "I'm just getting shed of a little congestion. You have to get it out. Just let me hack."

I put my ear to her back and listened while she struggled to fill her lungs to capacity. I was worried beyond all rational thought, for I had heard those breaking, cracking sounds in boys who had pneumonia. I would not send her to the hospital, because of a recent outbreak of measles. Quincy had said he was grateful that we had taken in soldiers, so I would stay home during the course of the illness. I sent word to Quincy to come see after Clarice. There was nothing he could do to divert the course of the symptoms she was presenting, a fever and a clamminess in addition to the rattling in her chest. Still, I wanted him to rescue the woman I had always trusted to be invincible.

I did not believe I could exist without Clarice. From my experience with boys at the hospital, I knew what was ahead for her, the way she would feel, as though her heart and lungs and throat were being strangled. The illness was ruthless, vicious. I despised mortality. And while I prayed for her, for a miracle, I had to ask God why He had to make me see this, why she could not pass after me. She and I had, I believed, been punished enough. I did not feel brave, and I was not stoic. I was broken.

She resisted changing into a proper resting gown and did not want to stay in bed. She did not trust the other servants to keep the kitchen going. Over and over, I tried to convince her, "They know what to do."

"No, they don't," she said, sitting on the end of my bed after consenting to let me undress her.

"What they don't know, I'll teach them."

"That might be the funniest thing I ever heard," she answered hoarsely. "You teach somebody in the kitchen? Most of these boys can't swallow popcorn."

I imagined myself telling Martha that she was about to overstimulate broth with peppers, and wondered indeed what I would do if any household duty was left to me. When the furniture was dusty, I knew to clean it. When the windows were dirty, I knew to scrub them with water and vinegar. But that was it. My mother had spoken of cooking as a mystery fathomable only by Negroes. I was incapable of lifting heavy irons from the fire, even though rolling heavy men over to change their linens had strengthened my arms. In the main, I felt myself too weak and ignorant to function in the kitchen. My experience was calling out receipts from a cookery book, asking Clarice if this or that might be tasty, and that is a long distance from actually doing anything. I liken it to driving a carriage. Although Charlie or Quincy had taken me the route from our house to the hospital hundreds of times, the first occasion I had to make the circuitous journey alone, I became hopelessly lost and had to stop and ask a little Negro boy to hop in and get me to the Fair Grounds. You can watch something being done all your life, but the brain does not always fully engage.

I told Clarice she could not worry. To ease her mind, I had to call Martha, Mavis, and Charlie each to the bedroom to assure Clarice that they knew how to manage, that she could sleep without wringling back and forth with worry.

Clarice told Charlie he smelled like carrion.

He replied, "It must be on account of I ain't washed since I been cleaning squirrels for two days."

She told him to go wash. All my time with her, she had been telling people what to do and they had obeyed without question, as did Charlie now. When he returned with the proof of his clean self—for she often required evidence that her mandates were taken to heart—she was asleep. I called Maureen in to help me fan her until Quincy arrived.

Maureen was worried at Clarice's labored breathing. "I am sorry, truly sorry, when I see her every few minutes, that I did not treat her better when we were at Seven Oaks."

"Do not nurse worry," I said. "You were a child when Clarice and I left. Just help me nurse her now. Mavis and Martha can attend to the soldiers. Charlie can cook." We would be with Clarice through a long night. I told my sister she had nothing to regret, but her youth did not fully excuse her. Even when she was tiny, she refused to obey Mother when she bade us treat the servants with respect. Maureen would likely go to sleep that night guilt-ridden. When people are very ill, others are bound to recall every slight, every instance of thoughtlessness. Guilt is the precursor of fear—we obsess about the past and grow afraid that our culpability will never abate and will hound dreams, waking and sleeping. Maureen had given Clarice and all Negroes at Seven Oaks wide berth, had not honored them as God's people. Clarice, nonetheless, treated Maureen with love and tenderness, even after her efforts to soothe a stomachache or help sew a torn doll were spurned. Maureen had not returned Clarice's affections, and now that she needed to make amends, she did not have words enough or time. Clarice was asleep and did not look as though she would be able to travel back to Virginia with Maureen and reassure her that those instances of neglect were healed, forgotten.

Indeed, Clarice was beyond all effort. She would give in to her body, its failing, because she had no choice. She did not have the strength to fight, and she was wise enough to know that any attempted struggle would be futile. Maureen realized Clarice lacked the energy to assuage her guilt. "Oh, Emma Garnet," she said. "I waited too long." Then she kissed Clarice on the forehead. She sat on the slipper chair in the corner and cried, her bitter fruit for having treated Clarice as a Negro servant, not as a woman who made Seven Oaks a home.

I had been almost daily with death, borne its intrusion in my efforts to court favor with life, but I was not prepared for it to take Clarice. She was the strongest woman I had ever known, ever would know, and I include Varina Davis, Dorothea Dix, and three generations of Lee women. She had worked for and loved all of us, been our constant guardian. We knew what she believed to be moral, and while at the top of her list was eliminating slavery, she did not interfere in its flourishing. Her mission was not to change history but to help both white and black prevail over the circumstances of living in that place, the South, in our time. She worked with the consequences dealt her by others, in the travails of her race. She was not merely dignified, and to label her such would be not an error of judgment but one of degree. No, she was dignity itself. As I lay down beside her and held her, Maureen took over the fanning. I smelled years of "prespiration" coming off her body, although she had taken that morning what she called her lavender refresher. Too many people, to her mind, thought Negroes inherently dirty, and thus she made sure that "all the Lowell Negroes stay clean to the bone." Still, I could smell her being tired.

I untied the scarf from her head, and Maureen gasped. "Her hair! It's completely white!"

I was surprised but not perplexed. Clarice had never let me see her hair. She looked, suddenly, old. Quincy soon entered and put his stethoscope to Clarice's chest and back without waking her. I moved to the window, so I would not have to see his face when he finished, but his words were laden. "It's bad," he said quietly. "There's something about that's moving quickly. If she were younger, maybe. If she were not so exhausted, maybe."

"Maybe what?" I snapped.

"Maybe she would hold out for a few days."

"Make her," I told him. At my tone, Maureen slipped out of the room.

Quincy told me that he had only so much power, and I knew that. "Her body is no different from anyone else's."

"But her spirit is," I reminded him.

He told me that many spirits were broken by high fever, that I should stay with her and make sure she got the love and care she deserved.

He met Maureen in the hall, where she was awaiting word of whatever she could do to help both Clarice and me. "Those two," I overheard my sister say, "have carried on a lifelong love affair with one another." I did not hear Quincy list the particulars of Clarice's care, but soon Maureen arrived with cups of rabbit broth—after Gettysburg's contributions to the hospital and our home, we would not have thought of taking beef or poultry from the soldiers—and asked me to drink mine while she sat Clarice up and found some way to make her take even a few spoonfuls. I did not want to move, not with Clarice resting so peacefully, not with my feeling, founded on no actuality, that I had caused her congestion to clear by love and will. But Maureen said, "Quincy left me with orders. You will do as I say. Just don't either one of you start bleeding."

She saw me turn my head to listen for sounds of the girls, who should have been in their rooms doing their lessons. She told me they were downstairs watching a couple of soldiers who were now ambulatory and playing lice. That meant that they had taken advantage of my disappearance, and Clarice's, to tap lice into their plates and place bets on their speed while they moved from rim to rim. These soldiers would bet on anything.

Taking the broth from Maureen, I told her to tell those boys to go out back and have Charlie wrap their heads in lard and to have Mavis and Martha remove all the sheets the afflicted had rested on and boil them with milkweed. "And check the girls," I said. They had been sent home from school many times since the soldiers' arrival, once with a hastily scribbled note from a teacher:

"Crawling heads. Please talk to them about these bets they place. Horrific." Clarice made them give Christ Church the money they won from other girls, those they had hired out lice to when the girls got tired of watching them and had to join in the fun.

Clarice had always given most of her salary to the church, and now, when I called her name and she came to half-wakeness, I asked if she wanted to see the rector. "I ain't near dead yet," she answered, and then fell into a coughing frenzy.

But she was almost gone. Pneumonia is so often the final punishment for a life of unrelenting work and strain, and as I helped Clarice drink the broth, I wondered why she would have to die in a fevered misery, why she could not simply ease away in her sleep after spending as normal a day as was to be had during the War.

Taking nourishment taxed her to exhaustion. Every move she made was burdensome, brutal to her in this weakened state. When I made her take the tepid bath Quincy prescribed to lower her temperature, I was afraid that she would lose consciousness in the water and drown. I held her up in the tub, as a mother would an infant, and poured water over her neck. When I dried her and settled her back in bed, she motioned for me to bring my face close to hers.

"It ain't going to be long," she said. "I can feel the wind die down in me. Go get Martha and Mavis and Charlie."

Her voice, though at a hint of its strength of the day before, was not to be ignored. I rounded up the servants and brought them to Clarice's bedside.

Charlie tried to tease. "You need to go on and get out from under these covers. It's daylight outside."

She shushed him with her finger. She wanted to sit up, so Charlie and I bolstered her.

Martha spoke to me as if Clarice could not hear her. "She got this and it's taking her quick."

"I heard you," Clarice said. "But it don't matter. Listen. If something has to be quick, it might as well be me, on account of my air." More coughing. Then, "The three of you—I don't own you. Nobody don't. Sit down here and let me tell you how you need to act."

I had meant to tell them in my own time and in my own way. One of the great shames of my life is that I had let them work under the delusion of bondage, a condition no different from reality in its oppression on the soul, its damning of one's esteem. But always, I had told myself that the three of them lived much better than any truly free Negroes I had experience with, save Clarice. I had never intimated that they were bound by any strictures against their movements. I had paid them well. I would go for months without regarding their freedom, and in the middle of the night, when I felt I could do nothing to change matters, I would work my stomach into a knot, rehearsing time and again my announcement, their reaction. And then, the more time passed, the more convenient became an easy disregard for the truth, a forgetfulness. With the War, if I had freed them, they would have been in great danger, such was the animosity against uncontracted Negroes. Of this last fact, Quincy and I had sometimes regarded Mr. Lincoln's anticipated proclamation as the instrument that would release us from the obligation to tell them the truth. Quincy once said, "We have to tell them, but what would we do? What would they do? In time, this will all be taken care of. In time." And now Clarice was about to assume my unpalatable responsibility from me. I feared that they would leave me at the mercy of my incapable self. They would loathe me for perpetrating upon them a basic fraud.

The servants glowered at me. I told them I was sorry. "But now you know," I said.

"Don't do somebody much good now," Charlie said.

Martha sighed. "Leastways, I been saving my money."

"I ain't," Mavis said, and began crying into the handkerchief Charlie gave her.

I told them that they would not hurt for money, that I would set them up in trades or buy properties and furnish houses. If they wanted to settle in their old home, Warren County, Quincy and I could make that possible.

I should be grateful that they were not outwardly wrathful, but I deserved any ire they sent my way. When Charlie did look as though he might fume, Clarice placed her hand on his and said, "You listen to me. She did not go to do it. It was my notion. Let me be the one you blame."

"Then so tell us, what are we supposed to do?" Mavis asked.

"You, all three of you," Clarice said, "will go downstairs and fix the kitchen. I need to finish what is happening to me. I have no choice, or I would help you. What I want you to do is teach

Miss Emma Garnet and her sister how to cook. Then you go home, or wherever it is you dream of going—you know where the real money is—and leave if you have to. There won't be nobody to stop you."

By their looks, I could tell they were not thoroughly satisfied that I had not been part of Clarice's conspiracy to keep them in our house. But they left without a word to me. "Thank you," I told Clarice.

"I have to set matters right," she said. "Now you be the one who comes here. You have to be the one who listens."

I lay down facing her and waited until she had ample breath for talking. Her lips were becoming purple. "Listen to why your father was who he was," she finally said.

I told her to go slowly, to take her time; she responded that she had very little time.

She spoke of the hidden truth: It was a Saturday night. Her sixteenth birthday was the next day. Her mother, a freedwoman who made her living by tending kitchen gardens for white people, wanted to decorate the house with flowers, but it was too early for anything but one lonely crocus to come up in the yard. Her mother was "jubus" of the woods because of the fairies. Clarice went out flower-picking by herself. Darkness was taking the woods, so she foraged about quickly. She was picking along fine when she heard a shot. "I knew that a drunk and a little boy lived in the woods, in a sorry cabin, and I knew that the drunk beat his wife. I sometimes heard her screams"—a tear spilled from Clarice's eye, for she must have been hearing again the woman's agony——"and then I heard people coming through the trees." She hid behind a tree and watched. "The little boy, your father, had a woman by the arm. He was helping a man drag her." Father, she said, looked to be about eight. The boy and the man dropped the woman at a clearing and the man lifted the woman's skirt and pulled out a spade and a broken-handled shovel. "I had to wide my eyes to see. The night was fast coming." The man and the boy dug at the hard dirt, and when the man wore himself out——he didn't look to be made of much—— the boy had to keep going. He was crying hard, and his father would jab him in the back when he didn't move fast enough. Clarice stood watching until they covered the woman. Father's father told him to stay out there all night and guard against wild dogs. "I knew he didn't suddenly take a care to his wife. He just wanted to punish the boy some more, for what I did not know."

When the man staggered off and was far enough away, Clarice went to where Father sat crying. She placed her birthday flowers on the grave. She picked him up and carried him home with her. On the way, she asked, "Why'd he kill her?" Father told her that he, he his little self, had been the one. His father had made him do it. "Oh, he was so come apart," she told me. He said his mother sighed too much to suit his father, and since he was always taking sides against his father in arguments with his mother, the old man had "got about all he said he could take from the both of us and made me shoot her." I must have appeared incredulous, for Clarice swore she was telling me the truth. She took him home with her, and her mama said she needed to leave her home and go look after the boy. Clarice's mother had been wanting to move in with her brother anyway, but he had not wanted Clarice to join her. "He always said I had too much mouth." So she went to that sorry cabin and cooked and cleaned and drove them to Alexandria the day Father saw the nice rugs on the floor and the silver money. And she helped him pull Seven Oaks up out of the swamp. "I was there the day he brought his bride home. Oh, she was a beautiful girl."

She told me then about the time he robbed a turtle of its back to make a Lancelot shield, how she knew he would be marked because of all he had seen and done and been party to. Then she asked for rest. "I've said what I needed to. Now everybody's free."

She spit up a bolus of congestion into a handkerchief that I held to her mouth. As I wiped her lips, I thought of what inadequate repayment I was making for the life she had given me. Without her, I would have grown reclusive. I would have had a dismal existence, but with her, I had become a woman. She taught me, as she did everyone else, how to live.

She died after an hour, with a great heaving and retching. I lay with her until I had cried as much as I needed to, until my eyes were nothings. I kept thinking of how she would want me to be brave, but that belief gave me little comfort. I was as a bank that subsides into the James during a freshet—there was a slow falling away, the disappearance of my soul.

I lay there and wondered what she would want me to do next. I knew she would want me to go to the kitchen, but I could not, not yet. And I could not bring myself to cover her sweet face with the blanket. I tucked her in like a baby, and as I closed her eyes, I thought that although God had not sent down a saving miracle, He had given us the benefit of her daily miracles of patience, virtue, and love. I knew that on her grave marker, beneath her name, would be the words I felt most true: *Kind Mother.* Then I left to follow her instructions, to learn to feed those hungry boys and my family.

What did assuage my grief was cooking all night. When I told Maureen that Clarice was gone, and went with her into the kitchen, my sister pushed aside the vegetables the servants were chopping and laid her head on the table and wept.

Charlie said, "I'm sorry about Clarice's time. We all are. But we need to do what she told us to do. Then we've got to be going. We took just enough money from the cellar. Don't worry. Nobody robbed you."

I told them I was not worried about being robbed. I was worried about feeding the soldiers and my family. "And," I said, "I'm concerned about the three of you."

Charlie threw a potato peel into a basket on the floor, missed, and did not pick it up. I was meant to. I did. I let him defy the stricture of servitude, for in the act of bending to the floor, I traded places not only with Charlie but with Mavis and Martha as well.

He spoke their common destinies: "We will go and do, like Clarice said. She also said don't blame you, but we can't be that dumb. It was good of you to pay, and it was decent money. And we know you and your husband and Clarice thought we were better off. But you ain't better off until you get in your own house. We won't look back. You can rest on that tonight, but we're going to be on the home-road to Warrenton, trying not to get hung. The last thing we need off you is a letter we can show. And we will need to take the big wagon that your sister came in."

Martha and Mavis had been silent, staring at me, while Charlie spoke for them. I answered their glowering. "I'm sorry. I have no excuse."

Martha said, "Oh, yes ma'am, you do. The excuse is not being able to look after yourself and depending on colored folk all your life. Mr. Lincoln means to teach y'all ladies how to suffer by. I read it in the newspaper." She sighed. "And us free all the time. Jesus."

Again, I told them I was sorry. I promised to send them monthly allowances that would make it unnecessary for them to work another day. They did not argue. They looked at one another for a moment, ruminating upon my promise, and then Charlie said, "We thank you. My mama and papa need me to look out for them. And these two women need to have some babies before Nature comes. Leastways you'll be giving back part of what you took, even if you can't make up time."

Mavis handed me a long knife and said, "Now we need to work. You need to. Here. Cut up this duck. Charlie already scalded it, but he can tell you how to do it yourself while you make it into pieces. Since there ain't no chickens, he went and borrowed a few ducks from Miss McKimmon's yard. Listen to me tell the both of you what to do."

Maureen and I stayed in the kitchen all night, but each taking turns to sit with Clarice until Quincy came home. As I walked with him up to see Clarice, I told him that the servants would be gone before the morrow's noon. He said that he had figured Clarice would tell them, that he was glad to have off his conscience that burden of facing the servants with the truth. "We can live alone," he assured me. I showed him the burn marks on my arms and said I was not so certain. But he was, and, as said, I trusted him with every thought, every emotion. I laid all fears and timidity at his feet.

We buried Clarice in our plot at Oakwood Cemetery. I had not wanted to put Father there. He needed his Virginia, so Quincy had arranged for him to be transported on a military train. I had sent the bishop a note with the body: "Please place him a safe distance from my mother." When Quincy and I were walking home from Clarice's burial, I told him Father's story. He said, "Now all you have is this war to fight. Let the one with him be over."

fourteen

Everywhere I turned, I needed Clarice. I thought of her with especial longing the afternoon I arrived home from the hospital and found Maureen reading the just-published Gettysburg Address to the soldiers. Clarice would have thought the words healing, the length and tenor of the speech a perfect expression of the horror of the recent past and the hope for an endless peace to come. She would have thought that Mr. Lincoln had redeemed himself from what she called the missing-bite Emancipation Proclamation. When the mandate was issued, applicable only to slaves in territories under the control of the Confederacy, with the desired effects negated because it freed slaves where it could not be enforced, Clarice offered a prediction: "Unless Mr. Lincoln reaches his long, bony arm down to the South and scoops up Negroes, they won't be free for a hundred years. They're trapped. A whole class of men like your father have to die off," she told me, "then their sons have to die, and then enough memories

might be gone. Then you will see some change. All that proclamation will do is make white folks worry again, the way they did
over Nat Turner and John Brown."

To those boys hearing the Gettysburg Address, the president's
words meant that he had the capacity for great compassion.
When one asked Maureen to define "consecrate" for him, she
said, "It means that he thinks the bloody ground should be
blessed and made holy." There were twenty or so boys in the two
parlors, one on either side of the foyer, where Maureen and I
were standing, and they all grew quiet at the shared memory of
futile charges, of gore and pulp where faces had just been, of a
stench so far-reaching that snipers in trees, left at the scene to
pick off stray Yankees, vomited onto the strewn bodies.

Among the surviving snipers was one of Lavinia's brothers.
He had asked to be transferred from the hospital to our home.
He had the qualifications to be an officer but had chosen to enlist
as a private—a dangerous selection that he made at the behest of
his father, who did not want his son to get above his raisings. The
boy, Frank, told me that he felt he owed something to his father,
who felt inferior to his educated children, and had followed his
wishes. "I wanted to satisfy him," Frank told me late one night,
as I changed the bandage on his right arm and adjusted the
splint on his left. When he heard Maureen read the speech, he
said, "It needs to be over. Why will it not stop?" His question led
to the boys' favorite conversation—how things might be different if Stonewall Jackson had lived. Without that great tactician
and leader, they believed, the War would drag on interminably

and bury thousands more boys beneath more ground that would beg for consecration.

While Frank thanked me for helping Lavinia conquer the odds of her survival to the extent that she lived long enough to love learning, their father was still contemptuous of Quincy and me; he blamed us for coercing her out of the house where she belonged. He expressed that sentiment to me when he came to visit Frank. He wanted to take his son home, but I would not let him go, for fear that his injuries would be corrupted. I had to listen to talk of how I thought I was better than folks in the flats: "You think you're piling up credit in Heaven by sending the nigger over with squirrel stew when I bet that same nigger sits at the main table and eats tenderloin." I let Mr. Dawes exhaust himself, while Maureen stood by, perplexed that someone would, in these desperate times, despise a person who had helped his family and would continue to do so, regardless of what language was foisted on her. From Clarice I had learned how to refuse to give a fighter something to push against.

Mr. Dawes was almost a welcome distraction in what had become, after Clarice's death, a monotonous accumulation of days. Before the War, Quincy and I had loved the regularity of our life together, its sure predictability. We were in full control, and if we wanted a break in our rhythm, we satisfied that desire with an excursion to the shore if he had the leisure, or by doing something as irregular as attending the early church service instead of the noon one. We made our days. But once Clarice was not with me to keep the disorder of wartime life from overwhelming me, and to supply order, even if a rather loose one, by making certain that meals were taken on schedule, that the children got to school, that the dead boys were removed quietly and their beds quickly stripped and remade for more injured souls, I looked to Maureen to keep me from swirling off into the wind. Her skill at organization allowed the house to operate after a fashion, even if a routine was not rigorously observed. It could not be——not after Gettysburg, and indeed not after the spiritual decay of the soldiers, who were so very confused by the Fort Pillow massacre, nor after we took in boys from the Wilderness who got lost in the choking smoke in those acres of scrub brush and never found their way clear.

This is how I remember 1864—dark. I arose before sunrise, and by the time I could wash a corn dodger down with okra coffee and get to the hospital, the sun was just purpling the horizon. The first thing I did when I entered my ward was to fetch Leon to help me open the canvases to let in enough light to wake the boys and remind them that they wanted to live to see another dawn like this one. Then I would check on Quincy, who, after the Wilderness, spent most nights at the hospital, trying to repair the awful injuries of close fighting, the deep puncture wounds to the stomach that generally meant an agonizing death.

Stomach wounds were so common after the Wilderness campaign that Quincy had me make rounds every hour and inspect, for the first sign of mortification, the boys he sent out of his surgery. When I saw white rise from the stitches, I would immediately call for Leon, who now had several assistants to help him apply maggots. The boys always cried—if they were conscious— when I told them they needed that application. They could not believe something so gruesome was happening to them. They had done nothing in their lives to deserve having the foul things set to their bodies, and many times I would divert their attention while Leon worked, reminding them of when their bodies were whole and pure and they were running through green fields in the sunlight. They loved to remember playing out of doors. That and food and girl acquaintances whom they intended to know better once the War was over. One of them wondered to me: "Do you think Helen'll take me, in this here shape I'm in? What's she going to do with somebody with half a leg?" When their thoughts turned too much to dread and rejection, I took their minds to the woods and ponds of their homes, to those green fields. And when the maggots had worked—this took about an hour, for a normal case—I would pick the hideous things off the wounds with tweezers and say, "There. See? You're safe now." All they wanted was to be safe.

I spent mornings on the ward, took my dinner with Quincy, and then worked all afternoon assisting him in his surgeries. So many arms were fractured by the new rifles the Union was employing that Quincy resigned himself to the inevitable loss of limbs and began amputating at a furious pace. When the boys arrived so terribly mangled after Cold Harbor, he pushed himself to the edge of sanity, fighting exhaustion to stand by his table hour after hour and sometimes take from those boys what they often termed to me as their manhood. It was in those first scorching weeks of June that Quincy tossed aside his stated order that amputated limbs be taken away wrapped in cloth and promptly incinerated. He simply could not keep up. He propped open the window and pitched the limbs out onto a pile that the Negroes collected when they found a spot of time. His eyes were fiery with fatigue, but he would not come home and rest properly. When he could not stay upright to hold his blade steady, he would crawl onto a vacant stretcher and snatch some sleep. Sometimes I lay on top of him, so we could be close—I missed his warmth—and he slept anyway. After two or three hours he would awaken, wash his face, and call for the next patient.

Around supper I went home. I spent what time I could with the children, always promising to make it up to them. We had our meals together when I could, but generally I had to tend to the boys, who rested all over the front rooms, up and down the hallways, in the servants' rooms. When I had performed whatever nursing duties were required—changed bandages, given baths, made note of who needed to go to the hospital for another surgery, decided who could not survive the trip and required surgery the instant Quincy walked through the door—I called Maureen in from the kitchen and asked her to sing the boys to sleep. She nursed them while I was at the hospital, and so she had a notion of their likes and dislikes. They enjoyed anything she sang, and they expressed such glee when the girls accompanied her. They could hide their hurts in music, and while Maureen and the girls relaxed them with song, I would blow out the sweet-potato candles and kiss them good night. Maureen, the children, and I made sure that they knew we prayed for them. I did not read aloud from the Prayer Book or pray aloud, for I thought it best that they keep their worship a private matter, keep God in the heart, where He is best heard.

After the soldiers and the girls were headed to sleep, Maureen and I would start cooking for the next day. My sister was as tired as I was, but, she said, she could swallow fatigue because for once in her life she had a purpose. Sometimes my wits were frayed from lack of sleep, and I would nip my fingers cutting up the potatoes and the frail carrots that grew in back of the house. If we had had cow manure, we might have grown lovely vegetables, but the days were gone when every house bragged of two or three milk cows. Maureen and I cooked as Charlie, Mavis, and Martha had taught us—corn dumplings, corn pudding, corn dodgers, cornbread, corn, corn, corn, all that ever-loving corn. We had various types of greens, and we would put on a mess of collards at midnight and take it off the fire at three. That is how we knew when to go to bed—when the greens were tender. We baked everything else, fried almost nothing, because lard was becoming increasingly hard to find. Nobody had hogs to kill. This was not Seven Oaks, with its two hundred hams hanging in the smokehouse whenever you happened in.

Even with Maureen and me cooking until three in the morning, we barely kept the household adequately nourished. Because of the dearth of white lily flour, the children lost their complexions. They became sallow. We did have an abundance of wild-growing peppermint in the wood between our property and the

Mordecais', and Maureen and I made liberal use of it in teas that gave the boys and the children some energy. Whenever a patient complained of the tea's unfamiliar taste, I would say, "Drink it. A body cannot subsist on itself. You cannot eat and drink your own self. You ate rancid hardtack on marches. You can drink peppermint. Take it, and you'll have enough strength to walk about in the yard tomorrow and feel some sunshine again."

Around three, I would take a spit bath and then sleep as hard as I could for two or three hours, wake up ragged, try to will myself to believe that the burnt-okra concoction was coffee, and go to the hospital, open the canvases, and begin again. Over and over, and more of the same. And while this continuous coming and going may sound horrendous, the War, with its erratic pulsations, kept me functioning at a survivable level, right below the chaos.

The once helpful quartermaster became of little use, save to keep us stocked with sacks of meal and to maintain the basic store of medical supplies I kept in the kitchen pantry. But he was handy at making scuppernong wine from the grapes in our arbor. We served it to the boys when it was barely fermented, so eager were they for anything that approached the taste of spirits.

Sherman burned Atlanta in November of 1864, and if anyone was still foolish enough to court the dream of a Confederate victory, that dream had ended the minute Sherman took his first step toward the sea. Boys at the hospital and at our home listened to announcements of his movements with rapt attention. A soldier on my ward said, "He don't have to do this."

"He is compelled to," I replied. "He is a criminal."

When boys recovered enough to be sent back into the fighting, whenever I could I arranged to have their orders lost. I did that not only for their sakes but for mine, because in my heart I knew they might die in some general's blind, stupid rage against fate. I knew I could have been hanged, and now that I have confessed the fact that I disrupted military command and saved a few boys from dying, I might be banished in some circles in this town that still worship the Confederacy. But these veterans who march by my house in their tattered uniforms on Lee's birthday, on their way to the Capitol to hear rounds of speeches about that man's kindness, his courage, and his love for the common soldier, would not persecute me for misplacing orders. Among those veterans may be one I saved as a young man. Quincy was always my willing co-conspirator, often marking through another doctor's "Fit to resume service" and writing, "Permanently disabled."

We celebrated a sorry, makeshift Christmas that year, without Quincy. I traded a gold piece from the cellar for what oranges and walnuts the quartermaster could find, and that was all the merry Christmas treats the children and the soldiers had. There were no pig bladders to blow up and pop. There were no tin horns to toot. No powder for rockets and firecrackers. I made myself stay home on Christmas Eve, all day, and all the next. If the children could not have presents, they could at least have me. We read funny dialect stories to the soldiers, and Maureen sang carols while we should have been eating oysters and stuffed ham and boiled turkey, pickled beets and pickled okra. Oh my Lord, what everyone should have been consuming instead of song, which soothes the heart but does not lean against the backbone. Then, late on Christmas Day, after the boys had shared tales of happier times in the last valley of Nine Hills, a washerwoman name of Victoria appeared at the front door with a gunnysack full of live chickens—a gift from Governor Vance. Victoria did not seem over-eager to let those chickens out of her hands, and I divined that although she had been sent out in the cold to deliver them, she would not be eating any. The governor had, I assumed, given us all the decent food in his house, for he was famous for his generosity to everyone but his servants, who were forever running from my yard with hurriedly uprooted turnip greens, dashing from the outside cellar entrance with aprons full of potatoes. Thank goodness they did not know what lay beneath the false bottoms of those baskets!

Maureen and I had Victoria come in with the chickens, and when we announced the arrival of fresh poultry, the boys sent up a Rebel yell, the sort I had heard only from the fanatics who gathered at Capitol rallies. The three of us set to work on those chickens immediately. Maureen astounded me by wringing necks double-handed. I wished, in a burst of sudden nostalgia, that Mother were in my backyard to witness the comportment school graduate of years previous, the debutante in love with her delicate body, dealing so mightily with those chickens. In no time, the poultry was scalded, plucked, cut up, and fried, in lard that was perhaps on the rancid side, but nobody would care. The girls, at Maureen's instruction, made johnnycake and shaved-potato hash.

A couple of soldiers moved a patient off the dining room table, which could seat sixteen, and a few more boys pushed library tables together to form a length that could seat ten or eleven. With the breakfast table in the sun parlor, we had enough room for a proper meal. If they could move at all, the boys made themselves come to the table. The day had been redeemed by the governor and his washerwoman. We had cut up the chickens in a way irregular enough to give everyone at least one piece, even if it was only a wing. I had made count of just nine chickens, but we were all satisfied. One tender boy, who was recovering from the amputation of his right foot, went from room to room on his crutches and said simply, "Y'all pray. Y'all bless this house." And they did. They consecrated this room I now sit in, where I enjoy the bliss of a peaceful morning.

Although I remained in a state of fury about the senselessness of the War, a state of dread about the consequences either victory or defeat might have for the Negroes, I vacillated: Some days I believed things would soon return to normal, and on other days I realized I had forgotten what normal was. I forgot the way to be. There was no Clarice to tell me each day that things were going to turn back around just fine, as she had in the hard opening months of 1862 and until her death. And I had no mother to tell me that all would be well. Quincy was gone or busy, and what waking time we had together was spent over a quick meal or a slit-open body, so he could not assume possession of my woes. Maureen was grabblin'. And I could not reverse roles with the children. That left me to find a way through my own Wilderness, and I often felt I lacked the stamina to power that household and my ward through what Quincy, at the New Year of 1865, said was "it."

"Then let's stay home," I told him. "Let's not go to the hospital." I was not joking. I was ready to give in. I wanted our life back.

"You know we can't stop. They're everywhere." I was not sure whether he meant injured boys or rapidly advancing Union troops, and I did not ask, could not, for Quincy fell into his first sleep in our bed since before Thanksgiving. I did not awaken him the next morning. I closed the curtains to trick his sensitive eyes against the day. I made anyone moving about upstairs go as quietly as possible. And so Quincy slept, on what I believed to be a cliff overlooking unconsciousness, for thirty hours. When he did awaken, he was exasperated. I tried to calm him: "But you needed the rest." I had stayed home not only to nurse patients but to guard him from disturbance. He was happy that I had not gone to the hospital, yet as he splashed cold water on his face, he muttered, "Damn it, damn it. I have to work."

"You also have to sleep."

"No, I don't," he said. He was gone before I could ready myself to accompany him.

Those first months of 1865 were a living Hell, but I could see the end. On April 10, when I learned of Lee's surrender on the day previous, his boundless dignity and grace, my initial reaction was not one of happiness but rather this: What shall I do now? I fell into a void and was not shaken out of this haze of unreality until Maureen read aloud from the Raleigh *Register* the details of Appomattox to the boys at the house, to which they cried a great "Hurrah!" I went to the hospital, where Quincy already had the news but had not stopped working long enough to celebrate. I implored him to come home and leave his responsibilities to his assistants. "Surely God does not have the temerity to take any of your boys today," I told him. But God had taken enough over the past years that the brass plate on the end of our pew expanded into a second, a third, and then a fourth, which had to be tacked onto the back. Before we went home, we went to Christ Church, where I knew people would be gathering. As we took our places, just in time for vespers, I touched, as I did on each trip, my mother's name and that of Miss Clarice Washington (1800–1863).

When we were on our way out, Quincy was stopped by the mayor and asked to work with a delegation assembling that evening to decide how to arbitrate peacefully with Sherman. Quincy thanked him but would not oblige. "I have to go to work," he said.

He did return to the hospital, but I sent for him to come home immediately on the evening of the eleventh. Our house had been in a swivet all day. I had seen to the removal of our soldiers to the safety of the Mary Elizabeth Hospital, for I did not believe that with the ruckus I would be able to attend them adequately. Assistants from the Capitol were in and out of the house, bringing in armloads of documents. With the threat of imminent siege, we were asked to store many of the state's historical and legislative documents in our attic and cellar. The council of government hoped that with Quincy's reputation and his history in the North, our home would not be raided or torched. Everyone was on alert—nervous, worry-worn—but we were spared the horrors of violent invasion.

Quincy came home. He was worried that any of his four Lowell ladies might open their minds and mouths to the wrong person at the wrong time. The newspaper that morning had issued a series of warnings: "All citizens should be polite and courteous to the Union soldiers. Be cautious of children and Negroes who might slip and say something that might precipitate an infection of your homes. Enjoy this peace. Do not create trouble where there is none." We heard the sound of cattle stomping, troops moving forward, and we told the girls they could climb the ash tree to watch the activity but they were not to leave the property. When we had a true promise, not a giggly one, Maureen, Quincy, and I walked to the Capitol square. Before Sherman's arrival, an agreement had been reached that the city would fall without harm to citizens or property. Before I realized what was happening, the Confederate flag was descending. It was conveyed with quiet ceremony to Sherman, the only Unionist, besides perhaps Butler, who I believed would burn in Hell. As the United States flag was raised, Quincy said quietly, "Thank God." People began shouting, "Peace! Peace!" The Capitol lawn was soon a sea of blue, but that did not matter to me—we were whole again. Soon children would eat until their stomachs pooched out. Soon mothers would have their husbands and sons. We could all go home and stay there.

Over the next two months, Quincy continued to work without respite. I was free to roam the city as I pleased, for our family was granted a liberal pass, but I used it only to go to the Mary Elizabeth Hospital or to the Fair Grounds. We were given a guard, whom Maureen kept company throughout the day. She said many times, "Oh, he and I? We just sat there and talked about nothing and everything in the world." Quincy began to worry me, the way he seemed to work more feverishly than ever, as though the War were one gigantic loose end he had to tie up as swiftly as he could ligate an artery. He adopted the habit of sleeping while leaning against a wall. And then one morning he fell to the floor, and an orderly had to pull him to his knees. He dropped again.

Two attendants carried him home to our bed, and he lay there like a stone until Burke Haywood came and roused him with—I am still afraid when I consider it—digitalis. Burke told me that Quincy was suffering a slow, systematic metabolic degeneration. I begged him to tell me what to do. He said, "Let him rest. Feed him when he's up. Otherwise, he should sleep."

Quincy rested very much and ate very scarcely for three months. He was wasting away. The world outside our windows grew increasingly turbulent, bummers everywhere. Maureen ran the house. I sat by Quincy. We were quarantined against the

anticipated turmoil of the coming days of reconstructed government. Negroes were all in the streets, fear-inspiring, menacing
and jubilant at once. People did not know quite what to do with
themselves. But I did. I would nurse Quincy.

He was stirring around the house by autumn. I was pleased at
his progress. I was grateful that he was not in a heap on the floor,
depleted, gone from me. It was on a crisp late-September afternoon when Quincy and I were sitting on the back lawn, doing
nothing, saying nothing, that he slumped in his chair. I caught
him against my body, and with his full weight on me, we both
slipped to the grass. I rolled him over on his back, so that I might
press wind into him if I needed to. He blew a sigh into my face
and whispered, "Now. I think I want to go home."

I had never regarded Quincy as having a notion of home that
was not, by definition, the two of us, together, along with our
daughters and now my sister. And there was the memory of
Clarice. All that meant home. But Quincy had meant that he
wanted to go North. I arranged for Maureen to stay in our house
with the constant guard, and then, within a week, I put myself
and the girls and Quincy on a train headed for Boston. The girls
were too concerned about their father to see the trip as any sort
of grand adventure. They were helpful to me and not at all resentful at leaving school and friends. I will always credit them
for their thoughtfulness.

I told them that when we stopped along the way they could
buy trinkets they had heard about from other traveling girls. I sat
with Quincy, who had drawn into himself and did not care to

talk. He looked out the window and said quietly: "A white house." "A cow." "A small boy." "A clothesline." Then he leaned his head on my shoulder and slept. I was leafing through a magazine when Leslie arrived at our seats and asked, "What's the matter with Father?" She grabbed my arm. I looked at Quincy—oh, I thank God—in time to see his sweet smile before his eyes rolled back and he fell over on my lap. The smile, the eyes, the falling—all in one fluid motion. So easy, so natural. My husband slipped away as gently as he had lived.

We buried him in Boston, in that New England ground that I will soon know. For eternity. I shall know it a great deal better than I did in those years I spent in the Lowell home, an unfamiliar widow in an unfamiliar place. I stayed there for four years. His brothers tried every brand of solace imaginable, but I could not overcome the loss, the sheer emptiness. When they met the train at the station and asked me, as Quincy was taken off the car, how he had passed, I replied, "He worked himself to death," and then I sat on the dirty platform and cried until the girls comforted me into leaving. At that moment, they were of much stronger constitution than I.

We had a simple Episcopal service. The organist played "That Sheep May Safely Graze," as I had asked, and I instinctively felt the side of the pew, searching for names, all those names. There was another hymn: "As angels gave poor Lazarus from all his ills release, so may they give you welcome to everlasting peace." When Quincy's coffin was lowered, I bit the back of my hand until it bled. The scar is with me still.

Quincy's mother had died in 1863, and his father thereupon gave up his medical practice and retired to his bedroom, where he spent all day doing nothing but read the newspaper. Mornings I went to his room and tried to cajole him into talking about Quincy, anything about Quincy, but he was beyond any class of conversation. His nurse told me that the War had ground him to his present condition. Dr. Lowell was worn out. I said that it had done the same to my husband. He enjoyed seeing the girls, and although they explained to him who they were, the familial bond never registered. Many times, he would gaze at them and say, "I have grandchildren." Then he would wander back into the news of the day. Once, Louise took a photograph of herself from his desk, held it up beside her face, and said, "My name is Louise Lowell. I am the girl in this picture. I am your granddaughter." Dr. Lowell smiled sweetly and told her that she did indeed put him in mind of his son's youngest daughter. "And the others? How old would they be?" Mary and Leslie told him their ages. "Oh," he said, "you are in the middle passage. These are turbulent years. Be careful. I need to write my granddaughters, who are exactly your ages, and warn them. Let me read the paper first." He had retired from the world. The girls, at first frustrated by his apparent dementia, gradually accepted the fact that he would never make a connection to them. But they still visited him every day, hoping that the ravages of accrued years of exhaustion would give him enough reprieve to see his son in them.

The girls would leave his company each morning and begin their days. They went to school and to art and music classes, ballroom dancing, and horseback riding. Quincy's brothers engaged an extra driver to take them to and from their activities, and thus I did not worry over their safety. When classes were filled before I could register them, the Lowells would peddle a bit of influence, and I would receive a note: "The Boston Fine Arts Society welcomes . . ." They were able to busy away their loneliness for Quincy, but grief was my days' close companion. During my first months in Boston, I moved only to visit Dr. Lowell's room and to walk to the churchyard where Quincy was buried. I stayed each day until nightfall, regardless of the weather. He was present there. Now, when I am very still, he is present here as well. Those whom we love are everywhere. I wore the black of full mourning until the day I looked in the mirror and said to myself, "He's gone. Do I need to wallow in this abject signal of loss?"

When I felt capable, I allowed Quincy's brothers to introduce me to ladies they thought would be of benefit to me. They wanted me to know people who might help me come back to life. Had it not been for my daughters, I would have had no quest for life. Of those ladies I met, I felt the most instant kinship with Miss Charlotte Seymour, who ran a cooking school. She helped me devise a plan for living, and I followed it closely for the next two years. I wanted a rhythm, craved it. I accepted that I would not be able to dictate when the girls married, whom they married, where they lived, yet their movement into adulthood was the bit of change I felt I could withstand.

By spring, I was on a schedule. I arose at seven. I was served breakfast by a lovely Irish maid named Anna. After visiting Dr. Lowell, I dressed in a starched white dress and walked down Marlborough Street, through the Public Gardens, up the few blocks to Massachusetts General Hospital, where one of Quincy's brothers was administrator and the other a pediatrician. They let me nurse in the post-operative ward. I knew exactly what to do. What perplexed me, however, was how to arrange my features when a veteran looked up at me through a hung-over fog of ether and said, "I guess you hate me." He, like others, thought that to know my accent was to know who I was. I always responded, in Quincy's spirit, "I don't hate anybody." Colonel Shaw's father, a great friend of the family, brought me luncheon in a basket one day, and we sat on a bench in the Gardens and talked, in the main, about hate.

"You have every reason to loathe Southerners," I told him.

"But Southerners didn't kill my son," he said, "the South didn't kill him. A wild attack, heavy fire issued by enraged, and probably drunken, soldiers on a rampage—that is what took him. Spite would eat me whole. I cannot let that happen."

I replied that, yes, it was unreasonable to hate a place. "My home is adrift now amongst vengeful men who think that the only way to make the South part of the Union again is to tear it completely apart, foundation and all, especially the foundation, and build it back up while beating it into submission. You can't accomplish both ends at once." I told him of my sister's frequent letters about the rampant corruption and graft. "I do not think I want to be there now," I said, "but I feel like such a foreigner here."

"But you will go home?"

"Eventually," I replied. "For now, I have to stay by Quincy. I have to check each day to make sure he's settled." I realize that I must have sounded somewhat delusional—a person is never more settled than when grass grows over his grave—but I felt perfectly reasonable, nothing less than when a mother walks with her child on the first day of school, sees that she knows where to stow her lunch pail, sees that her pencils are trimmed. But to Mr. Shaw, I must have appeared insane.

I worked at the hospital until about two o'clock, then returned to Marlborough Street and changed into day clothes for the long walk to Charlotte's school. There I stayed until supper, learning to cook things unknown to my palate—cream-of-radish soup, cream-of-celery soup, all those creamed soups, whereas in the South a cook threw rough-cut vegetables into a pot of water and waited until they were rid of the crunch. I learned to make *bouchées* and *rissoles*, fish potatoes, brown bread, stuffed artichokes, and *bonbons*. While I worked alongside the other students, I realized that I was attenuating anguish the way women had for generations before me—they went to the kitchen and worked and talked until things were ready to eat and they all felt better.

Charlotte asked what I thought of sharing some Southern ways with her students. The idea appealed to me, but I knew that the wartime cooking Maureen and I had done was not adequate preparation for such an endeavor. So I wrote to the young Landon Carter, who had bought Seven Oaks when Maureen and I chose not to rescue the property from the tax solicitor, and asked him to root around wherever he had stored what possessions had not been stolen and send me *The Williamsburg Art of Cookery*, the receipt book Clarice had used. So thoroughly were things catalogued that the book was not long in arriving. Charlotte gladly gave me a few months to study and experiment, and in that time I learned that a receipt is only as good as its alterations. And Clarice's alterations were copious. She even amended her own additions and deletions. All over were notes: "Miss Alice is wrong—not too much salt." "Miss Alice says add root beer for sweetening—no, cane." Reading that book, I was in the kitchen again with Mother and Clarice—Mother suggesting that last Saturday's egg pudding lacked enough sauce, and Clarice insisting, "It did not. Your mouth must be off."

I felt some of my joy returning, and by the time I had tested Clarice's receipts and found her generally right, I was able to present myself, my world, and my food to a roomful of Northerners. In the early spring, I had received from Maureen collard seeds, which I planted in the Lowell front yard because the back was taken up with a formal garden. A March in Boston is perfect for cultivating collards. Most of the students, mainly brides, thought collards odious. But they were pleased to learn that a chicken lasts longer if the stuffing is cooked outside the cavity. Nobody enjoyed an instant affinity for grits. I told the brides not to worry—that a pot of grits thrown at an adulterous husband was many a Southern woman's notion of ideal punishment. At the end of an afternoon's cooking, we ate. In the blessing, I forever thanked God for home. I knew I needed to be there. It was simply a matter of time.

After I was able to stand by Quincy's grave without leaning on the cold tombstone, I wondered if I was now in the short rows of grief. And when Mary entered Mount Holyoke College, I felt some heart's ease to know that she would be engaged in the intellectual pursuits her father had nurtured in her. The following years, Leslie and Louise also went off to school, and now, for the first time in my life, I felt wholly alone. I wondered if some brand of purpose awaited me. Maureen's letters told not only of the political havoc wreaked by carpetbaggers but of the dire want assailing freed Negroes and poor whites. And so I began to see myself at a confluence—a small measure of happiness was returning while there was that tug homeward, time and place and circumstance aligning themselves into something like the eclipse I had experienced as a child, the one that had intensified the seasons. My heart was changing seasons, as well. I was moving into the sturdy, proper respectability of my middle years.

There came a day when I was able to stand by Quincy's grave and talk to him without bending to the ground and whispering, "I do love you. I do. Help me. What will I do without you? I'm lonely." On that first day when I could speak dry-eyed, standing, I heard his response louder than ever before.

Go now, Quincy said. *Go there and pat things down the way you like to—I know you. See who needs some help. You know the fear of a loss of reason. Go to the asylum and help them. You've felt blind. Go to their school and find their needs. Go to the flats. The children there are hungry and they need shoes. A hundred Lavinias need you. Return to me, finally. Go home, hurry.*

It was late when the driver turned onto Blount Street. All the houses were turned down for the night, save mine. It was completely awash in welcome. Maureen asked if I was pleased with the new lighting—indoor gas illumination was commonplace in Boston but still a novelty in the poor, reconstructing South. I certainly was, I told her. I was pleased with the lighting, and with the condition in which she had maintained the home. The bloodstained carpets were now spotless, after the hours she had spent scrubbing them with a brick. The top of the piano had been restored. There was no evidence of the surgeries that had been performed on it, no marred places where soldiers' rough uniforms had rubbed away varnish. Nothing was out of place. I wondered if that house might again be a perfect refuge. Maureen and I did little but talk for a week. We spoke of the girls, and of her plans to use the old furnishings from Seven Oaks in a house she was trying to establish for women and orphans. She said that she would not be with me for much longer, that before she committed herself to the charitable house, she was using part of her bequest from Quincy to go around the world with a woman she had met through her work in the flats. She announced an intention to visit our brothers in Milan, where

Henry and John operated a textiles concern, with Randolph as their American exporter. I was heartened to know they had moved out from Father's shadow and made glad lives for themselves.

Off Maureen went, around the world, and deeper and deeper I dug into my small part of it, a corner of the South. I organized my days so that I was left no time to think about the past. That sort of thinking has been my occupation these past months, but back then, I saw something to do every time I left the house and crossed the square that separated the rich from the poor. Weeks, months, and years whirred past me; my chief effort was in holding myself steady enough to do Quincy's bidding.

On my first walk through the flats to see how Lavinia's brothers were managing, I was immediately surrounded by a band of pitiful children, begging for anything I might have. I gave them some coins, but I knew that the real need was work for their parents. Proceeding to the railroad depot, where I sat on a bench and entertained imagined stories of the passengers—this would become a habit—I formed the idea of setting up a clothing factory in one of the abandoned stores downtown. While I sat, reckoning the details, a Negro girl of about fourteen caught my gaze by hopping repeatedly on and off the scales. When she had me almost unnerved, I walked over and offered her a few cents to cease her activity. She took the coins, tied them in a hank of her ragged dress, stepped back onto the scales, and asked me to tell her how much she weighed. "It is right there," I said. "You weigh ninety-one pounds." She grinned and ran off. I could not bear the thought of a pretty girl so recently freed yet still bound by ignorance. She was on my mind when I hounded gentlemen for donations for the clothing factory. I also said I needed funds for a schoolroom for Negroes. This request was so repulsive to them that word of my homecoming was featured in a newspaper editorial, which began:

> Mrs. Quincy Lowell has returned, bringing her high-minded, high-handed, moralizing ideas along. She seeks to create a class of learned Negroes, but we already have enough literate Negroes installed in the legislature. Do we not? Turned away by every member of her class, she plans to use some specie from her late husband's fortune to teach Negroes in the old United States Bank building, which she bought for a song. Glad to have you with us once again, my dear Mrs. Lowell.

When the Ku Klux Klan organized in Raleigh, the schoolroom was turned inside out. Someone left a note for me in plain view on the floor: "Dere nigger-lover. A nigger that can rede is one that wil lord hisself over the wite man. Stop now. We no were you live." First I laughed. Then I made arrangements for the tutors I hired—boys from the Lovejoy School who agreed with me on the value of learning—to go to the students' shacks and teach them there.

Besides the tutoring and the factory endeavors, I became a partner, with Burke Haywood, in a bakery, a livery stable, a pottery, and a mortgage company. Men did not mind investing in any enterprise as long as I assured them that white people would benefit more than Negroes. My chief effort, over the years, was made on behalf of all the Lavinias I found. Christ Church adopted many of the girls, seeing to their thorough welfare. I saw to their education. Several of them write at Christmas, and some who did not leave Raleigh come by now and again. My books are on constant loan to these girls—women now, but still impressionable enough to be delighted over the adventures in *The Innocents Abroad.* A few years ago, I started a reading circle for ladies who were interested in expanding their minds beyond love serials. When Maureen brought some of her women from the charitable home to a discussion of *Bleak House,* the more snippety ladies made known their displeasure by staring at their feet. They did not return. Maureen's women filled the empty chairs.

I always enjoyed going to the charitable house, where Maureen lived, and seeing the intricately carved furniture from Seven Oaks put to good use. And the thought did cross my mind: How revolted Father would be by the typical scene of children teething on the backs of his Hepplewhite chairs. When Maureen was nowhere to be found one morning, I was told she had felt puny the night before. I found her in her room, unclothed, crumpled in the sliver between the bed and the wall. She had been dead for hours, so cold she was, and rigid. As I dressed her body, thinking all the while, "Don't hurt her," I cried over the fear and confusion that must have seized her at the end. Her mouth was pulled down on one side. At the hospital, I had seen bodies lose control before death. Her eyes were open and as full of terror as any soldier's I had closed, as I now closed hers. Death had spared the children, but the rest were gone. Although my mind was not set for a fight, I did want to attend to the items on Quincy's list before working became impossible.

I knew I was next. And so I rushed against time. My rest came on holidays, when my children and grandchildren would come and fill the house with a happy racket. Some of them have gotten along in life better than others, but at least someone could have carved on the tombstone in Boston: "None of Dr. and Mrs. Lowell's heirs was ever arrested on a morals charge." Quincy would be pleased that every one of our family is kind, thoughtful, and opinionated in the correct direction. We knew the sort of family we wanted to have, and so we spent much time and will and care raising the girls to be true to their hearts.

When my body could no longer endure long days at the clothing factory, the bakery, the pottery, I resigned myself to staying home and writing checks that would do my work for me. And I began looking in the mirror, not ever one of my pleasures, to see myself age, to see myself deteriorate. Mornings I felt especially old, I would send out more money than on those days when my joints felt loose, when I felt able to dance again, with Quincy. I have lived easily on interest, so what money I have not marked for my heirs, I have given away until my accounts have been emptied of what I will not need to keep myself going. I have felt a purging to give the money away in an almost gleeful disbursement that the newspapers have noted as being reckless. What do I need of money? I need to eat and run the house, but not for long, not long at all.

I feel my life closing—memories, pain, anger, frustration all now reconciled. The time is ripe. I need nothing now, no one but Quincy.

All day, I have been watching the arc of the sun in the sky. This is my favorite time—when the heat of early spring rises from the Earth and spreads, spreads wherever it will. I choose to finish my story here, at this time, because I am comforted by the blue sky out the window, and I am not afraid of letting myself go into it. I want to meet my husband.

On the occasion of my last afternoon, I feel no sorrow, feel no regret, for I have done what Quincy told me to do: *Face it all dry-eyed. Say it. Say it.* This has been such a glorious afternoon—my heart would not weep if I did not live to see another.